JACK IN THE BOX

A Brock and Poole Mystery

DCI Harry Brock is called to a murder scene on Ham Common early on a Sunday morning. But it is far from being an ordinary sort of murder. The victim has been stabbed to death, locked in a wooden box and set alight. Brock and his assistant, DS Dave Poole, believe that there might be a connection to a gang, which leads them on a journey through London's underworld...

*Graham Ison titles available from
Severn House Large Print*

Lost or Found
Drumfire
Working Girl
Whispering Grass
Kicking the Air

JACK IN THE BOX

A Brock and Poole Mystery

Graham Ison

Severn House Large Print
London & New York

This first large print edition published 2010
in Great Britain and the USA by
SEVERN HOUSE PUBLISHERS LTD of
9-15 High Street, Sutton, Surrey, SM1 1DF.
First world regular print edition published 2008 by
Severn House Publishers Ltd., London and New York.

British Library Cataloguing in Publication Data

Ison, Graham.
  Jack in the box. -- (A Brock and Poole mystery)
  1. Brock, Harry (Fictitious character : Ison)--Fiction.
  2. Poole, Dave (Fictitious character)--Fiction.
  3. Police--England--London--Fiction. 4. Murder--
  Investigation--England--London--Fiction. 5. Organized
  crime--England--London--Fiction. 6. London (England)--
  Fiction. 7. Detective and mystery stories. 8. Large type
  books.
  I. Title II. Series
  823.9'14-dc22

ISBN-13: 978-0-7278-7868-7

Severn House Publishers support The Forest Stewardship
Council [FSC], the leading international forest certification
organisation. All our titles that are printed on Greenpeace-
approved FSC-certified paper carry the FSC logo.

Mixed Sources
Product group from well-managed
forests and other controlled sources
www.fsc.org Cert no. SA-COC-1565
© 1996 Forest Stewardship Council

Printed and bound in Great Britain by the
MPG Books Group, Bodmin, Cornwall.

One

Murder victims are usually discovered out of office hours. Given the cynic I am, it's probably because their killers have decided to cause my colleagues and me the maximum inconvenience. It was ever thus, but in my case it was even more of a damned nuisance because I'm currently enjoying an intimate relationship with a gorgeous blonde actress. She's called Gail Sutton, and stands – or as often is laid – a statuesque five-ten in her bare feet. I don't know why she puts up with the constant disruptions to our social life that my job entails, but she does. Perhaps being an actress, and occasional dancer, she knows what working unsocial hours is all about.

This murder was no different. At nine o'clock on a Sunday morning in early September, we were in bed at her town house in Kingston when my mobile rang.

Swinging her long shapely legs on to the floor, Gail muttered a most unladylike obscenity, but actresses have a reputation for earthy language.

'Harry Brock,' I said into my little all-

5

singing, all-dancing mobile phone, with enough venom in my voice to deter all but the most resolute caller. Perhaps I should explain that I'm a detective chief inspector on the Homicide and Serious Crime Command. At least, that's what it was called last week. Maybe our masters have changed it yet again; the boy superintendents at New Scotland Yard take a great delight in changing things. Just to show us poor plebs how clever they are.

We work out of Curtis Green, a grim grey eight-storied building tucked away behind Richmond Terrace Mews just off Whitehall, and most people don't know we're there. Including quite a number of police officers. Our core task, as the *wunderkinder* are fond of describing it in the strangulated language they learn at Bramshill Police College, is to investigate murders in that chunk of the great metropolis that stretches westwards from Charing Cross to the boundaries of civilization. Or, in other words, to the perimeter of the Metropolitan Police District. But not *all* murders. Some are the preserve of other specialized squads, one of which is called Operation Trident, and has the politically incorrect task of dealing with 'black-on-black' gun crime. The simple murders are dealt with on division, but we get the dross, which usually means the most difficult.

'It's Colin Wilberforce, sir,' said the sergeant who ran the incident room.

'Yes, Colin?'

'The fire brigade was called to a burning box on Ham Common at eight o'clock this morning, sir. The box contained a dead body.'

'Are you sure, Colin?'

There was a pause. 'Yes, sir. There's no doubt.'

'But are you sure it was Ham Common?' It was a valid question arising out of self-interest; Ham Common is at the very edge of that area for which my section of Homicide and Serious Crime Command is responsible. A few yards nearer Kingston and it would have fallen to HSCC South, and some other poor DCI.

'I'm afraid so, sir. DI Ebdon spoke to the commander and he said it was down to you.'

'Was this box a coffin, by any chance?'

'Not as far as I know, sir. First reports suggest it was a crate. And it was padlocked.'

'How very interesting. Was the victim perhaps a fire-eating escapologist who wasn't very good at the job?'

Even after working with me for some years, Colin sometimes has difficulty in recognizing what passes for my sense of humour. 'There's nothing to indicate that that is the case, sir,' he said stiffly.

'Has Dave Poole been notified?'

'Yes, sir. He's on his way to the scene as I speak. So are DI Ebdon and her team.'

'Good. Give Dave a call and tell him I'll meet him there.' Dave Poole is my bag carrier – what DCIs call the detective sergeants who act as their right hand. And there's no one better at it than Dave Poole, who's saved me from making a fool of myself on quite a few occasions. 'And Colin, rustle up the usual support team.'

'Meet who where?' As I cancelled the call, Gail returned to the bedroom carrying two cups of coffee. My attempt to switch to a macho operational mode was not helped by the fact that she was still naked.

'Ham Common, to examine a body. Dave Poole's on his way already.'

Gail put the coffee on a bedside table, and sighed.

Murder is a funny old business. Half the time you're rushing about the length and breadth of London in a vain attempt to discover the murderer. And the other half is spent not knowing what the hell you're doing, but that's usually when you're trying to put together the report. I had a nasty feeling that this topping would be no different.

Despite it being Sunday morning, a small crowd had gathered behind the blue and white tapes on the distant periphery of Ham Common, a few acres of greenery that straddles the road between Kingston and Richmond. Some of these morbid sightseers were obviously residents from the twee houses on

8

the far side, confirmed by the copies of the *Sunday Times* they were clutching. I imagine they all read the *Sunday Times* in this part of the world.

A small canvas structure had been erected in the centre of the common, doubtless housing the subject of my latest investigation. There were four police cars – God knows why there were four – and a couple of fire appliances drawn up on the edge of the grassland, their blue lights still lazily revolving. A little convoy of white vans containing the scientific support had already arrived. They were emblazoned with the latest slogan to emanate from Scotland Yard: Evidence Recovery Unit. Oh, well!

As I alighted from my car, a black BMW drew up and Dr Henry Mortlock got out. He was muttering to himself, and clutching a leather case that contained all the ghoulish instruments of his trade as a Home Office forensic pathologist.

'Good morning, Henry,' I said.

'What's bloody good about it?' demanded Mortlock. 'I was supposed to be playing golf this morning.'

'Happy camping,' I said, as Henry disappeared through the opening in the canvas screens.

An ageing inspector, with Falklands and Long Service and Good Conduct medal ribbons on his tunic, approached, clipboard at the ready. 'May I have your name, please?' he asked politely.

Having told him who I was, I said, 'Once the pathologist and crime-scene people have finished, Inspector, I shall want the common scoured. Would you arrange for a team of officers to start on that as soon as possible?'

The inspector tucked his pen into his breast pocket, and looked glum. 'We're a bit short of men, being a Sunday, sir, but I'll do what I can.'

'Good. And make sure that none of that lot encroaches on the area.' I waved at the on-lookers.

'Of course, sir.' The inspector looked affronted by that request, as if I were telling him his job, but I've known the public to foul up a crime scene before.

Dave Poole was in earnest conversation with the fire chief, and I strolled across to join them. Dave is black, six foot tall, and weighs in at about fifteen stone. His grand-father, a doctor, came to England from the Caribbean in the fifties and settled in Beth-nal Green to the north-east of the capital. Son of an accountant, Dave graduated in English from London University, but then decided to join the Metropolitan Police. He frequently says that this decision made him the black sheep of the family, a statement that seems to disconcert our diversity-con-scious commander. But Dave has a weird sense of humour; it goes with the job.

'Are you the station officer?' I asked the

fireman with the white helmet.

'We're not called that any more. They like us to be called watch managers now. It's supposed to soften our image.' And just to demonstrate that it had done no such thing, he bellowed at a fire fighter. 'Mind what you're doing with that bloody thing, you idiot. They cost money.'

'Tell me the story,' I said.

'Got a shout at oh-seven-fifty-six to a smouldering crate,' said the watch manager, now giving me his full attention, and waving at the canvas shelter. 'When we arrived on scene, we doused it, just to make sure, but then we noticed that there seemed to be human remains contained in the box. As we don't deal with cremations, we called your lot.'

'Thanks a bundle,' I said. 'Any idea as to the cause of the fire?'

The watch manager grinned. 'Well, it sure as hell wasn't spontaneous combustion.'

I always knew that the fire brigade shared a macabre sense of humour with the police.

'Initial examination,' continued the fire chief, 'indicates the presence of petrol or a similar accelerant. We're treating it as arson.'

'Oh, good.' I hoped that didn't sound too sarcastic because it wasn't meant to be. When the fire brigade treats an incident as arson, it means that they treat it with a view to preserving evidence. 'My sergeant will want a statement from you.'

'I've already taken a preliminary, sir,' said Dave, flourishing a handful of official paper. He always called me 'sir' in the presence of the public. When he called me 'sir' in private it was usually an indication that I'd made a fatuous comment. 'I'll get someone to go to the fire station and take a detailed statement.'

'Which nick covers this area?' I asked. I don't often deal with dead bodies in burning boxes on Ham Common.

'Richmond,' said Dave, who always had such information at his fingertips.

'Any joy with that lot?' I gestured at the rubberneckers on the far side of the common.

'Miss Ebdon's got some of her people checking them out, sir,' said Dave.

We crossed to our victim's funeral pyre just as Henry Mortlock emerged from the canvas structure.

'What d'you think, Henry?'

'Can't tell until the post-mortem,' said Mortlock, but he always said that. 'The body's quite badly burned. Whoever set fire to this man made a good job of it.'

'It is a man, then.'

'I just said that.' Mortlock put down his case of instruments. 'I think you'll be able to get one or two fingerprints from the cadaver, Harry, and from a cursory examination, I'd say he was probably under thirty years of age. But if you're going to ask me if he was

12

dead before the fire was started, you'll have to wait until I've carved him up. Usual place.' By which, he meant the Westminster mortuary in Horseferry Road.

'Any clothing?' I was immediately thinking in terms of identification.

'It would appear not. It looks as though he was naked when he was barbecued.' And with that irreverent comment, Mortlock picked up his case and strode towards his car whistling some obscure aria.

Dave and I went to have a look at what we were dealing with, and ventured inside. As Henry Mortlock had said, whoever had set fire to our corpse had made a good job of it. Although much of the body had been badly burned, the face was virtually untouched, and one of the hands on the body that the fire brigade had found in the crate might, if we were lucky, yield a set of fingerprints. But if there were no criminal record with which to match them, we wouldn't be much further forward in identifying the dead man.

Linda Mitchell, the senior forensic practitioner, made a timely appearance in her sexy all-white outfit. 'All right for me to do the necessary, Mr Brock?'

'Yes, go ahead, Linda. Fingerprints would be a help, and a photograph of the face, as well as all the others you usually take. ASAP.'

'Of course,' said Linda, rather curtly, I thought. I shouldn't have said what I needed; Linda knows her job.

13

'G'day, guv.' Kate Ebdon, the DI in charge of the 'legwork' team, walked across holding a clipboard. Kate, a flame-haired, ex-Flying Squad officer, is Australian, and invariably dresses in jeans and a man's white shirt. Rather than disguising her figure, this outfit tends to emphasize it, and it's strongly rumoured that she had seduced more than one detective. Of the male species, of course. Unfortunately, Kate's mode of dress disturbs the commander, but he hasn't got the guts to tell her he disapproves. A man of fixed and outdated ideas, he thinks that anyone promoted to inspector rank automatically becomes a gentleman. Or in Kate's case, a lady.

The commander was visited upon us some time ago by a genius in the Human Resources Directorate who thought that a Uniform Branch senior officer could become a detective at the stroke of an official pen. I can tell you that it ain't necessarily so. It's also rumoured that upon his own distant promotion to inspector, our beloved chief embarked upon a course of elocution lessons. But that might just be a malicious story put about by the inferior ranks. And, when the mood takes them, the inferior ranks can be pretty malicious, believe me.

'What've you got, Kate?'

'There was just one bloke you might like to have a word with, guv.' Kate glanced at her clipboard. 'Name of Robert Walker. He was the one who called the fire brigade.'

14

'I don't suppose he saw anyone dumping a coffin, did he?'

'You suppose right, guv.'

'So what did this upstanding member of the community do next, *ma'am*?' asked Dave, grinning at Kate.

'At first, he thought that someone had dumped some rubbish,' said Kate, ignoring Dave's sarcastic formality. 'Apparently they have had trouble with fly-tippers recently, and he considered telephoning the council about it. But then he realized that it was Sunday and there'd be no one there.'

'God help us!' I said.

'After a great deal of soul-searching,' continued Kate caustically, 'he decided to call the fire brigade. On account of smoke coming out of the box.'

'Perhaps we should arrange for him to get a letter of commendation from the Commissioner,' suggested Dave.

'Which one is he, Kate?'

'The one holding the *Sunday Times*,' said Kate, with an evil grin, 'and talking to the PC.'

'They're all holding the *Sunday Times*,' I muttered.

Dave and I crossed to where an unshaven man in a rugby shirt, jeans and brown loafers was standing on our side of the cordon. He looked to be about forty and had brown, wavy hair and rimless glasses.

'Mr Walker?'

15

'Yes, I'm Bob Walker, Inspector.'

'Chief Inspector,' I said. '*Detective* Chief Inspector.' That's the trouble with television. The writers of TV police soaps always allow their chief inspectors to be called 'inspector'. Some of these actors even introduce themselves as 'inspector', which just goes to show that the writers and actors know nothing about the coppering lark. The difference between an inspector and a chief inspector is about eight grand a year, and no one gets away with demoting the real ones, even verbally.

'Oh, sorry, old boy,' said Walker, which pleased me even less.

'I'm told that you called the fire brigade, Mr Walker.'

'Absolutely. Right thing to do, what?'

'When was this?' I knew that the call reached the fire brigade at four minutes to eight, but I like to be certain.

'Um, just before eight, I suppose. I'd driven down to get a paper.' Walker flourished the *Sunday Times*. A large amount of advertising rubbish fell out of the newspaper, and he bent to pick it up. 'It's amazing the amount of junk they put in these things,' he said. 'Anyway, when I got back, I saw this box in the middle of the common, and I thought to myself, that's damned funny. It's disgraceful the sort of stuff people leave lying about. We often find old mattresses here. But then I noticed it was smouldering,

16

so pulled out my mobile and called the fire brigade.'

'Was the crate there when you left to get the paper?' I asked.

'I'm not sure,' said Walker.

I could see this guy was going to be a great help.

'Did you see anything, or hear anything, Mr Walker?' asked Dave. 'Earlier, I mean. Like a vehicle, or voices. Any sort of commotion.'

'No, I'm afraid not. My partner and I sleep at the back of the house, you see.' Walker gazed across at the screens surrounding the crate. 'Is it a murder, d'you think?'

'We're not sure,' said Dave, who never committed himself without hard evidence. 'Could be suicide, I suppose.' But neither of us thought that our victim had locked himself in a box and then set fire to it. If he had, it would be the most bizarre suicide I'd ever come across.

'One of my officers will be across to take a statement from you, Mr Walker,' I said. 'Which is your house?'

Walker provided us with his address and telephone number, and we left him to bask in the glory of having been the first to notice our charred corpse.

It was gone midday by the time everything was wrapped up at the scene, and the crate, still containing its gruesome contents, was removed. The duty inspector from Richmond police station had managed to rustle up seven PCs who had fanned out and meticulously criss-crossed the common in search of evidence. They didn't find any. The tapes were removed, and the gawping residents were left with a topic of conversation that would doubtless dominate their dinner parties for weeks to come.

There were two pieces of news awaiting us when we got back to Curtis Green that afternoon.

The first, from Linda Mitchell, was that there was no trace of the victim's fingerprints in the Criminal Record Office. That meant that he didn't have any previous convictions, and so we still didn't know who he was.

The second snippet was, however, more encouraging, but could yet turn out to be a wild-goose chase.

Colin Wilberforce, that paragon of administration, had already embarked on cataloguing statements, such as they were. Photographs of the scene of the murder, and the crate itself, were already displayed on a huge board at the end of the incident room. And, I have no doubt, entries on the computer were already logged in. We shall definitely be in trouble if Colin is ever promoted and posted.

'We've had a message from the CID at Fulham, sir,' said Colin.

'What about? If it's another murder, give it to someone else. I'm busy.'

Colin smiled. 'It might just be the same one, sir. The DI at Fulham was called by one of their instant-response units at ten this morning.' He glanced down at his message pad. 'A Miss Sasha Lovell rang the police at nine-forty to report that the man she shares a flat with had gone missing. She was alarmed to discover what she thought were bloodstains on the carpet, and smears of blood on the inside of the front door.'

'Why did the Fulham police think we were interested, Colin?'

'No idea, sir, but they passed on the information in case it had anything to do with the Ham Common job.'

'How did they know about that?'

'Their Q car picked it up on the force radio, sir.'

'And I suppose they thought they could unload it on us.' I sighed, but I'd tried unloading jobs a few times myself in the past. Without a great deal of success, I might say.

19

Two

I telephoned the DI at Fulham, and asked him for more details. He told me that Sasha Lovell, a twenty-eight-year-old model, shared a basement flat in Fulham with an artist named Jack Harding to whom she was not married. She had left him at the flat on Saturday afternoon to take part in a photo-shoot session at a studio in Chelsea, but when she returned on the Sunday morning, Harding wasn't there. She noticed signs of a disturbance, and then saw what she thought were bloodstains on the carpet, and on the inside of the front door.

There was no way out of this. Fulham to Ham Common is only about seven miles, and early on a Sunday morning could be travelled in not much more than quarter of an hour. But this was all speculation. The problem for me was that the missing man *might* be my victim, but if he wasn't, I'd be wasting my time. On the other hand, if I ignored it and it was him, I'd be pilloried for not looking into it immediately. Who said a detective's life was glamorous? Sure as hell he wasn't in the Job.

'What's the address?' I asked the Fulham DI.

'Five Badajos Street, guv'nor. Not far from World's End. You can't miss it.'

'Chance'd be a fine thing,' I muttered. 'I'll see you there.' Nevertheless, I had a feeling that I was being drawn into something that was none of my damned business.

The Fulham DI was parked outside the house when Dave and I arrived, and a uniformed PC was standing guard on the pavement near the opening in the railings that led down to Harding's flat. The three of us descended the basement steps, and into an area full of empty beer tins and poly-styrene boxes that had been thrown there by passing overnight gourmets whose idea of the high life is to eat a burger on their drunken way home in the small hours.

Although she was a model, Sasha Lovell was not a particularly beautiful girl, at least, not in the conventional sense. But she was attractive, was the right shape, and had a bit more meat on her than the usual matchstick clothes' horses that adorn the pages of fashion magazines. Looking tired and drawn, she was attired in tight-fitting jeans and a loose, black woollen sweater with a cowl collar.

'This is Detective Chief Inspector Brock from Scotland Yard, Miss Lovell.' The Fulham DI obviously shared my view that Homicide and Serious Crime Command

21

West was too much of a mouthful.

'Come in.' The girl led us into a dank, dark corridor, and opened the door to a huge room on the front of the flat. 'It used to be the kitchen when one family occupied the house,' she explained. She turned on the light, and indicated worn armchairs and a threadbare sofa, all set on an equally threadbare carpet that covered only half the room. 'It's only light in here in the middle of the day,' she said, peering round at the detritus that was Harding's workshop. 'I don't know how Jack manages.' She nodded towards an artist's easel on the far, uncarpeted end of the room, and a wooden table that was littered with pots, palettes, brushes and paint.

'I take it Mr Harding is an artist, then,' I said, confirming what the Fulham DI had told me. I noticed a slight aroma of cannabis in the air, but decided not to mention it. Not yet, anyway. Nevertheless, I was struck by the detached attitude of the woman. Her answers so far had been slow, and she had a vacant look on her face, as though she were in another world.

'Of sorts,' said Sasha. 'He doesn't make much money at it. I help out with my earnings, and Jack does a bit of bar work at the local pub in the evenings, and he gets income support.' Realizing what she'd just admitted, she gave me a guilty glance, and giggled. 'Oh, I shouldn't have told you that, should I?'

'I'm looking into the possibility of a serious crime, Miss Lovell,' I said, hedging my bets, and forbearing to mention the dreaded word 'murder'. After all, I didn't yet know that it was Jack Harding whose body we had found on Ham Common that morning. 'I'm not interested in social security fraud. Perhaps you'd go through the sequence of events. I understand from this officer,' I continued, indicating the Fulham DI, 'that you last saw Mr Harding yesterday.'

'Yes. I left here yesterday afternoon to do a photo shoot in Chelsea.'

'On a Saturday?'

'We often do them on a Saturday,' said Sasha. 'Weekdays are usually taken up with live modelling and catwalk work. If I'm lucky enough to get an engagement.' She sat down in one of the armchairs, suddenly, as though tired of all the questions.

'What was the exact time that you left here, Miss Lovell?' asked Dave.

'About three o'clock, I suppose.'

'And what was Mr Harding doing when you left?' Dave scribbled a few lines in his pocketbook.

'Doing?' Sasha looked at Dave, again with a vacant expression.

'Yes. Was he painting, or sleeping? Or watching television?'

'Oh, I see. He was painting. That, as a matter of fact.' Sasha pointed to a canvas on the easel that portrayed a woman in a long diaphanous robe holding a Grecian urn on her shoulder. 'That's me, actually,' she added.

'Very nice,' murmured Dave. 'And when did you return here?'

'This morning, at about half past nine, maybe a little earlier. I'm not sure.'

'It was an all-night photo shoot, as well as all-afternoon, was it?' asked Dave mischievously, but guessing the answer.

'No.' Sasha lifted her chin defiantly. 'I spent the night with the photographer. We're old friends.'

'Am I to understand that your relationship with Mr Harding is purely platonic, then?' Dave asked.

'No,' said Sasha, and left it at that.

'Tell me what happened when you got home this morning,' I said.

'I let myself in and shouted Jack's name, as I usually do. But there was no answer. I looked in the bedroom and the kitchenette, but he wasn't anywhere. I thought he might be in the shower, but he wasn't. Then I came in here. That table was overturned.' She pointed to a small side table with a lamp on it. 'But there was no sign of Jack, and no note to say where he'd gone.'

It was interesting, but probably irrelevant, that she had looked into the living-room-cum-studio last of all. 'You stood the table up, and replaced the lamp, I take it?'

'Yes. But then I noticed that stain on the

floor.' Sasha pointed to a dark red mark on the carpet. 'It hadn't been there before.'

'It tested positive for blood, sir,' said the Fulham DI, repeating what he had told me on the phone. 'As did the smears on the inside of the front door.'

'I thought he might have gone out for a paper,' Sasha continued. 'He sometimes does that on a Sunday morning. But the newsagent's shop is just round the corner and he'd only have been gone ten minutes at the most. But he never turned up.'

I didn't particularly want to put Sasha Lovell through the trauma of viewing the charred body of our victim – who quite possibly wasn't even Harding – and decided on an alternative course.

'If you've no objection, Miss Lovell, I'd like to have fingerprint officers examine your flat. It is your flat, is it, rather than Mr Harding's?'

'No, it's in his name. He was already here when I moved in with him.'

'And when was that?'

'About six months ago. The end of March, I think.'

'And how did you meet Mr Harding?' asked Dave.

'He's a friend of the photographer who did my photo shoot on Saturday. Jack was looking for a model and couldn't afford to pay for one. As I said, Dominic's an old friend and he asked me if I'd do Jack a favour by posing for him occasionally. I finished up moving in.'

'Dominic's the photographer, is he?'

'Yes, Dominic Finch.'

'And how long have you known him?'

Sasha Lovell looked resentful at what she probably interpreted as an intrusion into her private life, but she didn't understand about police investigations. 'Five or six years, I suppose,' she said eventually.

'And so you agreed to model for Mr Harding. And this was in March, was it?'

'No, last year.' Sasha stood up and crossed the room to pull a canvas from a pile stacked against the wall. 'That's one he did of me. Rather good, isn't it?' she asked, displaying a full-length painting of herself in the nude.

'Very good,' said Dave, allowing his glance to linger on the portrait. He pulled out his mobile phone. 'I'll give Linda a call, sir. Get the fingerprint team over.'

'Perhaps you'd hang on here and point them in the right direction?' I said to the Fulham DI. 'In the meantime, we'll have a word with the people upstairs.'

It was a three-storeyed Victorian house, and in its heyday must have been the residence of an affluent family. Certainly Harding's living and working area would have been a kitchen large enough to cater for a big family and a sizeable staff of servants. But now, in its years of decline, the old house had been

26

divided into four flats, of which the basement was one. All in all, it looked pretty sorry for itself, with its paint peeling from the window frames and the front door.

Mounting the cracked and broken steps, I found that the front door was open. The first door we came to in the hall had a bell push over which was a label bearing the name 'Smith'. I rang the bell. Twice.

Eventually a woman answered the door, opening it to the limit of the security chain, the wise woman.

'Yes? What d'you want?' The voice was croaky, commensurate with her age, which was probably about seventy-five.

'We're police officers, madam,' I said, and held up my warrant card.

The woman put on a pair of glasses that had been suspended from a cord round her neck, and peered closely at the document. 'What d'you want?' she asked again, having satisfied herself that my identification was genuine. But I doubt she'd ever seen a police warrant card before.

'We'd like to talk to you, madam.'

'What about?' This woman did not give in easily.

'About the couple who live downstairs,' I said, wondering whether we'd ever be allowed to cross the threshold.

'Oh, them. Well, you'd better come in.' It took the woman several seconds to disengage the chain, but eventually she opened the door wide, and escorted us into a living room that was immediately above Harding's studio.

'What is it? What's all the fuss?' A man appeared through a doorway from one of the rooms that led off the living room. Attired in a blazer, grey flannel trousers, and a white shirt with a regimental cravat tucked into the collar, he inched himself forward on a Zimmer frame.

'It's the police, dear,' shouted the woman.

'The police? What do they want?' The man – he must have been a good eighty years of age – fiddled with his hearing aid. 'There's no need to shout, Cynthia.'

'It's about the people downstairs, dear,' said the woman in a normal voice.

'What did you say, Cynthia? Speak up, woman, for God's sake. You know I'm deaf.'

'Mr and Mrs Smith, is it?' I asked, when at last we had managed to introduce ourselves.

'*Colonel* and Mrs Smith,' corrected the man sharply. 'And it's time you did something about that couple that live in the basement. They're not married, you know.'

'Really?'

'Disgraceful,' muttered Colonel Smith, his hearing apparently restored at the mention of his downstairs neighbours. He tweaked at his snow-white moustache and ran a hand over his bald pate. 'She takes off all her clothes, and he paints her, you know.'

I hoped that my English language purist of

28

a sergeant would not point out that what Harding actually did was to paint a *portrait* of Sasha Lovell, rather than painting the girl herself. On second thoughts, however, the colonel might have been right; the people who live in the Chelsea and Fulham areas have some very strange practices.

'How d'you know that, sir?' yelled Dave.

'They never pull the curtains, young man,' bellowed the colonel in reply. It's funny how deaf people always seem to think that everyone else is deaf too. 'To tell you the truth, I don't think they've got any curtains. Probably spend all their money on drugs. They're all the same, the younger generation. The government ought to do something about it.' His complaining degenerated into a disagreeable mumble.

I wondered briefly how a man on a Zimmer frame could possibly have positioned himself in such a way that gave him a view of the basement area of the house sufficient to see Sasha Lovell posing naked.

'Mr Harding has gone missing, Colonel Smith,' I said loudly. I had no intention of telling him that Harding might be a murder victim. 'Some time between yesterday afternoon and early this morning. I was wondering whether you'd heard anything. Any noise of a disturbance, perhaps, or shouts or screams. Or perhaps had seen anyone leaving the flat.'

'Not last night,' said Smith. 'Never hear

anything. Always take my hearing aid out, see? Did you hear anything, Cynthia?' he asked, turning to his wife.

'Not last night,' said Mrs Smith. 'Why, was there a party?' she asked, turning to me.

'Not as far as I know. We think that Mr Harding might have been abducted,' I said, taking a chance on that being the truth.

'We had a fellah abducted when I was in Malaya, you know,' volunteered Smith. 'District officer, he was. Been in the Punjab as a young man, so he said. We got him back though. Hadn't been abducted at all, damn fool. Wandered off into the jungle somewhere and got lost. I think he finished up as our ambassador in Turkey. Was Turkey, wasn't it, Cynthia?'

'No, Norway, I think,' said Smith's wife.

'Well, thank you,' I said, deciding that nothing would be gained by questioning this pair of geriatrics any further.

'What rank d'you say you are?' Colonel Smith moved his Zimmer frame a fraction.

'Detective Chief Inspector, Colonel.'

'What's that equal to in the army, eh?'

'I don't think you can compare army ranks with police ranks, Colonel,' I said, and Dave and I took our leave.

There was a white van outside the house, and I rightly assumed that the fingerprint team had arrived. We went back to Harding's flat.

'We've collected quite a few prints, Mr

Brock,' said Linda Mitchell. 'We'll get them back and process them as soon as possible.'

'Why are you doing all this?' asked Sasha Lovell, gazing in dismay at the powder that the team had spread liberally over those surfaces where they expected to find finger marks. 'And why did they have to take my fingerprints? D'you think I had something to do with Jack disappearing?'

Dave gave the girl an understanding smile. 'It'll help to have Mr Harding's fingerprints on record,' he said. 'If we have to circulate details of him, it sometimes enables the police to make a positive identification.' It was all gobbledegook, of course, but Dave was shrewd enough not to mention the possibility that our roasted corpse might be that of Sasha's partner. 'And we need your prints to separate them from those of Mr Harding.'

'Oh, I see,' said Sasha. But I don't think she understood anything that Dave had said. Mind you, I have the same problem at times.

'One other thing, Miss Lovell,' I began.

'Yes?'

'Is anything missing from the flat? Anything that might have been stolen?'

Sasha Lovell put her hands on her hips and looked around, an exasperated expression on her face. 'Are you joking?' she asked. 'How the hell am I supposed to know if anything's missing from this mess?'

'I'll take that as a no, then,' said Dave. 'But if you do notice that anything's gone adrift,

31

perhaps you'd let this officer know.' He nodded towards the Fulham DI.

There was not much we could do until we received the result of the fingerprint examination of the flat that Harding shared with Sasha Lovell. And if our Ham Common body turned out *not* to be that of Harding, we'd have wasted a great deal of time.

We returned to Curtis Green and launched ourselves into the paperwork that necessarily goes with every murder investigation.

Then we went home.

Monday morning proved that we'd not wasted our time. Linda was on the phone first thing.

'Some of the prints we took from Harding's flat match those of the Ham Common body, Mr Brock,' she said. 'And Sasha Lovell has no previous convictions.'

'Did you find any others there that might help, Linda?' I asked.

'We're still checking, Mr Brock. I'll let you know as soon as possible.

'We're up and running, Dave,' I said, as I replaced the receiver. 'It's him.'

The next visit was to the forensic science laboratory. I've always found that a personal visit lets the people there know that you're taking an interest. Well, not really; it actually helps to speed things up.

'It was a fairly new wooden trunk, Mr Brock,' said Heath, the scientist who was examining what was left of the crate in which Harding had been found. 'Looks like the sort of trunk that hardy travellers take on world cruises, or the military on a posting abroad.'

'Any indication where it might have come from?' I asked.

'I'm afraid not.' Heath gestured at the remains of the crate. 'As you can see, it was quite badly burned.'

'Get hold of an artist, Dave,' I said.

'There's a few in Montmartre, in Paris, sir,' said Dave. 'Will one of them do?'

I ignored this typical example of Poole humour. 'I want an artist who can produce a sketch of what this trunk might've looked like before it was set on fire, Dave,' I explained patiently. 'We can then circulate it to the press. Someone might have remembered seeing it, or even having sold it to our murderer or murderers.'

'What a good idea,' Dave said. 'But computer graphics would probably do a better job.'

'Well, whatever,' I said. I hate computers and don't really understand them. Years ago, the police relied on an artist, and pencil and paper. And got results.

'How about the padlock, Mr Heath?'

'I doubt you'll have any better luck there, Mr Brock,' said the scientist. 'It's a standard galvanized iron padlock. Child's play to open it.'

'But not from inside the crate,' observed Dave.

'Probably not,' said Heath, giving Dave a puzzled glance.

Linda Mitchell had already told me that there were no discernible fingerprints on the padlock, so that looked like a dead end. To coin a phrase.

'So a key, if we ever found one, wouldn't necessarily belong to that lock,' I said.

'I doubt it,' said Heath. 'There's a limit to the number of permutations you can have for a two-lever padlock. And that's what that is.'

Back at Curtis Green there was a message from Henry Mortlock awaiting me to say that the post-mortem examination would take place that afternoon.

I hate autopsies, and even more do I dislike the businesslike way in which Henry approaches his job. But don't misunderstand me; there's nothing slapdash about the manner in which he does it. It's just that he's opened up so many dead bodies that he no longer thinks anything of it.

'Well, Henry, what's your opinion?' I asked when Mortlock had laid down his scalpel for the last time.

'He was dead before he was set on fire, Harry. I would say that death was caused by a single stab wound to the heart, probably at the flat you mentioned, some time between

34

say midnight on Saturday and eight o'clock Sunday morning. At a guess whoever did for him bundled him into the crate post-mortem and carted him off to Ham Common. There's evidence that petrol was poured over him *before* the crate was locked, and they probably poured a bit more over the outside just to make sure. Then, I suppose, they lit the blue touchpaper and retired immediately.'

As I have often mentioned, Henry Mortlock has a bizarre sense of humour.

Dave and I went for lunch at our favourite Italian restaurant in Westminster, and ate our way through spaghetti bolognese.

'Someone obviously had it in for our Mr Harding, Dave,' I said, finishing off the meal with vanilla ice cream.

'That is a truism, sir,' said Dave, putting two spoonfuls of sugar in his coffee.

'It looks like whoever topped him knew that Sasha Lovell wasn't going to be there on Saturday afternoon.'

'So far that looks like two people, guv. First there was Sasha herself, and then there was Dominic Finch, the photographer.'

'I reckon we can rule out Sasha,' I said. 'She was the one who alerted the police.'

'Could've been a double bluff,' said Dave crushingly. 'But we'll need to have a word with this Finch guy.'

Three

As Dave and I were going to tell Sasha Lovell that her flatmate had been murdered, we thought it might be wise to take a woman police officer with us. We drove from Henry Mortlock's carvery direct to Fulham police station, and asked the superintendent for the services of an officer from his family liaison unit. One who could stay with Sasha and provide the necessary support after we'd left her, just in case she had a touch of the vapours. It would save tying up one of my own officers.

The policewoman who eventually appeared was in her forties, and told us she'd been doing the job for five years. Although she appeared to be as tough as old boots, it turned out that there was no small element of sympathy beneath that hard exterior. When we explained what we were about to do, she just nodded, took off her uniform cravat, and put on a civilian anorak.

'Better go and do it, then, sir,' she said.

If anything, there was even more rubbish in the basement area of Harding's flat than there had been on the Sunday.

Sasha Lovell answered the door, and looked at us with a strained expression. I sensed that she knew what we were about to tell her.

'May we come in, Miss Lovell?'

Sasha didn't answer, but just turned from the door and left us to follow her into the living room.

'I'm afraid we've bad news,' I said.

'He's dead, isn't he?'

'Yes.' I'd lost count of the number of times I'd told people that their nearest and dearest had been murdered, and it got no easier with the passing years. The worst occasions were when our arrival snuffed out parents' last vestige of hope, and we told them that some depraved bastard, who should've been put down at birth, had killed their missing young child. It was made worse when you knew that, despite all the bogus promises about suppressing crime that came so glibly from the mouths of our beloved politicians, the killer would be out of the nick in a few years' time.

'What happened?' Sasha sat down on one of the worn armchairs, but remained dry-eyed. 'Have you got a cigarette?'

Dave produced his packet of Silk Cut, and his lighter.

'He was the man found on Ham Common,' I said. The newspapers had already described, in lurid detail, the discovery of the body in a burning crate on Ham Common, and I hoped that she had read about it, or seen the brief report on television. Fortunately, she had, and that saved us from having to go over it again.

'Oh God, how awful. I saw a bit about it on television last night. I never realized...' Sasha sat bunched up and tense in her chair, and puffed hungrily at her cigarette. Then the tears came. 'Why?'

'I'll make a cup of tea, love.' The family liaison officer departed in search of the kitchen to prepare the standard police panacea for all crises.

'Who would want to do such a thing?' asked Sasha.

'That's what I have to find out,' I said. 'Do you know of anyone who might've wanted to harm Mr Harding?'

'No.' Sasha stared at me, a look of bitterness on her face, as though it were the fault of the police that this had been allowed to happen. 'He didn't have any enemies, if that's what you mean. At least, none that I knew of.' But, it transpired, she did know of at least one particularly nasty enemy.

'Is there anything you can help us with? Did he owe people money, for example?' I asked, even though I thought that Harding's brutal murder would have been an extreme measure for debt. Unless it happened to be associated with drugs. Drug dealers can be very spiteful if they don't get their money.

Sasha laughed scornfully. 'He owed money all over the place,' she said, 'but I doubt if

38

the guy who runs the pub on the corner would have killed him for a few quid.'

'If you do think of anything at all, Miss Lovell, perhaps you'd give me a ring.' I handed her one of my cards, and we left her to the tender ministrations of the family liaison officer.

From Fulham, Dave and I drove the short distance to Dominic Finch's photographic studio not far from Sloane Square. But unlike Jack Harding's ramshackle place of work, Finch's studio was in a smart converted shop, the windows of which were blanked out by closed vertical blinds.

The entrance was in a small lobby, the door at right angles to the street, thus shielding whoever answered it from public gaze. It didn't take us long to find out the reason.

A young woman answered the door. She was a blonde in her twenties, and her shapely figure was covered in a flimsy sort of robe. And nothing else. She was too well-built to be a typical fashion model, and I soon discovered that she wasn't.

'I'm looking for Dominic Finch,' I said.

'You come for a session, love?' enquired this vision, looking directly at me. 'You're a bit old,' she said, and then glanced admiringly at Dave. 'He looks like he's got the body for it though.'

I sensed that Dave was about to make a facetious reply in response to these curious remarks, but fortunately he said nothing.

'No, we're police officers.'

'Oh Gawd!' The girl turned, but still held on to the door. 'Dom, there's some coppers here to see you,' she yelled, presumably, from what we saw a minute later, to give him time to stop what he was doing. But, as we also found out a minute later, he didn't care.

'Bring 'em in,' came a shout from somewhere inside the building.

The girl left us to close the door and sashayed through to a studio at the back of the premises. We followed.

'Won't keep you a moment.' Finch was lying on the floor, his camera angled up at about forty-five degrees. In front of him, on a low platform, was a naked girl in an explicit pose. 'I'm just trying to get this bloody woman to arrange herself so that I can get a half decent shot of her. Or should I say an indecent shot?' He looked up from his viewfinder. 'For God's sake, Miriam, put your hands behind your head, get your legs further apart and stick your boobs out,' he yelled. 'You're supposed to be erotic. Try to look as though you're wanted. Or even wanton.'

The model pouted and did as she was asked. 'You don't have to shout at me, Dominic,' she complained. 'And my name's Michelle.'

'Yeah, whatever.' Finch took three or four shots in quick succession. 'God alone knows how I'm supposed to create seductive art out of the sort of material I have to work with,' he muttered. He let out a sigh of cxasperation, then stood up. 'That'll have to do, darling. For Christ's sake go and put some clothes on. You'll probably look sexier covered up.'

The model poked out her tongue, stepped down from the platform on which she had been standing, and, none too hurriedly, donned a robe. Retreating to the far corner of the studio, she lit a cigarette and began complaining vociferously to the girl who'd admitted us.

'Now then, what can I do for you?' Finch switched off some of his floodlights, stood up, and turned to face us. He wore scruffy chinos and a checked shirt. Around his neck was a chunky medallion that must have hit his camera every time he bent over it. But who am I to make judgements about someone else's profession?

'I'm Detective Chief Inspector Brock of Scotland Yard, and this is Detective Sergeant Poole.'

'And what brings the long arm of the law to my humble workshop?'

'D'you do much of that?' I asked, waving a hand at the two models.

'It's not illegal,' protested Finch. 'Don't tell me that two guys from Scotland Yard have come round here to ask questions about my business. Porn Squad, are you, or just sight-seeing? If you are, you came on the wrong day. Those two are bloody useless.' He gestured towards the two models. 'Last Friday's were much better.'

'Not at all. But I was told that you were a fashion photographer.'

'Yeah, I do those too. But I have to do stuff for top-shelf girlie mags, otherwise I'd go broke.' Finch laughed savagely. 'Then I'd have to work for a living. Well, if you haven't come about my porn shots, why are you here?'

'Jack Harding,' I said.

'Oh, and what's Jack been up to?'

'You don't know?' I was surprised that Sasha Harding had not been on the phone to him, even though we had left her less than half an hour ago.

'What are you talking about?'

'He's been murdered.'

'Christ! When did this happen?'

'Sunday morning. His body was found on Ham Common.'

'Bloody hell!' Finch pulled out an old pipe and began to fill it. 'Are you saying that Jack was the guy who was burned to death in the crate? It was on the telly.'

'Yes.' I decided not to tell him that Harding was already dead when his makeshift coffin was set on fire, or that he'd been stabbed. You never tell suspects how someone was murdered. You wait for them to slip up and tell *you*. And right now, Finch was a suspect,

42

as was everyone else I spoke to.

'Who the hell would've wanted to do that?'

'That's what I'm trying to find out, Mr Finch.'

'Well, it's no good asking me. I don't know a damned thing about it.'

'We've just come from his flat in Fulham,' said Dave. 'I understand that you and Harding shared Sasha Lovell between you.' He never believed in mincing his words.

'So what? This is Chelsea, man.'

'Was there any needle between you and Harding? About the girl, I mean,' I asked.

Finch laughed. 'No. Why should there be? She's a free agent, and Jack didn't mind. Anyway, I knew her first.'

'Did she pose naked for you?'

'Yeah, of course she did. Quite a few times.' Finch leaned across and picked up a magazine. He thumbed through a few pages and showed me a revealing photograph of Sasha Lovell. 'One of my better efforts,' he said.

'And Harding didn't mind about that sort of thing?' asked Dave.

'Why should he? After all, she did the same for him, except that he put her on canvas. Bloody hard work, I call that. And in his case without much profit.'

'Can you think of anyone who might've wanted to kill Harding?' I asked.

'Not offhand.' Finch dropped the magazine on the floor, and put his unlit pipe on

43

top of it. 'She was shacked up with a guy in Docklands for a while, though,' he said thoughtfully.

'D'you know his name?'

'No. It was about a year ago that she split from him. God knows why. Apparently he'd got pots of cash, and he drove a bloody great Bentley.'

'Have you any idea where in Docklands he lived? Or where his money came from?'

'No. You'll have to ask Sasha.'

'Miss Lovell told me that she spent Saturday night with you.'

'Yeah, she did. She came round on Saturday afternoon. We did a few shots, and then spent a pleasant couple of hours in the sack. That evening we went down to a bistro in King's Road for a meal, came back here and went to bed.'

'What time did she leave?'

'I don't know. Must've been about half past nine on the Sunday morning, I suppose. She got up, made a cup of tea, and went. I couldn't understand why she wanted to split so early.'

I couldn't understand it either, but the alibi that Finch had given her more or less ruled out her participation in Harding's murder. Unless it was the other way round: that she was giving Finch the alibi, and he was responsible for the death of the man with whom she shared a flat.

I decided that we'd done enough for one

44

day, and would leave interviewing Sasha Lovell again until the following day. It proved to be a mistake.

On Tuesday morning, we arrived at Harding's basement flat at about nine o'clock. I hammered on the door several times, but got no answer. And when I peered through the windows that gave a view of the studio, there was no sign of life.

'Bugger it!' I said.

'Yes, sir,' said Dave. 'I wonder if she's with Dominic Finch.' Without waiting for my answer, he pulled out his cellphone and rang the photographer. 'She's not there, guv,' he said as he concluded the call. 'And he said he hasn't seen her since last Sunday morning when she fell out of his bed. So what do we do now?'

'It's a waste of time talking to Colonel and Mrs Smith again. Let's try one flat up.'

We climbed the stairs to the first floor, and rang a doorbell that was labelled 'Maitland'. Being nine o'clock on a Tuesday morning, I didn't expect to get a reply, but we were in luck.

'Yes?' The woman who opened the door was probably in her late thirties. She gave the pair of us a curious look, but the combination of a reasonably well-dressed white man in his forties and a scruffy black giant sometimes has that effect on people.

'We're police officers,' I said, producing my

warrant card. 'Mrs Maitland, is it?'

The woman put on a pair of glasses and peered closely at the document. 'No, it's *Miss* Maitland, actually,' she said, in a tone that implied that her marital status was none of our business. 'Davina Maitland.'

'We're enquiring into the murder of Jack Harding,' I began, as the woman finally let us in.

Davina Maitland stopped and turned so suddenly that I almost cannoned into her. 'Murdered? My God! When did this happen?' Although the newspapers and television news broadcasts had carried lengthy reports about Sunday morning's bizarre scene on Ham Common, I had deliberately not released the victim's name.

I explained the circumstances. 'We're anxious to have a word with Miss Sasha Lovell, Miss Maitland. She lived with Mr Harding in the basement.'

'Yes, I know. She was his model, wasn't she?'

'Yes, she was,' said Dave. 'Did you pose for him, by any chance?'

'No. I don't think he was into painting consultant structural engineers,' Davina said, with a crushing smile. With a wave of her hand, she invited us to take a seat. 'You're not the first to come here making enquiries about them.'

'Oh? What was that about?'

Davina sat down opposite us and crossed

her legs. 'It was about ten days ago, I suppose. Two men knocked on my door, and said that they were private enquiry agents working on behalf of a finance company. They weren't very specific, but mentioned something about debt collection. It was all a bit vague.'

'What did you tell them?' I asked.

'Nothing. They were very polite, but I don't much care for discussing my neighbours' affairs with complete strangers.'

'Did they show you any identification, Miss Maitland?'

'Not exactly. They sort of wafted a piece of official-looking paper in front of me, and then started talking.'

'What did they look like, Miss Maitland?' asked Dave, pocketbook at the ready.

'They were both about your height, I suppose, but white.' Davina Maitland looked apologetic at having to mention Dave's colour. 'One of them spoke with a foreign accent – well, actually, he was the only one who spoke – and said something about Jack Harding being in debt. It was all so vague that it made me suspicious.'

'But you sent them packing, I suppose.'

'Yes. They were quite persuasive, but they didn't get anywhere with me. I just told them I hadn't heard of Sasha or Jack. As a matter of fact, I told them I didn't know the names of anyone else who lived in the house.'

'Were Sasha Lovell and Jack Harding friends of yours, then?' asked Dave.

'No, not really. But I'd been down to their flat once or twice for a drink, and they came up here a few times. But it was nothing more than a neighbourly thing.'

'Did they ever mention anything about being in debt?'

'You only had to look round the flat to work out they hadn't got much money. After all, he was an artist, and she was a model.' Davina paused before adding her final assessment of the couple's wealth, or lack of it. 'And I'm sorry to say the wine was awful. As a matter of fact, I think it came out of a box.'

'How dreadful.' Dave nodded sagely, as though he were a wine connoisseur. But I knew he preferred Scotch and beer.

'You wouldn't know whether she's gone out, I suppose?' I asked. 'It is rather urgent that we get in touch with her.'

Davina Maitland looked from one to the other of us. 'She's left. She came up here yesterday evening and told me she was moving out straight away, and that she'd tell the letting company.'

'Did she say where she was going, Miss Maitland?'

'No, she just said that she'd had enough of living in Fulham, and that she'd found somewhere else. I can't say I'm surprised. These arty-crafty people are a bit odd, aren't

48

they?'

'I wonder why she came up here instead of telling the Smiths,' mused Dave.

Davina laughed. 'Have you met the colonel and his lady? It's no good telling them anything. They're practically gaga.'

'Yes, we've met,' I said guardedly. 'D'you have the address of the letting company?'

Davina Maitland walked across to a bureau, and scribbled a King's Road address on a piece of paper. 'I imagine she's given them the key,' she said. 'She certainly didn't leave it with me.'

I don't like estate agents. They have the audacity to regard themselves as 'professional', as though they were doctors or lawyers, and whenever you ask them for information, they talk blithely about client confidentiality.

A power-dressed young woman rose from her seat behind a desk near the door, a winning smile on her face. 'How may I help you?' she enquired.

I introduced myself, which had the effect of wiping the smile from her face. 'I'm making enquiries about Five Badajos Street, Fulham,' I said.

'We're not in the habit of discussing the affairs of our clients...' the woman began.

'For which we'll need to speak to the manager,' I said.

Without a word, the woman turned and engaged in a whispered conversation with a middle-aged man seated in a position of power. I knew it was a position of power: his desk was isolated at the far end of the office.

'How may I assist you?' asked this artificially urbane individual.

I started again, and got the same response that the woman had trotted out.

'We are conducting a murder enquiry,' said Dave, with a modicum of quiet menace in his voice. 'And we wouldn't like to think that we were being obstructed in so doing, because obstructing the police is an offence. And that would create an unnecessary diversion, because we'd have to arrest you. And we've got quite enough to do already.'

'Ah, quite so.' The manager capitulated. 'What is it that you want to know?' Then, as an afterthought, he added, 'Perhaps it would be better if you came into the office.' And without further ado, he led the way into an enclosed cabin, the walls of which were decorated with photographs of very expensive properties.

'I understand that the basement flat was rented to a Jack Harding.'

The manager opened a filing cabinet and took out a slender folder. He thumbed through it, and then looked up. 'That's correct, Chief Inspector.'

'Mr Harding was murdered last Sunday,' I said, 'as a result of which I understand that the tenancy has been terminated by Miss Sasha Lovell. Miss Lovell, as I'm sure you

50

know, shared the accommodation with Mr Harding.'

'Most irregular,' muttered the manager. 'We had not been advised that Mr Harding was sharing the flat. He should have told us. In fact, we knew nothing of this until Miss Lovell came here late yesterday afternoon and handed us the keys.' The manager glanced at his file. 'There was also the question of rent. It was in arrears to the tune of two months. We had sent several letters demanding payment.'

'You could try suing him,' said Dave, 'but I doubt you'll have much luck.'

The manager shot Dave an acid glance. 'We're going to have to make up the shortfall to our clients,' he complained. 'Unless we can open successful proceedings against this Miss Lovell.'

'Did you employ the services of a debt-collection agency?' I asked, mindful of the story that Davina Maitland had told us about the two men who'd called on her.

'Certainly not.' From the tart way in which the manager replied, the idea was clearly anathema to him. 'But we have now instructed this agency's solicitor to seek an eviction order.'

'Bit late for that,' commented Dave.

'Did Miss Lovell give you a forwarding address?' I asked.

Once again, the manager sought refuge in his paperwork. 'She gave us an address in

Earwold Avenue, Orpington.' He obligingly wrote it down for us on a small sheet of paper bearing the name and address of his agency and a meaningless logo that must've cost thousands to design. 'I hope that Mr Harding's murder won't attract unwelcome publicity for our company,' he said.

'I don't suppose it will,' said Dave. 'Unless it was you who murdered him.'

'We'd like to borrow the keys for an hour or so,' I said. 'We need to have a look round the flat.'

'Don't you need a warrant for that?' asked the manager hesitantly, his hands fluttering nervously in front of him.

'No,' said Dave, somewhat aggressively I thought.

The manager obviously thought it was aggressive, too. He moved quickly across the office to a keyboard and handed them over.

'Thank you for your assistance,' said Dave, and smiled disarmingly.

Four

I didn't know what I expected to find in Harding's basement flat at Badajos Street, but right now we were clutching at straws. And there weren't too many around to clutch at.

We started with the studio, looking for things we hadn't noticed on our two previous visits. The same unfinished portrait of Sasha, posing as 'Woman with Grecian Urn', was still on the easel.

'Harding doesn't seem to have had much luck selling these,' commented Dave, as he looked through the stack of six or seven canvases that rested against a wall. All but one were completed depictions of an unclothed Sasha Lovell in various artistic poses; the other was of a young woman neither of us recognized. I made a note to have it photographed; if we were able to find her, she might just give us another lead.

There was a small bureau against the wall behind the door, and Dave leaped at it with enthusiasm. There is often much to be learned from a victim's paperwork, but, unfortunately, in this case we learned very little.

The bureau was as untidy as the rest of the flat. Dave pulled out a clutch of unpaid bills, two of which were demands from the letting agency. As the estate agent had promised, there was a threatening letter from a firm of solicitors warning Harding that unless arrears of rent were paid within twenty-eight days proceedings would be taken. There was also a letter from a credit card company advising that credit facilities were being withdrawn until the outstanding balance of £2,304.71 was settled.

I enjoy jousting with credit card companies, and I was going to enjoy telling them they weren't going to get it.

Next, Dave produced a 'red' demand from the electricity company, and another from the telephone company.

'This might mean something, guv,' said Dave, holding a letter.

'What is it?'

'It's a letter from someone called Sofia, and it's addressed to "Dear Jack".'

'What's it say?' I asked.

'Just some drivel about how she's getting on, and how she's missing him. She hopes his painting is going well, and asks when he's likely to return to Rome.'

'Is there an address on it, Dave?'

'No, it's just headed Rome, and the English isn't too good. I suspect that the writer's probably Italian.'

'Any correspondence relating to Sasha?' I

asked.

'Nothing, guv, and looking at this lot, I reckon our friend Harding was on his beam-ends,' said Dave, as usual understating the glaringly obvious. 'But this doesn't make much sense.' He held up a slip of paper.

'What is it?'

'It's a cheque for twenty-five quid from a Chelsea art gallery, presumably for one of his paintings. But it hasn't been paid in. Now why would a guy in desperate need of cash not pay in a cheque?'

'What's the date on it, Dave?'

'A month ago, guv.' Dave put the cheque back into the bureau.

'No, hang on to it,' I said. 'We might have a word with that gallery. See if the owner can explain it.'

'It looks as though those two guys that Davina Maitland told us about could have been genuine debt-collectors after all,' said Dave. 'And judging by the state of Harding's finances, they could've been acting for almost any one of a dozen creditors.'

We moved on to the couple's bedroom, a small, untidy room at the rear of the flat. The bed was unmade, and clothing was spread about. Surprisingly, much of it was female attire, and it seemed to indicate that Sasha had left in one hell of a hurry. Unless it belonged to another woman; the unidentified woman in the other portrait perhaps?

The shower room and the tiny kitchenette

55

were also a mess, but told us nothing that we didn't already know: Jack Harding and Sasha Lovell were unlikely to win a good-housekeeping award.

'We shall go to Orpington,' I announced.

'What a good idea, *sir*,' said Dave.

The eighteen miles from Chelsea to Orpington do not constitute a happy experience, but it had to be done. It was not improved by the pouring rain, nor the fact that the windscreen wipers on the Job car needed replacing.

I wanted to know why Sasha Lovell had suddenly upped sticks and left Fulham in such a rush, and I also wanted to know the identity of the mysterious Docklands resident with whom she'd been living until a year ago. It could also be that Sasha might shed some light on the two heavies who'd posed questions about Harding's debts when they had called on Davina Maitland.

The house in Earwold Avenue (where the hell do they get these names?) was a typical three-up-two-down semi in the heart of dormitory Kent.

I was surprised that a woman answered the door. Not so much that it was a woman, but that anyone at all was at home in the middle of the day on a Tuesday. Orpington is an area of suburbia where the wives have to work as well as the husbands in order to pay the mortgage. And to pay the instalments on the four-by-four. And the fees for second-rate private education for the children. And the subscription to the golf club.

'We're looking for Miss Sasha Lovell,' I said.

'No one of that name lives here.' A mocking smile on the woman's face implied that there were two idiots on her doorstep. 'I think you must have the wrong address. What was it about?'

'We're police officers, madam. I was led to believe that Miss Lovell had moved in here either today, or late yesterday.'

'I'm sorry, but I've never heard of her.' The mocking smile remained, confirming what she had always thought about the bumbling police.

I handed the woman one of my cards. 'Perhaps you'd ask her to call me if she does turn up.' Not that I harboured any illusions that she would. 'It's a murder enquiry.'

Unfazed by this announcement, the woman took the small piece of pasteboard, glanced at it, and tucked it in the pocket of her denim skirt. 'I can't imagine that she will. We don't take paying guests,' she added, somewhat haughtily, and shut the door. Presumably she was anxious to get rid of us before the hidden eyes behind the twitching net curtains of Orpington wondered what this black and white duo was doing on her doorstep.

'Well, that was a blow-out,' said Dave, 'but

it doesn't surprise me.'

'Nor me, Dave,' I said as we drove off.

'Either she doesn't want to be found by us, or she's running from creditors. Or both. But whichever way it is, I reckon she just plucked that Orpington address out of thin air.'

The computer graphics wizard had made a good job of producing a depiction of what our partly burned box might have looked like before it and Jack Harding had been set alight. I'd enlisted the aid of the Yard's public relations branch, and on Wednesday morning a photograph of the box was published by most organs of the national press, and broadcast by television stations.

In the meantime, I set DC John Appleby the task of doing General Register Office searches on Sasha Lovell and Jack Harding. And, just for good measure, Dominic Finch, the photographer.

The picture of the burned box produced a result rather quicker than I'd expected. A man called Middleton telephoned from Tooting, and told Colin Wilberforce that he was in the woodwork business and made boxes like the one published in the press.

'Yeah, I'm Ted Middleton. You come about the box, have you?' asked the carpenter when we arrived at his workshop not far from Tooting Common. The place was a shambles. Lengths of wood stood against the walls, or lay higgledy-piggledy in assorted piles, and the floor was covered in sawdust. It appeared to my untutored eye that the tools of his trade were littered about all over the place, but I've no doubt he knew the location of every one of them.

'What can you tell us about it?' I asked, once introductions had been effected.

'It looks very much like the ones I make. I made one for a gent in Southwark a couple of months ago. He was off on a trip up the Amazon or somewhere, and wanted a box to stow all his technical gear in. It had to be five foot by three foot by two, with handles at both ends, so he said. Anyway, I thought there might be a market for 'em, so I chanced an advert in the press, and I've been turning 'em out fairly regular ever since.' Middleton ran his hand over a similar box that had almost been finished. 'They're a bit of a work of art, them is,' he said proudly.

'How many have you sold?' asked Dave.

Middleton scratched his head. 'About a half a dozen, give or take.'

'Do you have a list of the people you sold them to?'

'Yeah. This bleedin' VAT's a nightmare, I can tell you. Have to write everything down these days, or the inspectors will turn the place upside-down.'

'I thought they had,' said Dave, glancing around the workshop.

Middleton wiped his hands on his apron, crossed to an old desk and pulled open a drawer. 'Here we are. Seven I've knocked out. Want the names?'

'Yes, please.' I took the list, and handed it to Dave to copy.

'No way to treat a decent bit of joinery, putting a body in it and setting fire to it,' complained Middleton.

'There's one on here that's got no name against it,' said Dave.

'I remember that bloke,' Middleton replied. 'He paid in readies, but never give me no name. Between you and me, I knocked off the VAT for cash, so I only charged him two hundred and fifty quid. But you're not interested in any of that, are you, guv'nor?'

As a law enforcement officer, I deemed it impolitic to reply, even though I couldn't have cared less. 'Is there a date for that anonymous transaction, Dave?'

'Yes, sir. The fifteenth of August this year.'

I turned back to the carpenter. 'Can you describe the man who bought that box, Mr Middleton?'

Middleton sucked through his teeth. 'I dunno as I can,' he said. 'About your height, I s'pose, with black hair and a thin moustache. That's about all I can tell you. Oh, and he was wearing sunglasses.'

'Sounds like a Mafioso,' commented Dave.

Although Dave had intended it as a joke – I think – I had to admit that he might be right. Had Harding been involved in something that we knew nothing about as yet? If it was drugs, then he couldn't have been doing too well at it. I've not come across a penniless drug dealer before.

'Did you deliver this box?' I asked, hoping for the hopeless.

'Nah! Anyone who wants any of my stuff has to collect it themselves.'

'How did he take it away, then?'

'In a car.' Middleton gave me a look that implied that the purchaser's manner of transportation was obvious. 'He wouldn't have been able to carry it on his back,' he added, with a throaty chuckle.

'You didn't happen to note the number, I suppose?' ventured Dave, knowing full well what the answer would be.

'Nah! I give up collecting car numbers when I was a kid.'

'Well, what sort of car was it?'

'A black Volvo estate,' said Middleton promptly. 'Got one meself, see. Last year's model, I reckon.'

'Yours, or his?' Dave always had to get things right, thank God.

'His, of course. But I'll tell you something...'

'That'd be useful,' Dave commented drily.

'Its lights never come on.'

'What d'you mean, it lights didn't come on?'

'When you turn on a Volvo's engine, the

headlights always come on, automatic like. You'll notice it next time you see one. Always got their headlights on.' Middleton picked at his teeth with a matchstick. 'They're Swedish, see. I reckon the Swedes must be a bit short-sighted, or something. Can't see another car unless it's got its lights on,' he added with a cackle. 'But you can have 'em fixed so's they don't come on, and I reckon that's what he'd had done.'

I issued another of my little cards. 'If this man should come back, perhaps you'd note the number and give me a ring,' I said. 'Without letting him know we're interested in him.' Not that I thought it likely that the man who'd bought the box would be planning another burning corpse job. Well, I hoped not. Or, if he were, that he'd do it in another police area.

'Well, that shouldn't be too difficult, guv,' said Dave, on the way back to Curtis Green. 'All we've got to do now is find a black Volvo estate with lights that don't come on, driven by a black-haired bloke with a moustache and sunglasses.'

I gave DS Tom Challis the task of checking out the list of named purchasers of Ted Middleton's boxes.

'I don't think there's anything in it, Tom,' I said, 'but if you get the chance, take a look at their boxes yourself. Invent some fanny about why we've taken a sudden interest in wooden boxes, but if they're fly enough, they'll know why. Oh, and ask if they own a Volvo.'

John Appleby had been busy on the computer to the General Register Office at Stockport, and had come up with a surprising piece of information. Sasha Lovell was married.

'Let's have the details, John,' I said.

'Born Sasha Lovell, sir, she's twenty-eight years of age, and four years ago she was married to a Georges Gaillard, three years her senior. His occupation was shown as a golf professional of Le Touquet.' Appleby looked up. 'That's in France, sir.'

'Yes, John, I know.' Some years ago, I'd visited the resort on the north coast of France, just south of Boulogne. I knew it boasted several golf courses, and they'd even named a road the 'Avenue du Golf'. Not that I've ever played the game; it seems a bit pointless to me. 'Was there an address for him?'

'Yes, sir. Twenty-seven rue Gascoigne, Le Touquet.'

'I suppose it's possible he's still there now, and she might be there with him,' pondered Dave. 'Worth a trip, guv?'

I laughed. 'I can just see the commander giving the okay for that. No, Dave, we'll have to rely on the French police to make some enquiries for us.'

Interpol is all very well, but it takes forever

63

and a day to get an answer. However, I had a friend in the Paris Police, *Inspecteur* Henri Deshayes, who could probably be persuaded to point me in the right direction. I always use the old boy net whenever I can. Unfortunately, a visit to Paris was out of the question, but maybe just as well. The last time I was there, my girlfriend Gail got into a discussion with Henri's wife Gabrielle, a former dancer at the Folies Bergère, about the best Paris fashion houses at which to buy clothes. Need I say more?

'Colin, send one of those computer letters you're so good at.'

'What about, sir?' Colin Wilberforce turned to the computer, tapped a few keys and brought up something called 'Create Mail'.

'Ask Inspector Henri Deshayes in Paris who I should talk to in Le Touquet about this golf professional that Sasha Lovell is married to. If she still is.' I turned to Appleby. 'Did you check in the divorce registry, John?'

'There was nothing to indicate that they'd been divorced, sir, but as she's using her maiden name again, I suppose that they could have got a decree in France. I don't really know what the law is now, what with the European Union.'

'Nor do I,' I muttered.

'I wonder if this guy who bought the box is the mysterious Docklands resident who was

64

mentioned by Dominic Finch,' said Dave. 'Or even the French golfer.'

'I did a check on Dominic Finch too, sir,' said Appleby. 'Born thirty-seven years ago in Bermondsey. Married and divorced.'

'By the way, sir,' said Colin Wilberforce, 'we've received the report from the fire brigade.'

'Anything startling in it, Colin?'

'The accelerant is confirmed as petrol, poured liberally over the body and the box,' said Colin, reading from the report. 'The fire investigator is of the opinion that there was a slight breeze that morning which, rather than fanning the flames, tended to extinguish them.'

'Well, that doesn't really tell us anything we didn't know,' Dave concluded.

Dominic Finch was not pleased to see us. Once again he was in the middle of taking a series of risqué shots of a naked bimbo who doubtless thought that this sort of exposure was the first rung on the unstable ladder to stardom.

'Be nice to be able to get on with this,' Finch complained. 'I'll be with you when I've finished.'

He spent the next few minutes trying to persuade his pouting model to adopt a more explicit pose, giving instructions that were larded with obscenities. Finally he declared himself reasonably satisfied and dismissed the girl whom he called 'Trish', although that was probably not her name.

'Now then, what can I do for you, Chief Inspector?'

'Did you know that Sasha Lovell was married, Mr Finch?'

'Yeah. To some French guy, but she left him about two or three years ago, I think. Apparently he was in the habit of beating her up.'

'It would have been helpful if you'd mentioned that last time we were here,' said Dave, who was never happy with reticent witnesses.

'Didn't think it was relevant,' said Finch dismissively.

'Did you ever meet him?' I asked.

'No. Saw a pretty poor photograph of him though. Whoever took it got the light all wrong.'

'Yes, but I'm not here to discuss the photographer's lack of professional expertise. What did he look like in this snapshot?'

Finch appeared to be offended by the term 'snapshot'. 'Seemed to be a tall, well-built guy with a thin moustache and slicked back hair. Looked a smarmy sort of git to me.'

'How was he dressed?' Dave had his pocketbook out.

Finch laughed. 'He wasn't. It was taken on a beach somewhere and he was wearing poofy little swimming trunks that tied up at the sides with bootlaces. Typically French, what there was of it.'

'D'you know if he ever came to this country? Or did Sasha live in France with him?' I knew he must've been here on at least one occasion; Appleby's research had shown the couple to have been married in Wandsworth.

'She said that he had a place in somewhere called Paris-Plage, wherever that is.'

'It's Le Touquet,' said Dave. 'Full name Le Touquet Paris-Plage.'

'Well, fancy that,' said Finch sarcastically. 'You learn something every day.'

'Did she ever say how they met?' I persisted. It was hard work getting answers out of Finch.

'No, she never talked much about him, except to say that when they split she came back to England. It wasn't long after that she got into a relationship with this rich guy in Docklands who I mentioned the other day.'

'And you don't remember anything about him.'

'It's not that I don't remember,' said Finch. 'I didn't know anything about him *to* remember.'

We left Dominic Finch to his enviable task of photographing nudes, and made our way to the art gallery that had paid Jack Harding twenty-five pounds for one of his paintings.

Having explained the reason for our visit,

John Clarke, the man who owned the gallery, had taken us into a storeroom, switched on overhead floods, and dragged a full-length portrait of Sasha Lovell from behind a stack of canvases. Because Dave and I had viewed Harding's other paintings in his dimly lit basement flat, we didn't appreciate just how bad they really were. But here, in the harsh light, it was apparent how poor this one was. And I'm no art expert.

'I understand you paid twenty-five pounds for it,' I said, taking the gallery's cheque from Dave and showing it to the owner.

'Sometimes you take a chance in this business,' said Clarke. 'I could see that it had been painted over another one, and I wondered whether the one underneath might be worth more than the one on top. But I had it x-rayed, and it wasn't. In fact it was probably one of Harding's earlier efforts.'

'Have you any idea why Mr Harding didn't cash the cheque, Mr Clarke?'

'Yes. I rang him up, and told him I'd cancelled it. Having had a good look at his daubing, I realized that it wasn't even worth five quid, let alone twenty-five. But I did tell him that if I ever sold it, he'd get whatever I got for it, less my commission. I do occasionally get people in here who aren't connoisseurs and might buy something like that just because it's a nude. I should care.' Clarke let out a hollow laugh. 'Mind you, now that he's been murdered, it could fetch

68

quite a bit. I might even put it up for auction – once you've caught the bloke who did it.'

'How did you come to meet Harding?' I asked.

, 'It's the sort of thing that happens all the time. Ask any gallery owner. The guy just strolled in here one day, said he was a painter, and wanted to know if I'd be interested in any of his work. I told him to bring something in for me to look at, and he brought that.' Clarke gestured at the painting. 'Sometimes you discover an unknown talent, but not in this case. To be honest with you, Chief Inspector, Jack Harding would've been better off painting houses rather than portraits.'

'Did you ever meet his model?' asked Dave. 'That's her,' he added, pointing at the canvas.

Clarke shook his head. 'No, and if I had to rely on that, I doubt I'd recognize her if I met her in the street.'

Having had enough of dead ends for one day, we returned to Curtis Green.

'There's an email from Inspector Deshayes, sir,' said Colin Wilberforce, flourishing a printout.

I scanned the message. Apart from suggesting that we meet again in the near future for a few cognacs, Henri told me that the man to talk to was *Inspecteur* Alain Leduc of the Le Touquet police. He was apparently an old golfing friend of Henri, and would be happy to assist.

But that, I decided, was a job for tomorrow.

Five

I reached home at about seven-thirty – early for a detective – and decided to ring Gail and suggest dinner somewhere.

There was yet another note from Gladys Gurney, my cleaning lady. Gladys is an absolute treasure, and I don't know why she puts up with me.

> Dear Mr Brock
> There are some of your shirts what need buttons putting on. I had a good look round for your button box but I don't know where you've hid it. If you leave it out for me I'll sew them on. If I've got time.
> Yours faithfully
> Gladys Gurney (Mrs)

I set aside the problem of not having a button box, rang Gail, and got the okay for dinner. I left my car where it was, and walked to her townhouse in Kingston, secure in

70

the knowledge that I was going to have a few drinks. I had no desire to be caught by the Black Rats – otherwise known as the traffic police – who would like nothing better than to catch a CID officer with a positive breathalyser reading.

Gail, who was wearing a pair of what she called 'bootleg' jeans and a hip-length, grey roll-neck sweater with a loose-fitting belt, insisted on our having a drink before we went in search of food. But eventually we got under way.

It was a beautiful September evening, and we strolled along the Thames riverbank into the town centre.

'I like your anorak,' I commented, nodding at her sleeveless jacket. I do like to curry favour with my girlfriend.

'It's not an anorak,' said Gail, with a sigh at my ignorance of haute couture. 'It's a quilted gilet.'

'Oh well, whatever,' I said.

'And how are you getting on with your body in a box?' Gail had become far more blasé about my job since our first meeting a few years ago. Living the fantasy of the theatre, as she was then, I think it had come as a shock to her that someone she'd known actually got murdered for real. But the brutal killing, a few years ago, of her chorus-line colleague Patricia Hunter had dragged her into the sordid world of violent crime.

'Not very well,' I said. 'The woman he was

shacked up with has vanished, and we haven't a clue where she's gone. The address she left with the letting agent turned out to be false, so she could be anywhere. I just hope she doesn't turn up dead too.'

Gail stopped briefly to watch a school rowing eight going upstream. 'What gorgeous young men,' she sighed, and turned to face me. 'In my experience,' she said, 'girls who are in trouble usually make for their parents' place.'

Once again my lovely actress had proved that she would have made quite a good detective.

I pulled out my mobile and called Gavin Creasey, the night-duty sergeant in charge of the incident room. 'Gavin, see if you can find out where Sasha Lovell's parents live, preferably by first thing tomorrow morning.'

'Can we now get on with the business of finding somewhere to eat, darling?' said Gail impatiently, once I'd finished my call.

We made small talk over dinner, and returned to her place. I had far more brandies than was good for me, and then we went to bed.

I arrived at the office with a hangover, and rang through to the incident room. 'Is there anyone in this outfit who speaks French, Colin?'

'Yes, sir. Sheila Armitage.'

'Good. Send her in. And ask her to bring

some coffee.'

'By the way, sir, Gavin left details of Sasha Lovell's parents' address on your desk. At least, it was the one that John Appleby turned up on her birth certificate. It's a long shot, I know, but I suppose they might still live there.'

'Thanks, Colin. I'll deal with that once I've got Sheila to have a word with this French copper in Le Touquet.'

'You wanted me, sir?' DC Armitage appeared in the doorway bearing a cup of the much-needed coffee. She was a rather plain girl with short, blonde hair, and was a damned good detective.

'Colin tells me you speak French.'

'Yes, sir.' Sheila placed the coffee on my desk. 'One sugar, sir,' she said. 'That's right, isn't it?'

'Thank you.' I drew the coffee towards me, and stirred it before ferreting around in my desk for an aspirin. 'I want you to ring Inspector Alain Leduc of the Le Touquet police, Sheila. Tell him that our mutual friend Inspector Deshayes of the Paris police suggested I get in touch.'

'What d'you want to know, sir?'

'Ask him if he would be so good as to make enquiries about a Georges Gaillard at...' I shuffled through the bits of paper on my desk until I found the piece with his address on it. 'Twenty-seven rue Gascoigne. This guy's a golf professional and is – or was –

73

married to Sasha Lovell. I'm interested to know if they're divorced or, more to the point, whether she's with him now. As you know, Sasha's disappeared, and I need to talk to her again.'

Sheila looked up from the notes she'd been making. 'If she's there, sir, d'you want this inspector to ask her any questions?'

'No, and I'd rather she didn't know of our interest. That's a bit of a tall order, but if he can fabricate some duff story about work permits, or something of the sort, it might stop her from doing a runner again.'

'She wouldn't need a work permit in the European Union, sir,' Sheila said rather smugly, 'but I'll get on to it straightaway.'

The address that Appleby had turned up for Sasha's parents was in Wandsworth, and she'd been married to Georges Gaillard at the register office there. It looked hopeful. But despite what Gail had said about wayward girls rushing home to their parents, I decided to await any information that might be forthcoming from *Inspecteur* Leduc.

Surprisingly, Sheila Armitage returned twenty minutes later with an answer.

'You were quick, Sheila. Was he out?'

'No, sir, he was there. He knew the name Georges Gaillard as soon as I mentioned it. Gaillard is dead.'

'Oh! Did someone murder him?' I asked jocularly.

'Not exactly, sir. He died about two years

74

ago. It was an accident that Inspector Leduc investigated. It seems Gaillard was out on the golf course when he was struck on the head by a golf ball. Killed instantly. M'sieur Leduc said that Gaillard apparently had a thinner skull than average.'

'I wonder if Sasha Lovell played golf,' I mused.

Denver Street, Wandsworth, a turning off Garratt Lane, consisted of pokey little terraced council houses, circa 1950. Number fourteen looked like all the others. Unwashed curtains hung at dirty windows, but there was a satellite television dish screwed to the front of the property I hoped was Sasha's parents' house.

The man who answered the door was attired – if that's the word – in jeans and a filthy singlet. He was, I suppose, about fifty-two years of age. For a moment or two, he stared at us suspiciously. I sensed that he knew instinctively that we were police officers, and that the arrival of the law on his doorstep boded ill. I also sensed that his bulging pectorals were the result of weight training in one of Her Majesty's prisons.

'Mr Stanley Lovell?'

'Yeah? Watcha want? Whatever it is, I ain't buying it.'

Amazing! After twenty-eight years, Sasha's parents still lived in the same house.

'We're police officers, Mr Lovell,' I said, a

statement that probably came as no surprise.

'Oh yeah.'

'I'd like to talk to you about your daughter Sasha.'

'Watcha want to know about that little bitch?' As an apparent afterthought, Lovell invited us in, albeit reluctantly.

'Is she here?' I asked, once we'd been escorted into the front room. It was not the most salubrious of living rooms: untidy, dirty and furnished with cheap armchairs and a sofa. In one corner of this tip, however, a state-of-the-art plasma television dominated the room.

'No, she ain't, and she ain't welcome, neither.'

'Oh? Why's that?'

'She got married to some golf-playing Frog bastard. Never invited us to the wedding, neither. Even though it was here in Wandsworth down the registry office in the town hall. The missus, God rest her soul,' said Lovell, glancing briefly at the photograph of a harridan on the sideboard, 'was quite cut up about it.' He took a half-smoked cigarette from behind his ear, lit it, coughed, and sighed. 'Then she took up with some artist geezer. Quite happy to take all her clothes off and stand around naked while he painted pictures of her. Downright disgusting, I call it.'

'When did you last see your daughter, Mr Lovell?' asked Dave.

'About six weeks ago, I reckon. She come round here trying to touch me for a few quid. The bloody nerve of the girl, me working on the railways as a track worker, an' all. Think I'm made of money, does she? I sent her packing. I told her she'd made her bed and she could lie on it. Or anyone else's bed for that matter.' It suddenly occurred to Lovell to ask why we were there. 'Watcha want her for, anyhow?'

'The man she was living with was murdered.'

'D'you think she done it, then?'

'We know that she didn't, Mr Lovell,' I said, even though I hadn't ruled out the possibility that she might've had something to do with it, 'but we need to speak to her urgently. She may have some information about the man that will enable us to catch his killer.' I didn't mention that we'd already seen her, but that she'd disappeared before we could talk to her again. That would sound like sloppy police work, and these days we get enough criticism without asking for it.

Lovell ran a hand round his chin. ''Ere, it wasn't that Eyetie she was shacked up with, was it?'

'What Italian?' This was new information.

'Some bloke she had a fling with. Lived down the East End, I think she said. But that was about a year ago. Seems to go in for foreigners does our Sasha.'

'Have you any idea of this Italian's name,

Mr Lovell? And might it have been Docklands where he lived?'

'Sorry, squire, I can't help you there. And I've no idea where she is now.'

'D'you know where she was living when she came to see you six weeks ago?'

'Nah! She never said, and I never asked. Not interested, see.'

'How did you know she was working as an artist's model, then?'

'She told me. Sounded quite proud of it, an' all. Model, my arse. I reckon the silly little cow's on the game.'

'Aren't you working at the moment?' asked Dave. He was always interested in the activities of men who looked as though they'd been in prison, or were likely to be in the near future.

'Nah, I'm nights, see.'

'I hope we didn't wake you,' I said, aware that policemen on night duty usually went straight to bed when they'd finished their tour.

'Not this time, no. I'm day off tomorrow, so I'll likely stay up all day. Probably have a pint or two and a game of darts down the local before I turn in.'

The next step was to place Sasha Lovell's name on the Police National Computer, and circulate her details to all ports and airports. I was beginning to think that her disappearance might be more sinister than merely

78

escaping from her creditors. Although she had attempted to borrow money from her father, I was not altogether convinced that shortage of funds was a sufficient reason to vanish. Perhaps I was right in my original theory that she and Dominic Finch, the photographer, had been responsible for Jack Harding's death, and they provided each other with a mutual alibi. Maybe Sasha was fed up with Harding, but that Harding had threatened her with violence if she left him. However, that didn't call for a killing that smacked of a gangland show murder.

I was regrettably drawn to the conclusion that we were getting nowhere, and that there was more to Harding's character and background that we'd not even remotely discovered. It was time to start digging. Finding this mysterious Italian that Sasha's father had mentioned would be a start, but, as Dave pointed out, that was a needle in a haystack job. Italians in the East End of London weren't exactly thin on the ground.

'Did you turn up anything on Harding when you did the searches at the General Register Office, John?'

'Yes, sir.' DC Appleby seemed surprised at the question; surprised probably that I hadn't asked for them until now. 'The details are filed in the incident room with Sergeant Wilberforce. I'll get them.'

Seconds later, Appleby was back. 'He was

twenty-five years old, born in Liverpool the son of Frank and Marcia Harding.'

'Ask the Liverpool police if they're still at the address shown on the birth certificate.'

It took about half an hour.

'The Hardings' house in Liverpool was demolished fifteen years ago as part of a redevelopment, sir,' said Appleby. 'There's no way of finding out where they went from there.'

Well, that came as no surprise.

I glanced across the incident room to where Tom Challis was sitting.

'Any results from your wooden box enquiries, Tom?' I asked.

'Yes and no, guv,' said Challis. 'I traced all six of Ted Middleton's other customers. Five of them still had their boxes, but the sixth guy – according to his housekeeper – went abroad on the thirtieth of August, and isn't expected back until next week. I've arranged to follow it up just in case he's spinning a fanny. Oh, and none of them own Volvos.'

And that looked very much like another avenue of enquiry closing down.

On the basis that Davina Maitland might have been at work all day – although our last visit seemed to indicate that she worked at home – we left it until half past six before returning to Badajos Street to see her.

'I've not been in very long,' she said, confirming what I'd thought. But she'd been in long enough to change into a kaftan, and pour herself the glass of red wine she was holding when she answered the door. 'Do come in.'

We followed her into her sitting room, accepted a seat, but refused her offer of wine.

'When we spoke to you previously, Miss Maitland, you told us that you'd occasionally socialized with Jack Harding and Sasha Lovell.'

'That's right. We had drinks or a meal together from time to time, either up here or down there.' Davina added a defensive rider. 'But there was nothing more to it than that.'

I suppose she was wondering whether I suspected her of some sexual relationship with Harding, or even with Sasha. As if the police would be interested in that.

'Did Jack Harding ever mention anything about his background?' I asked. 'We know he was born in Liverpool, but beyond that we've learned very little.'

'I know he spent some time in Rome.'

'You're sure it was Rome ... or was it perhaps Paris-Plage?' I asked, mindful of Sasha's previous connection with the place.

'No, definitely Rome.' Davina inclined her head and gave me a strange, almost pitying look, as though I had a hearing problem.

'Did he say when he was in Rome?'

'It was some years ago, I believe. He said he'd always wanted to be an artist, and as he

81

was interested in the Italian school, Rome was the place to go. Personally, I would've thought Venice would've been better. He was terribly enthusiastic about it, and went on at some length about the Renaissance period. Once he got started, he'd bandy names about like Raphael, Michelangelo and Leonardo, and describe their work. It got quite boring at times. However, that said, I got the impression that he didn't fare too well over there because he told me he came back to this country just over a year ago.'

I dismissed the idea of enlisting the help of the Italian police; getting information about an itinerant English artist in Rome who'd left there twelve months or more previously would be impossible. There was, however, the letter headed Rome and signed Sofia that we'd found among Harding's papers, but that was no use without an address.

'Did he ever mention his parents, Miss Maitland?'

'No, not really. I seem to recall him telling me that they lived in Guildford, but apart from that he had nothing to say about them. I sensed that he didn't get on with them because when I asked him about them, he changed the subject.'

'Did Sasha Lovell ever mention anything about knowing an Italian, Miss Maitland?' asked Dave. 'Or having an affair with one?'

'An Italian?' Davina raised an eyebrow and

smiled. 'No. All she said was that she'd met Jack through a photographer friend of hers a year or two back.'

'I don't suppose she's been in touch with you again since she left, has she?' I asked.

'No, she hasn't. I gave her my phone number, but I've heard nothing. But then I didn't really expect to. She and Jack weren't bosom friends of mine. We were just ships that pass in the night.'

'If she should happen to ring you, Miss Maitland,' I said, 'perhaps you'd dial one-four-seven-one when you've finished speaking to her, and then let me know the number she called from. It might help us to trace her, and we need to speak to her again.'

Davina Maitland seemed a little mystified by my request, but agreed to ring me if she did get a call from Sasha.

I had little hope that Sasha Lovell would ring Davina Maitland, or that Davina would remember to trace the number if she did. Furthermore, there was always the possibility that Sasha would ring from a 'withheld' number or, more likely, a cellphone. But when the road you've taken turns out to be a cul-de-sac, you've got to go back to the crossroads and start again.

Next was the problem of finding Jack Harding's parents. But trying to find people called Harding living somewhere in the Guildford area would be a nightmare, apart from which they may have moved again.

I had not authorized the release of Jack Harding's name, so his parents wouldn't have heard of his murder through the media.

We had carried out a thorough search of the basement flat at Badajos Street, but despite sifting carefully through all Harding's paperwork, we had found nothing to indicate where his parents lived. We didn't even know if they were still alive. It is not pleasant for parents to learn of a son's murder from the newspapers or television, but I could see no alternative.

Back at Curtis Green, I telephoned my contact in the Department of Public Affairs and asked him to reveal Harding's identity to journalists.

Six

The details of Jack Harding's murder had been released early enough for them to appear in Friday morning's newspapers. They also carried a plea for Harding's parents – believed to live in Guildford – to contact police as soon as possible.

It brought a result almost immediately, but one that merely complicated our administrative procedures further.

At eight thirty, a man named Ian Carter telephoned the Yard. He explained that he was on a train on his way to work, and had just read the account that identified Harding. He claimed to be a next-door neighbour of the Hardings in Guildford, but went on to say that they were in Portugal for three weeks' holiday.

His message was relayed to our incident room, and Colin Wilberforce took a note of Carter's address, and that he would be at home from seven that evening onwards. Ever thorough, Colin then checked the electoral roll and confirmed that Ian Carter did indeed live next door to a couple called Frank and Marcia Harding at Scat's Hill Avenue, Guildford.

Ian Carter was a grey man in every way: grey suit, grey hair, and a pallid, greying complexion. Even his spectacles had grey frames. By contrast, his wife Yvonne was a vivacious, attractive blonde, who looked to be some fifteen years or so her husband's junior.

'This is a terrible business,' said Carter as we settled in the spacious sitting room of his elegant house. 'May I offer you a drink?'

'No thank you, sir,' I said.

'You don't mind if I do, do you?'

'Not at all.'

I waited while Ian Carter crossed to a sofa table and poured himself a sherry and prepared a gin and tonic for his wife. Alongside the bottles and glasses, I noticed that the Carters had displayed photographs of a young man and a young woman. Each was suitably gowned, and pictured at what I imagined to be a university graduation ceremony.

'When did the Hardings leave for Portugal, Mr Carter?' I asked.

Carter glanced at his wife, raising a questioning eyebrow. I got the impression that he deferred to her in most things.

'It was last Monday,' said Yvonne Carter. 'From what I've seen in the paper, that was the day after young Jack was killed. Is that right?'

'That would be correct,' I said. 'Have you any idea where they are in Portugal?'

'The Algarve, I believe, somewhere near Albufeira. It's where they usually go.'

'Do you have any way of getting in touch with them?'

'I don't know where they're staying, but we have their mobile phone number. Is that any help?'

'Maybe,' I said doubtfully. I didn't much care for the idea of giving Harding's parents the news of their son's shocking death by so impersonal a method as a cellphone.

Dave made a note of the number in his pocketbook. 'The Portuguese police might be able to locate it with direction-finding apparatus, sir,' he said. I hoped he was right, but Dave knows far more about these technological gadgets than I do. 'On the other hand, they could just ring and make an appointment to see them.'

It does help to have a clever sergeant.

'Would I be right in thinking that Mr and Mrs Harding didn't have very much contact with their son, Mr Carter?' I suggested.

Ian Carter glanced at his wife again, and again it was she who answered.

'No, they didn't, Chief Inspector. I think there was some sort of rift between them. We didn't enquire too deeply. After all, it was none of our business, but I believe he went to Rome some years ago with the idea of becoming a painter. As I understand it, they've not heard from him since. I rather got the impression that they didn't even know if he was still there.' Yvonne Carter thought about that for a moment. 'But obviously he did come back,' she said.

'Was Jack their only child?' I asked.

'As far as I know,' said Yvonne.

'What's Mr Harding's profession, Mrs Carter?' asked Dave.

But this time it was Ian Carter who replied. 'He's a civil servant,' he said. 'Must be pretty high up, I should think. These houses don't come cheap.' It was a comment that brought a frown from his wife.

'I take it you're *not* a civil servant, then,' said Dave, as ever keen to record facts, even if they were irrelevant to our enquiry.

Carter laughed. 'No, I'm what they euphemistically call "something in the City". Stocks and shares, and all that sort of thing.'

'What exactly happened to Jack?' asked Yvonne.

'The report in this morning's papers tells the whole story,' I said. 'His body was found in a box on Ham Common early on Sunday morning. It had been set on fire.'

'My God, how awful.' Yvonne put a hand to her mouth. 'I thought that was the press sexing up the story. So it's true?'

'Yes, I'm afraid so.'

'But who could have done such a thing?'

'That's what we're trying to find out, Mrs Carter,' volunteered Dave. 'Did Mr and Mrs Harding ever mention any trouble their son might've been in? Drugs, or that sort of thing?'

The Carters looked at each other, and then Yvonne replied. 'If he was, they never mentioned it. But we were little more than neighbours really. We went in there for drinks at Christmas, and they came in here, but beyond that, our relationship was confined to saying hello over the garden fence. And keeping an eye on their house when they were away.'

I thanked the Carters, promised that we would inform the Hardings of their son's death, and left. We'd learned a little more, but not much.

'If the Hardings' house is anything like the Carters',' I said as we drove away from

Guildford, 'it could be that Jack Harding is the sort of pseudo, left-wing artist who despised the Establishment – of which his father is a part – and spurned what he probably called materialism.'

'Blimey!' said Dave.

On Saturday morning, I sent for DC Nicola Chance, the Spanish-speaking member of Kate Ebdon's legwork team.

'I need to contact the police in Portugal urgently, Nicola.'

'I speak Spanish, sir, not Portuguese. There's quite a difference.'

'I appreciate that,' I said, at the same time noticing the smirk on Dave's face. 'But I was wondering...'

'Not any more,' said Dave quietly.

'It's possible that quite a few Portuguese do actually speak Spanish, sir,' Nicola said rather tartly. 'On the other hand, many of them probably speak English, given the amount of tourism there. I'll see what I can do.'

'According to the Hardings' next-door neighbours, Frank and Marcia Harding are currently on holiday in the Algarve, and they think it's probably near a place called Albufeira.'

'I'll give it a try, sir.'

Nicola Chance's 'try' turned out to be successful. Twenty minutes later, she returned.

'I spoke to a Carlos da Silva, sir. He's what

they call a *Chefe de Esquadra*, a sort of inspector. Fortunately, he spoke very good English. I gave him the Hardings' mobile phone number, and he said he'd try to contact them. He'll ring us back as soon as he has any information.'

The question of the Portuguese police officer and his attempt to make contact with the Hardings was put out of my mind within five minutes.

Colin Wilberforce's head appeared round my office door. 'I've just had a call from Chelsea nick, sir. There's been a fire at Dominic Finch's place. The brigade reckon it's arson, and the CTC's there too.'

'What's the Counter-Terrorist Command doing there? Was there an explosion?'

'I'm not sure, sir. All Chelsea said was that it was a fire.'

'Any injuries?'

'None reported, sir.'

'I'd better go and have a look, I suppose. Where's Dave?'

'Getting some coffee, sir.'

'How unusual,' I said.

Colin opened a folder. 'The photographs of the painting found at Harding's place have come through, sir. The one that featured a model who was not Sasha Lovell?'

'Probably another dead end, Colin. But give it to Dave, and we'll take it with us, just in case Finch knows her.'

* ★ ★ ★

The street outside the premises where Finch
had his studio was a tangle of fire hoses. The
red and white tapes of the fire brigade vied
with the blue and white ones of the police. I
suspected there might have been a bit of a
turf war over that. The television people had
somehow heard that the CTC was involved,
and outside-broadcast units had set up their
cameras. A few cliché-ridden reporters were
gabbling into microphones, and one enter-
prising broadcaster was attempting a 'vox-
pop' interview with a deaf pensioner and,
predictably, getting nowhere. In other words
it was the usual chaotic scene of what the
police are pleased to call 'an incident'.

An officious young constable puffed himself up with piss and importance and demanded to know which newspaper we were
from. Dave does not take kindly to being
mistaken for a journalist, and promptly read
the PC's fortune for him.

The DI from Chelsea crossed to where
Dave and I were standing.

'Bit of a mystery, guv,' he said.

'What's the SP?' I asked, culling a useful
piece of shorthand from racing terminology.
To aficionados of the turf it means 'starting
price', but it's what the police say when they
want to know what's happened, and what led
up to it.

'That young woman was the one who
found the device, guv.' The DI gestured

91

towards the model known variously as Michelle or Miriam whom we had last seen posing naked for the photographer. 'She said that she heard the noise of the letterbox and, thinking it was the postman, went into the hall and found a jiffy bag addressed to Dominic Finch. She picked it up and put it on a worktop against the wall in the kitchen. But as she put the kettle on to make some tea, the package suddenly exploded and burst into flames.'

'Much damage?'

'Not a great deal, sir,' said the DI. 'The fire, such as it was, was apparently confined to the worktop it was standing on, and there are a few scorch marks up the wall. But the young woman fled in some panic and called the fire brigade on her mobile.'

'Where's Dominic Finch?'

'I haven't seen him,' said the DI. 'Not that I know him by sight.'

I crossed to where Finch's model was standing, barefooted, and shivering in a silk wrap. 'As a matter of interest, is your name Miriam or Michelle?' I asked.

'It's Michelle, but Dom always gets our names wrong.'

'Tell me what happened.'

'I've just told him,' said Michelle, pointing at the Chelsea DI. 'And I'm freezing to death out here.'

'Well, now you can tell my guv'nor,' said Dave impatiently. He glanced at the CTC duty officer, a chief inspector. 'Okay to go in, guv?' he asked.

'Yes, but don't go any further than just inside the front door. The forensic people are still working in there.'

I followed Dave as he escorted the shivering girl into the entrance hall of Finch's studio. 'So what happened?' he asked.

Michelle wrapped her robe more firmly around her voluptuous body, and directed her reply to me. 'I went through to the kitchen at about nine o'clock,' she began, 'and was just going to put the kettle on to make some tea when I heard the post.'

'How did you get in?' demanded Dave.

'Dom let me in last night.'

I didn't altogether blame Finch for spending the night with her; she was an attractive girl, if a touch coarse. 'Okay,' I said, 'so what happened next?'

'There was this package in a jiffy bag. It was addressed to Dom, so I picked it up and put it on the worktop against the wall.'

'How big was it?' asked Dave.

'About the size of a book,' said Michelle. 'I didn't pay any attention to it at first, but then I heard this fizzing noise, and then a bang. I turned round and the package had burst into flames. And there was lots of smoke. It frightened the life out of me, so I ran out here, into the street, and dialled nine-nine-nine to get the fire brigade.'

'Did this jiffy bag have any stamps on it?'

Dave asked.

'I don't know. I didn't notice. I just assum-ed it had come in the post.'

'And where is Dominic Finch now?' I asked.

'He's gone out for breakfast like he always does. He's a lazy sod is Dom. Never does anything for himself if he can possibly help it.'

'Why didn't you go with him?'

'I was still in bed when he left, but I don't eat breakfast anyway.' Michelle smoothed a hand down her stomach. 'I'm on a diet.'

'And how long does Dominic spend eating breakfast?'

'Usually about an hour, maybe an hour and a half. There's a coffee shop in the King's Road where he meets up with some of his mates. They sit there putting the world to rights.' Michelle followed this statement with a surprising flash of earthy philosophy. 'Which is probably why the world's in such a bloody awful mess.'

'Has anyone called him? I presume he's got a mobile,' I said.

'I never thought of that. I s'pose I should tell him.' Michelle took a cellphone from the shoulder bag she'd grabbed on the way out of the studio, and called him. 'Dom,' she said, 'there's been a fire in the studio. I think you ought to come back.' She terminated the call and put the phone back in her bag. 'He said he'd come.'

'Decent of him,' murmured Dave.

A few minutes later, Dominic Finch appeared on a bicycle. He dismounted, threw the machine against a wall, and joined us in the hall.

'Can't I leave you alone for five minutes, you silly cow?' demanded Finch furiously. 'Christ, I go round the corner for a bite of breakfast, and the next thing I know is that you've set fire to the bloody place. Is there much damage?' he asked, turning to Dave.

'Not really, Mr Finch, and it would appear that your girlfriend was not responsible for the fire.' Dave's comment was remarkably restrained. For Dave. He did not take kindly to men who abused women, even verbally.

'Well, what did happen? And what's that lot doing here?' Finch gestured towards to the explosives officer's vehicle.

I repeated what Michelle had told us about the delivery of the package, and how it had caught fire.

'Where the hell did it come from, then?' Finch turned to his model. 'Did you take it in?'

'No,' said Michelle. 'It came through the letterbox. It was the postman, I suppose. After you'd gone out.'

'Have you any ideas about this, Mr Finch?' asked Dave. 'Were you expecting a package?'

'No, I don't know the first thing about it. I've no idea where it could have come from.'

'Is there anyone you can think of who

might have it in for you, Mr Finch?' I asked.

Finch ran a hand round his chin. 'Not offhand, if you discount people who don't like me taking explicit photographs of birds in the nude.'

'One other thing, Mr Finch,' I said, displaying the photograph of the painting of the mystery nude we'd found in Harding's studio. 'D'you know who this girl is?'

Finch studied the photograph briefly. 'Yeah, she's called Kerry. She's a mate of Sasha Lovell's.'

'Any idea where she lives?'

'Same place as Sasha, I think. Sasha brought her round some weeks ago, and I did a few shots of her. Good-looking girl.'

And that seemed to be as far as we were going to get with the fire. I wasn't sure whether this pathetic attempt at firebombing Finch's studio had anything to do with Jack Harding's murder. For the time being I left it with the Chelsea police to deal with on the understanding that if anything of interest to me did turn up, they'd let me know.

In the meantime, I would pursue the matter of Kerry. It certainly wasn't a pseudonym for Davina Maitland. She had denied posing for Jack Harding, and the painting looked nothing like her anyway.

The Portuguese policeman in Albufeira called the cellphone number that Nicola Chance had given him. It was answered almost immediately.

'Mr Harding?'

'Yes.'

'This is *Chefe de Esquadra* Carlos da Silva of the *Policia de Segurança Publica*. The Public Security Police in Albufeira, sir.'

'Yes?'

'It is necessary that I come to see you, sir. Perhaps you will tell me where you are staying.'

'We have a villa at Quinta da Saudade. It's about four miles from where you are,' replied the mystified Harding, and furnished the precise address.

'Yes, I know it, of course.' Da Silva glanced at his watch. 'I shall be with you in about one quarter of an hour, sir.'

'Can you tell me what it's about?' asked Harding.

'It is better I tell you upon my arrival, sir.' Da Silva replaced the receiver, donned his cap, picked up his gloves, and summoned his driver.

The Quinta da Saudade was a small, exclusive estate of private villas and apartments built on a hillside. Nestling in the picturesque Vale de Parra, among olive and orange trees, the estate had its own swimming pool, restaurant and tennis courts. It was clearly the preserve of the well-off seeking a quiet, relaxing vacation.

Frank Harding, a man in his late fifties, was waiting anxiously at the door as da Silva arrived. Next to him stood his wife, Marcia, a gaunt woman with short, grey hair and an air of the academic about her.

'Is there some problem?' asked Harding, as the policeman saluted courteously.

'It is best I come inside, sir,' said da Silva.

Still curious as to why they should have a visit from the police, the Hardings escorted da Silva into the cool, tiled sitting room of the apartment.

'I have been asked by Scotland Yard to inform you of a tragic occurrence, sir,' da Silva began hesitantly.

'What tragic occurrence?' With an expression of increasing anxiety, Harding invited the Portuguese official to take a seat.

'You have a son called Jack Harding, sir. This is correct?'

'Yes, that's so,' said Harding, as he and his wife sat down opposite da Silva.

'It is with the greatest regret that I have to inform you of the death of your son, sir.'

'Dead?' Marcia Harding's face registered an expression of dismay, but beyond that there was no sign of grief. In fact, it was almost as if the death of their son was an inconvenience that would interfere with their vacation. 'Was it a traffic accident?' she asked.

'No, madam, I'm sorry to have to tell you he was murdered. It happened last Sunday, according to the Scotland Yard official I spoke to.'

'But that was the day before we left home,' exclaimed Harding. 'Why have the police in London waited until now to tell us?'

'I am told that they did not know where you lived, sir.'

'Did this happen in Rome?' asked Marcia Harding.

Da Silva referred to his pocketbook. 'The only information I have, madam, is that he was found on a place called Ham Common. It is near somewhere called Richmond.' He looked up. 'You know this place, perhaps?'

'Yes, of course,' said Frank Harding. 'But what happened?'

'Unfortunately, I do not know this, sir. I was only asked to tell you of this sad event.'

Harding stood up and shook hands with the Portuguese policeman. 'Thank you for telling us, Inspector,' he said, glancing at the two silver bars on da Silva's cuff, and taking a guess at his rank. 'We shall fly home immediately.'

Seven

We drove straight to Badajos Street and called, once again, on Davina Maitland.

'Sorry to bother you again, Miss Maitland,' I said, 'but do you know a girl called Kerry who might've lived here at any time?'

'There's a Kerry Porter who lives upstairs.'

Dave produced the photograph of the painting found in Harding's studio. 'Would that be her?' he asked.

'Well, well, well!' Davina smiled wryly at the photograph. 'She's not backward in coming forward, is she?' she said. 'Yes, that's Kerry. She lives in the flat above this one. She's got a good figure,' she added enviously.

Why is it that women always think other women have better figures than they have themselves?

'D'you know anything about her?' I asked.

Davina Maitland gave that some thought. 'I do know she goes out to work some days,' she said. 'But it seems to be at odd hours. When she does go out, I've known her to leave at around eight, and get in at just after six in the evening. Other days, she'll go out at midday, and return late at night. Oh, and she's divorced. She told me that she'd only recently split up from her husband. Well, when I say recently, I suppose it was about a year ago now. We don't have much to do with each other, but if we meet on the stairs, we'll stop and have a chat.'

'Was she very friendly with Jack Harding and Sasha Lovell?'

'She certainly had more to do with them than with me. As a matter of fact, she was there when I went down for supper one evening. Yes, they seemed to know each other rather well.' Davina paused. 'I suppose she must have known Jack pretty well, if she's prepared to take all her clothes off and pose for that,' she said, and gestured at the photograph.

'D'you know if she's in now?'

'I've no idea. You don't hear people moving about in these old houses.'

As we were already in the house, I decided to try. We thanked Davina and mounted the stairs to the second floor. And we were in luck.

The door was opened on the chain. The woman who peered nervously at us through the gap appeared to be in her twenties, perhaps early thirties. Her hair was cut stylishly short, and was jet-black.

'Yes, what is it?'

'Are you Mrs Kerry Porter?' I asked.

'Yes. Who are you?'

'We're police officers, Mrs Porter.' I showed her my warrant card.

'Is it about Jack's murder?' The woman released the chain and opened the door wide. 'You'd better come in.' There was no doubting that she was the woman in the painting, and Davina was right: she did have a good figure. To me the likeness was striking, and I wondered why Jack Harding had not been more successful in selling his work. But then, as I said before, I'm no art expert. However, I had to agree with John Clarke, the gallery owner, that the painting he'd taken was pretty poor. I certainly wouldn't have bought it.

The flat was much like Davina Maitland's in layout, but it was nowhere near as tidy or well furnished.

Kerry Porter shifted some magazines from a settee and invited us to sit down. 'I can't really tell you anything about Mr Harding,' she began nervously.

I was already beginning to think that she had something to hide.

'You knew he was an artist, of course,' said Dave.

'I believe so,' Kerry Porter replied hesitantly.

'And you joined him and Sasha Lovell for a meal from time to time.'

'Yes, once or twice, but it was only—'

'And I understand you posed for him occasionally.'

Kerry bristled at that. 'I don't know what gave you that idea,' she said, her chin lifting defiantly.

'This did,' said Dave, producing the photograph of the painting.

'Oh, my God!' Kerry's face reddened slightly. 'Where did you get that from?'

'It's a photograph of a painting we found downstairs in Mr Harding's studio,' said Dave. 'I believe you also posed for Dominic Finch.'

'This is terrible. I never thought anyone would find out.'

That seemed a remarkably naive thing to say. Any woman who poses naked for an artist or a photographer must expect the result to appear in the public domain, either at an art gallery, or in a smutty magazine. As far as Dominic Finch's interest in the girl was concerned, it was purely business – I think – and his work was supposed to sell. He was not one of the most charitable people I'd met, and certainly wasn't likely to patronize pretty women by taking photographs of them unless there was a profit in it.

'I don't see that it's anything to be ashamed of,' said Dave, adopting his art connoisseur's mode, and examining the photograph afresh.

'I needed the money,' said Kerry.

'Are you saying that Jack Harding paid you to pose for him?' I queried. Bearing in mind what we'd discovered about Harding's financial affairs, it seemed unlikely.

'Not immediately. But he said he'd pay me

once he'd sold the painting.' Kerry's admission was reluctant, and she avoided eye contact with both Dave and me.

There was something not quite right about all this. First of all, Kerry was saying that she didn't think that anyone would find out that she'd posed, but now she was admitting that she was expecting to be paid once the painting was sold.

'Mrs Porter, I'm investigating a particularly brutal murder, and I don't have the time to pussyfoot around. Shall we start again?'

'Jack and I had an affair,' Kerry blurted out.

'Did this affair with him start before or after your divorce?' It was not prurient interest on Dave's part. He might just have found a way into a murder that, so far, seemed to have been completely without motive. 'Mrs Porter?'

'How did you know I was divorced?' snapped Kerry Porter. There was anger on her face. 'I don't see what my private life has to do with any of this.'

But I was beginning to get a little annoyed too. 'Mrs Porter, you had a sexual relationship with a man who's been murdered. I therefore need to know everything about anyone with whom he had such a relationship.'

'It was before,' said Kerry softly, finally capitulating. 'It was the cause of the divorce.'

'I'm listening,' I said.

'Sasha Lovell's an old friend of mine.'

'How did you meet?'

'At night classes. We were both studying Italian. Jamie and I used to go to Italy for our holidays, and I decided—'

'Jamie was your husband, was he?'

'Yes.'

'Is that his real name?'

'No, it's James, but he's known as Jamie. Anyway, we were always short of cash, and Sasha said I could earn some money by posing for Jack. I assumed that he was an established artist, and wanted to paint a portrait of me – you know, head and shoulders – but when I arrived he asked me to take off all my clothes. Well, I refused at first, but Sasha said that Jack's work was tasteful and artistic, and she showed me a painting that he'd done of her. It wasn't until after I'd posed for him that I found out he hadn't any money, and that I'd probably never get paid. And I never was. In short, I was conned.'

Well, she said it just before I did.

'How come you posed for Dominic Finch, then?'

At last, Kerry Porter appeared resigned to telling the truth. It was only later I discovered that, even then, it was but a half-truth. 'After that, I posed several times for Jack, and, well, one thing led to another, and one day when Sasha was out, Jack and I finished up in bed.'

'And there were several occasions after that, I suppose,' I suggested.

'Yes. I bitterly regret it now, but it happened.' Kerry looked down at the floor, and played with the wedding ring she still wore. 'Somehow, Jamie found out. I suppose he must have followed me, or had me followed. There was a terrible row, and I made it worse by telling him that I'd only been posing. But Jamie was a suspicious man, and automatically assumed that I was doing nude poses, and that the natural outcome was that I'd finish up in the artist's bed. And of course he was right.'

'So you split up.'

'Yes. I admitted the affair, and he threw me out, and we eventually divorced.'

'When was this?'

'The divorce was finalized about a year ago. I hadn't anywhere to go, so Jack said I could move in with him and Sasha as a temporary measure. Then, as luck would have it, this flat fell vacant and I moved up here a few months ago. And, of course, the affair continued.'

'Didn't your friend Sasha object?'

'No. She's a very free and easy girl, and anyway she was having a fling with Dominic.'

'Ah yes, Dominic Finch. It was after the divorce that you started posing for him, was it?'

'Yes. I was absolutely broke. I got nothing

out of the divorce, so I started off by doing a bit of temping – I was trained as a secretary – but it hardly paid the rent, let alone anything else. It was then that Sasha told me she had this friend Dominic who would pay me quite well for posing for a magazine. I tell you, by then I was in no position to object, but I did insist on wearing a full-length blonde wig. Silly of me, really, but I didn't think anyone would recognize me like that.'

I think she was probably right. The sort of photographs that Finch took didn't exactly concentrate on the model's face.

'And did you have an affair with Dominic, too?'

Kerry looked down at the floor. 'Yes, but he had affairs with all his models,' she said, as though that justified it.

'Are you now in full-time employment?' asked Dave.

'Yes. I was lucky enough to get a job with a firm of solicitors.'

But she still wasn't telling the truth. The hours that Davina Maitland told us that Kerry worked didn't sound like those of a solicitor's secretary, but I let it pass. For the moment.

'Was your ex-husband angry about your affair, Mrs Porter?'

'That's putting it mildly,' said Kerry. 'He was furious.'

'Just furious enough to threaten violence against Jack Harding?' Perhaps at last we

107

were getting somewhere.

There was a long pause before Kerry answered. 'He did say he felt like giving him a good hiding,' she said eventually, 'but I think it was all talk. Jamie wasn't a violent man, and I guessed it was just a heat of the moment thing.'

'Where does your ex-husband live, Mrs Porter?' I asked.

'You don't have to see him, do you?' Kerry looked up in some alarm.

'Of course we do. Here's a man whose wife posed naked for a man with whom she later had an affair, and who spoke of giving that man a good hiding. And then that man winds up dead.'

Kerry Porter stood up and crossed to a table by the window. She opened a drawer and took out a file. 'This is all the paperwork connected with the divorce,' she said, thumbing through it. 'Jamie sold the flat we were living in at World's End, and moved to somewhere in Battersea.' She spent a moment or two finding the relevant letter. 'Here we are. This is the last address that the solicitor had for him. It's in Templars Road, Battersea. Number four.'

'What's Mr Porter's profession?' asked Dave.

'He's a car salesman.

'Where does he work?'

Kerry looked as though she wasn't going to tell us, but then she relented, and furnished the address of a car dealership in West London.

'Did Sasha Lovell say why she was studying Italian, Mrs Porter?' I asked.

'She said she had an Italian boyfriend, and that it would be nice if she could learn to speak his language. She told me about him when I was going through my divorce.'

'Did she tell you this boyfriend's name?'

Kerry played a little tattoo on the arm of her chair while she thought about that. 'I think it was Giovanni something,' she said eventually. 'She always referred to him as Gio, but I don't know his surname. In fact, I don't think she ever mentioned it.'

'Did she say where this Giovanni lived?'

'No, she never said.'

'Did she ever talk about having a boyfriend in Docklands, in the East End?'

'Not that I recall.'

'One other question, Mrs Porter. Sasha Lovell has disappeared from the flat downstairs. Have you any idea where she might've gone?'

'No, none at all. In fact, I was wondering why I hadn't seen her for a day or two.'

And that was that. We'd acquired a little more to add to our pathetic ragbag of evidence.

On Sunday morning a message had been received in the incident room from *Chefe de Esquadra* Carlos da Silva of the *Policia de*

Segurança Publica in Portugal. The message said that he'd contacted the Hardings and that they would be flying home immediately. They expected to arrive on Sunday evening.

The following morning I received an irate telephone call from Frank Harding, Jack's father, demanding to know why it had taken so long to inform him of his son's death.

I did my best to placate him, and promised that I would visit him as soon as I could get to Guildford.

'Ah, the police at last. You'd better come in.' When we arrived at Frank Harding's house in Scat's Hill Avenue an hour and a half later, his attitude was still as hostile as it had been on the telephone. He looked askance at Dave, and I got the impression that he was not altogether pleased that I was accompanied by a black detective.

'I'm sorry about your son, Mr Harding,' I said, as Jack's father ushered us into his sitting room, and introduced us to his wife Marcia.

'And I'm sorry that you didn't tell me about it before my wife and I left for Portugal last Monday, Chief Inspector.'

'I'm afraid that your son's body was not identified until that Monday, Mr Harding, by which time I imagine you'd already left the country. However, that wouldn't have helped much because when we searched his flat, we found nothing to indicate either your identity or your address. It was not until we circulatcd the details to the press that your neighbour, Mr Carter, telephoned us. After that, we were able to ask the Portuguese police to contact you.'

'Oh, I see,' muttered Harding grudgingly. 'But if only we'd known before we went,' he continued, 'we wouldn't have been in the position of wasting two weeks of our holiday. And I daresay we could have claimed on the insurance for cancellation.'

'We might even be able to do that now, dear,' suggested Marcia Harding, speaking for the first time since our arrival.

'Possibly,' said Harding. 'I'll get on to them this afternoon. But I don't hold out much hope. You know what these damned insurance companies are like. Do anything to avoid paying out.'

Over the years, I've heard some strange reactions to the death of a loved one, but this was strangest so far. The Hardings seemed far more concerned about the cost of losing their holiday than they were about the ruthless murder of their son. And that, perhaps, was a good enough reason for Jack Harding to have abandoned them.

'When did you last see your son, Mr Harding?' asked Dave.

'What?' Harding glared at Dave, almost as if he regarded being questioned by a mere sergeant as nothing short of insolence.

111

'It would be helpful if you answered my sergeant's question, Mr Harding,' I said mildly.

'Must've been three years ago, I suppose, just before he went to Rome. He had some daft notion about becoming an artist.'

'I take it you weren't much in favour of that,' continued Dave.

'Of course we weren't,' said Harding, including his wife in his condemnation. 'There's no money in that sort of thing. I told him to find himself a proper job, but he wouldn't listen. And I daresay he got in with the wrong crowd. These arty-crafty people are all on drugs, you know.'

'Did he communicate with you while he was in Rome?' I asked.

'Not a word,' said Marcia Harding, suddenly taking an interest. 'Not a phone call, nothing. Not even a Christmas card.'

'I presume that you were unaware that he was back in this country, then.'

'Came as a surprise, I must say,' mumbled Harding. 'Incidentally, how did you did you find out where he was living?'

'The woman he was living with—'

'He was living with a *woman*?' shrieked Marcia Harding, sounding scandalized at the prospect. 'D'you mean they weren't married?'

'No, they weren't,' said Dave quietly.

'Who was this woman?' demanded Harding.

112

'Her name's Sasha Lovell,' I said. 'The Sunday before last, she informed the police that Jack had gone missing. That's how were able to identify the body, by comparing his fingerprints with those found in the flat he shared with her.' I chose not to mention the bloodstains that had been found in the Badajos Street basement. Much as I'd taken a dislike to Frank Harding there was no profit in piling on the agony.

'If she was living with him, she must have known where he'd gone,' protested Harding.

'She wasn't there that night,' I said.

'D'you mean that my son was living with a woman who sleeps around?' demanded Marcia Harding, becoming haughtier by the moment. Clearly her perception of civilized behaviour did not accord with that of her late son. 'And where was this flat?'

'In Fulham.'

'Fulham!' Frank Harding screeched the word, and nodded knowingly. 'I might've guessed. Not a stone's throw from Chelsea. I don't wonder he went off the rails. The sort of people who frequent Chelsea wouldn't know civilized and decent behaviour if it jumped up and bit them.' He seemed intent on condemning his son's way of life.

'I presume that Mr Carter showed you the press report of the murder, Mr Harding?' I asked.

'Yes, he did. The whole thing seems quite bizarre. Who on earth would have wanted to kill him in that way?'

'That's what we're trying to find out,' I said.

'This woman you mentioned. How did he meet her?'

'I don't know, but she was his model.'

'His model?' exclaimed Marcia Harding. 'D'you mean she posed naked?'

'She did, as a matter of fact,' said Dave mildly, 'although that seems to us to be irrelevant.'

'Does it indeed?' snapped Harding. 'Well, it doesn't seem irrelevant to me. I'm beginning to see how this all came about. You want to be looking at these people he got in with, Chief Inspector. I think you'll find that drugs are at the bottom of this. Some drug dealer who didn't get paid will have murdered him, you mark my words. *Pour encourager les autres*, d'you see? It all fits.'

Oh, how I hate armchair detectives. They see a couple of police soap operas on television and think they know more about investigating serious crime than we do.

'It's early days to make any sort of assumption, Mr Harding,' I said.

'I don't understand it,' said Marcia Harding. 'We gave him the best of everything. He wanted for nothing. We sent him to a good public school, and we were prepared to pay for him to go through university. My husband knows some people at Churchill College, Cambridge, and there wouldn't have

114

been any problem about getting him a place there.'

And that, I thought, was probably the reason why Jack Harding broke away from his stifling family. Youngsters do hate being pointed towards a career in which they have no interest. I had no doubt in my mind that Frank Harding wanted his son to become a civil servant, just like himself. I still remember my father trying to persuade me to become a motorman on the London Underground, just like he'd been all his life. But I'd seen what it'd done to the old man, and I wasn't going down that road. Mind you, my dead-end job as a clerk with a water company didn't impress him too much, but that was nothing compared with my announcement that I was to become a policeman. He nearly threw a fit. But then my father was of a class and generation that always regarded the police with grave suspicion.

'I take it you know nothing of this woman Sasha Lovell?' I asked.

'Nothing,' said Harding. 'I presume she's a common tart of some sort.'

'Not all artist's models are,' said Dave.

'I'll keep you informed of any developments, Mr Harding,' I said as we rose to leave.

'I'm considering filing a complaint about not being told of his death,' said Harding. 'I may even have a word with my MP.'

'That of course is your right, Mr Harding.'

I turned to Dave. 'Perhaps you'd give Mr Harding the address of the Department of Professional Standards, Sergeant.'

'Very good, sir.' Dave scribbled a few lines on the back of one of his cards, and handed it over.

I hoped that Harding wouldn't bother. There was no doubt in my mind that such a complaint wouldn't get off the ground. But a hell of a lot of time and paper would be wasted in proving that there was no way that Harding could've been told of his son's death any earlier.

Eight

Because Dave was complaining that his stomach thought his throat was cut, I was compassionate enough to stop off at the Holiday Inn just outside Guildford to have lunch. It wasn't exactly on our route back to London, but the centre of Guildford's a hopeless place to try to park.

I'd decided that we had to see James Porter, Kerry's ex, as soon as possible, and in the afternoon we drove straight from Guildford to west London.

Dave was lucky enough to find a parking space right outside Porter's place of work.

'The sight of a Job car parked outside here should get up their noses,' he commented.

It was a glitzy showroom containing a number of highly polished cars, the prices of which were well out of the range of a mere detective chief inspector. That, however, did not stop me from dallying to examine one or two of them. The result was that Dave went ahead of me and, within seconds, an unctuous salesman appeared. It was apparent from his body language – and doubtless his racial prejudice – that he was wondering whether this scruffily dressed black man had the wherewithal to buy one of his expensive vehicles. He was soon disabused.

The salesman's lapel bore a little chrome metal badge engraved with the words 'James Porter', thus obviating the necessity of enquiring for him.

'Detective Sergeant Poole,' Dave informed him, and then turned to me. 'This is Mr Porter, sir,' he said loudly.

'Ah, good.' I dragged myself away from salivating over a chunky four-by-four, known locally as a Chelsea tractor, and joined them. 'I'm Detective Chief Inspector Brock of New Scotland Yard,' I said, just as another smarmy salesman homed in on me. He swerved away a touch smartly.

'Oh! Are you from the Stolen Car Squad?' Some of the artificial flamboyance vanished from Porter's demeanour, and he fingered his tie.

'No,' said Dave. 'Expecting them, were you?' He cast an eye over the nearest car as though assessing its legitimacy.

'I want to talk to you about Jack Harding, Mr Porter,' I said.

Porter glanced around the showroom with a hunted look, doubtless fearing that some affluent customer might have overheard me. 'You'd better come into the office.' Turning on his heel, he hurriedly led the way into a glass-fronted cubicle at the back of the showroom.

'What was that name again?' asked Porter, once he was safely ensconced behind the desk. 'A client, was he?'

'Mr Porter, you divorced your wife Kerry because she had an affair with Jack Harding, an artist for whom she posed. So don't pretend you've not heard of him. Apart from which, you probably read the account of his murder in the paper.'

'Oh, that Jack Harding,' said Porter lamely.

'Yes, Mr Porter, *that* Jack Harding. Now, shall we stop messing about? You threatened violence against Mr Harding when you discovered this affair, and Mr Harding was later found murdered.'

'I didn't mean it when I said that,' Porter blurted out.

'So you admit that much?'

'Yes. Well, wouldn't you have done? I discover that my wife is posing naked for some untalented dauber, and on top of that, I find

118

that she's sharing a bed with him. I don't know whether you know what it's like to discover that your wife's been unfaithful...'

You bet I know what it's like, but I didn't intend admitting it to Porter.

'When did you last see Jack Harding?' Dave asked.

'I never actually met him.'

'Really?' Dave let the question hang in the air like an accusation. 'How did you discover that your wife was having an affair with him, then?'

There was a lengthy pause before Porter replied. For a moment or two, he toyed with an ashtray in a rubber ring fashioned into the likeness of a motor tyre; doubtless some advertising material put out by tyre manufacturers.

'I saw a photograph of her in a magazine,' he eventually, and somewhat reluctantly, admitted. 'Although she was wearing a blonde wig, I recognized her immediately.'

'What sort of magazine?' Dave knew the answer, but was being his usual perverse self. He always enjoyed winding up the self-righteous.

'It was one of those girlie mags that you find on the top shelf of newsagents. The photo of her was quite shocking. Explicit, if you know what I mean.'

'You're into that sort of thing, are you?' Dave asked, out of sheer devilment. 'Read a lot of 'em, do you?'

'Not at all. I happened to find this magazine on the Tube. Someone had obviously left it there.'

The interesting aspect of Porter's statement was that Kerry Porter had told us she'd only posed for Dominic Finch *after* her divorce. Now it appeared that she had done so *before* her ex-husband had started proceedings. But I decided to let that go for the time being.

'What did you do about it?' I asked.

'Seeing that photograph made me suspicious that she was up to something.' Porter looked unhappy about having these admissions forced from him.

'I suppose it would,' said Dave, trying hard not to laugh.

'At the time, she was attending evening classes every Tuesday to learn Italian,' continued Porter. 'But when on a *Thursday* she said she was going to her Italian class, I was pretty certain that she was lying.'

'So you followed her?' I suggested.

'How did you know that?' Porter's hands twitched nervously on the desk.

'I guessed that's what you would have done,' I said. And I said it because Porter had struck me as a control freak who would want to know every damned thing his wife got up to.

'She always walked to the school where they held the classes,' Porter continued, 'and she set out on foot on this occasion. But

120

instead of going to learn a bit more Italian, she finished up at this basement flat in Badajos Street.'

'And she didn't spot you?' I asked. If she hadn't, this man obviously had the potential to be a first-class surveillance officer.

'I don't think so. If she did, she never said so afterwards. Anyway, I waited outside. Well, not right outside, but near enough to be able to see her when she left.'

'And she eventually came out and went home, I presume.'

Porter nodded. 'Yes. A couple of hours later.'

'You actually hung about in Badajos Street for two whole hours?' I asked incredulously.

'Certainly I did. I wanted to know what she was doing there.'

I had to admire this man's doggedness – if what he'd said was true – but not his motives. I doubt if I'd have gone to that much trouble when my ex-wife Helga was playing fast and loose. But then I'd done enough surveillance work in the Job without wanting to do it in what little spare time I had. Apart from anything else, Helga and I had already become estranged when she picked up with a doctor at the hospital where she was working.

'So when the pair of you eventually got home, you confronted her with what you'd seen, I take it.' I was having great difficulty in believing his account; somehow it didn't ring true.

'Of course I did,' snapped Porter. 'I asked her why she'd gone to Badajos Street and what she'd been doing there, but the infuriating thing was that she didn't deny it. She admitted posing for Harding, and for some backstreet photographer who took the sort of pictures that appeared in those magazines I mentioned. She told me that she had a good body and saw no harm in flaunting it. In fact, she said she was proud of what she'd been doing, and had no intention of giving it up. The last straw was when she told me that she earned more doing that than I did selling cars.'

This man was an enigma, but not an uncommon one. He freely admitted that he read girlie magazines, and was apparently content to leer at photographs if they were of other men's wives rather than his own. I certainly didn't believe his story about finding the magazine on a train. I was pretty sure that it was he who'd left it behind for fear that his wife would find it when he got home. In the circumstances, that was a rich irony.

'Did you accuse her of having an affair with Harding?'

Porter scoffed. 'I didn't have to. She threw it in my face. "You might as well know I'm having an affair as well," is what she actually said, and went on to say that Harding was much better in bed than I ever was. Well, that really infuriated me, I can tell you.'

'And it was at that point you threatened to do Jack Harding some physical harm, was it?' I asked.

'Yes, but as I said before, I didn't mean it. I was so furious when I found out what Kerry had been up to, and the way she taunted me about it, that I suppose I just flipped. Anyway, we had one God Almighty row, and I told her to pack her bags and get the hell out of my life.'

'No question of a reconciliation, then?' I queried, not that Porter struck me as the forgiving kind.

'Certainly not. What would I have said to other people – friends of ours for example – who might have seen her photograph? How would I have explained that away?'

'You could've asked them what they were doing reading porn magazines in the first place, I suppose,' Dave suggested mildly.

'I don't think we need to trouble you any further, Mr Porter,' I said, not meaning a word of it. 'But I hope you appreciate that when we're investigating a murder, we have to follow up every lead, no matter how tenuous.' He didn't know, of course, how near he'd come to having his collar felt.

'Of course, Chief Inspector.' Porter's confidence and superficial charm returned in an instant, and he let out an obvious sigh of relief. 'I do understand what a difficult task you have.'

But he wasn't off the hook yet, not by a long chalk. However, nothing would be gained by telling him that I was far from satisfied that he had spoken the truth. But I was also far from satisfied that Kerry Porter had been telling us the truth either. And that was something I would be pursuing.

Perhaps both the Porters were involved in Harding's death. And the principal reason I'd let him down lightly was that I didn't want him talking to his ex-wife before we had a chance to see her again. I didn't think he would, but if he did I was pretty sure that any such conversation would be larded with boasts on his part about how he'd talked his way out of the questions posed by the bumbling Old Bill. 'Dim cop' often works much better than the tired old 'good cop, bad cop' routine so beloved of television police shows.

'Personally, I'd have nicked him, guv,' said Dave as we drove back to Curtis Green.'

'What for?'

'Threats to murder,' said Dave, wrenching the steering wheel over to avoid a lemming on a bicycle.

'If his ex-wife is to be believed, Dave, he merely said that he felt like giving Harding a good hiding. That doesn't constitute a threat to murder, and he didn't make that statement directly to Harding.'

'I'd still have nicked him,' muttered Dave.

'Anyway, the threat doesn't have to be made to the victim; it can be made to a third party,' he added, not to be outdone in matters of criminal law.

Back at Curtis Green, there was a report awaiting me from the Counter-Terrorist Command's scientists who'd examined the debris of the explosive device that had caused the small fire at Finch's Chelsea studio.

The device, the report said, had been sent through the post, and was clearly the work of an amateur. In rather scathing terms, it went on to say that no efficient terrorist would have created a device so crude, and in the reporting scientist's opinion it was quite surprising that it had detonated when it was supposed to. He went on to state that the device was so volatile that it could have exploded at any time between posting and arrival. Further proof of the sender's ineptitude was the fact that a fingerprint had been found on an inside part of the packaging. The bad news was that there was no matching print in the collection at Scotland Yard against which it could be identified.

I handed the report back to Colin Wilberforce. 'You can file that, Colin,' I said. 'I don't think it had anything to do with Jack Harding's murder. Just one of those coincidences that crop up to confuse us.'

Davina Maitland had told us that Kerry

Porter didn't work settled hours, but I decided to call at her Badajos Street address on the off chance that she might be at home. I didn't like loose ends, and James Porter's statement that he'd seen a photograph of his ex in a pornographic magazine *before* the divorce was contrary to what Kerry had told us. It was probably irrelevant, but I fully intended getting to the bottom of that minor mystery.

We ascended the stairs to Kerry Porter's second-floor flat. There was no answer, but as we returned to the car, intending to leave the interview to another day, the figure of Kerry Porter turned the corner of Badajos Street. And a very nice figure it was too, even though it was power-dressed in a black suit with a white jabot, black tights and black stilettos. Presumably the solicitor for whom she had claimed to work insisted on it. He didn't know what he was missing. But I was pretty sure he hadn't missed out, because I was damned sure she didn't work in the legal profession.

'Good evening, Mrs Porter.' I stepped out of the car just as she drew level with us.

A brief look of surprise crossed Kerry's face, to be replaced almost immediately by one of concerned recognition. 'Oh, it's you.' She didn't sound pleased to see us.

'May we come in?' I asked. 'There are one or two points that you might be able to clear up for us.'

'I suppose so, but I warn you, the flat's a tip. I just don't seem to have the time to do anything before I rush out in the morning.' Kerry continued to speak as she mounted the stairs to the second floor, at the same time fumbling in her shoulder bag for her key.

When we reached the sitting room, she took off her jacket and invited us to sit down.

'We spoke to your ex-husband this afternoon, Mrs Porter,' I said.

'Oh!' An anxious look flitted briefly across the woman's face. 'What did he have to say?'

'He told us that it was a photograph of you he saw in a girlie magazine that first alerted him to your sideline. He claimed to have found the magazine on a train.' I noticed that Kerry smiled at that. 'But you told us that you didn't start posing for Dominic Finch until after your divorce.'

'I'm not proud of what I did,' said Kerry, but her facial expression, and the way she avoided looking directly at me, implied that she was still being evasive.

'Is that so? But Mr Porter told us that you boasted about it.' I turned to Dave. 'What exactly did he say, Sergeant?'

Dave opened his pocketbook. 'His actual words were: "She told me that she had a good body and saw no harm in flaunting it. In fact, she said she was proud of what she'd been doing, and had no intention of giving it up."' He put away his pocketbook. 'He also said that you told him that you earned more than he did.'

'Was that true, Mrs Porter?' I asked.

'Yes.' Kerry played with her wedding ring again; it seemed to be a habit of hers. She looked up, a defiant expression on her face. 'It's what I do,' she said. 'If you must know – although I don't see what it has to do with you – I'm a porn actress, but I also pose for Dominic Finch ... and for other photographers. There, satisfied?' she demanded arrogantly.

'Why didn't you tell me this in the first place?'

'Because you're a policeman.'

That had to be a joke. The police don't give a damn about adult porn any more. The people that we take a delight in prosecuting are the creeps who prey on children, and collect their images on their computers.

'Did your husband know?'

'No, he didn't.'

'Let me get this straight, Mrs Porter. It was not until Mr Porter saw this photo in a magazine that he found out. Is that the truth?'

'No, it's not. Anyway, he thought I was working as a secretary in a solicitor's office.'

I gestured at the woman's outfit. 'But you look as though you're a secretary.'

'D'you expect me to leave for work wearing nothing but a sexy G-string and a

128

bustier?' Kerry asked sarcastically. 'Of course I dress like this.' She swept a hand down her elegant suit. 'I don't want people like Davina – or, worse still, that damned retired colonel's wife downstairs – knowing what I do.'

That was fair comment. I couldn't see Davina Maitland or the Smiths viewing blue films, so they were unlikely to find out. That said, however, Colonel Smith might be tempted, but his wife would probably kill him if she found out.

'Well, Mrs Porter,' said Dave, 'Miss Maitland knows now, because we showed her the photograph of Jack Harding's painting that you posed for. That's how we tracked you down.'

'Thanks very much,' said Kerry sarcastically, and shot Dave a look that could kill.

'How long were you married?' I asked.

'Three years.'

'And were you a porn actress all that time?' I was amazed that she'd been able to maintain her double life without her husband finding out.

'Yes. But despite what Jamie may have told you, as far as I know he didn't see my photograph in a magazine, and he didn't follow me. One evening when I got in from work, he produced a blue DVD he'd bought. And guess who the star performers were.'

'You, I presume. And...?'

Kerry laughed, but there was no humour

in it. 'Yes. Me and Jack Harding. But what I said before was true. There was one hell of a row, and he threw me out. Not that I cared. As I told him, and he told you, I was making more money than he was. He's not very good at selling cars.'

Fascinating. If what Kerry was saying was true, James Porter admitted to reading girlie magazines, but not to watching pornographic DVDs. Why, I wondered, should he do that? It was a fine distinction that eluded me.

'If James didn't follow you to Jack Harding's place downstairs, how did he find out you were having an affair with him?' I asked.

'I told him after he played me the DVD. In fact, it was pretty bloody obvious from the DVD, wasn't it? So I told him what a fucking hypocrite he was. Can you believe it? He's buying blue DVDs, but complaining about me taking part in them.'

'Did you tell him who'd made the film?'

'I didn't have to. Dominic Finch's name and business address were on the case of the DVD.'

'You said that your ex-husband was furious when you told him all this. One hell of a row, you said just now.'

'Too right. He went up like a can of petrol.'

That was an unfortunate analogy, in view of the way that Jack Harding had died.

'What did he actually say to you about the affair, Mrs Porter?'

There was a long pause before Kerry answered. A vestige of loyalty to her ex-husband still remaining, perhaps?

'He said that, given half a chance, he'd kill Jack.'

'D'you think he was serious?' asked Dave.

'Absolutely. One thing about Jamie that I didn't tell you before is that he's got a vicious temper. And he harbours grudges.'

'To your knowledge, did your ex-husband ever meet Jack Harding? Or Dominic Finch?' It suddenly occurred to me that James Porter could have sent Finch the explosive device that was now occupying the minds of the Counter-Terrorist Command.

'I don't know. It's possible. He knew I'd come to live here, and it wouldn't have been too difficult for him to find out that Jack was in the basement flat. Anyway, the solicitor probably told him the address. After all, I was living with Jack for a few months before I moved up here.'

And there it was. Suddenly, Kerry Porter's original statement that she'd been posing for a 'tasteful' painting had developed into a very valid motive for murder. There was only one snag, apart from proving it, of course, and that was the bizarre way in which Harding had met his death. I didn't think that James Porter was capable either of devising such a murder, or having the ability to carry it out.

'My sergeant will now take a statement

from you, Mrs Porter, regarding what your ex-husband said he would do when he discovered that you'd been having an affair with Jack Harding.'

'Does that mean I'll have to go to court and testify against him?' asked Kerry.

'Yes, it does.'

'Good.' Kerry crossed her legs and smiled. 'Serve the vindictive bastard right.'

However, the Porters were married at the time of the threat, and I was unsure about the legal position of Kerry being competent to give evidence against someone who, at the time, had been her husband. But that would be a problem for the Crown Prosecution Service. If we ever got anywhere near a courtroom, that is.

'Where are we going now, guv?' asked Dave as we left Kerry Porter's flat.

'Your wish has come true, Dave. We shall go and nick James Porter. What was his address?'

Dave grinned, and reeled off the Battersea address that Kerry Porter had given us.

Nine

We arrived at James Porter's flat in Battersea at eight o'clock.

It was some time before the door was opened, and when it was, I was astonished to be confronted by Sasha Lovell.

'Oh my God, it's you.' It was not immediately apparent whether it was our arrival at Porter's door that surprised Sasha, or that she was not exactly dressed to receive visitors.

'Yes, it's us, Miss Lovell, and we want a word with you. And with Mr Porter. I take it he's in.'

'Er, well, I...' But that was as far as she got.

'Who is it, Sash?' came a voice from somewhere inside the flat.

'The police,' said Sasha, holding the edge of the door and leaning back.

'Oh, not again,' came the voice, and then Porter appeared in the small hallway, fastening the belt of a towelling bathrobe. 'You'd better come in.'

'I hope we're not interrupting anything, Mr Porter,' said Dave as we followed the couple into the sitting room.

'What d'you want now?' demanded Porter angrily. 'I answered all your questions this afternoon.'

'Not quite,' I said as we all sat down. I turned to Sasha. 'We called at the address in Orpington that you left with the letting agent, Miss Lovell. But to my surprise the woman who answered the door had never heard of you.'

'She wouldn't have. I made up that address. I'm amazed that it actually existed.'

'Why did you disappear, then?' asked Dave, who was still fuming over having driven to Orpington and back in the pouring rain for nothing. 'Because it's obvious you didn't intend to be found.'

'Money. The rent was outstanding, and I certainly wasn't going to pay it. After all, that flat was in Jack's name, so I didn't see why I should get caught.'

I was beginning to have grave doubts about this whole set-up. Dominic Finch had provided Sasha Lovell's alibi for the period when Jack Harding met his death, and I didn't trust Finch. She had then disappeared, having furnished a false address, and now she turned up in the flat of James Porter, a man who had threatened to kill Harding. At least, that was the story that his ex-wife had told us, and she was prepared to give evidence to that effect. It was beginning to look very much like a conspiracy. But who had conspired with whom?

I made a decision, not something I do often.

'I require you both to come to Charing Cross police station for further enquiries to be made.'

'What the hell for?' demanded Porter. 'I've told you all I know.'

'I suggest you both get dressed,' I continued, ignoring his predictable protest.

'And if we don't choose to "accompany you to the station", as they say in the worst TV cop shows, what then?' demanded Porter sarcastically.

'In that case, you'll leave me no option but to arrest you both,' I said.

'I want a solicitor,' said Porter.

'Yes, I think you probably do,' said Dave.

It was just past nine in the evening by the time we reached Charing Cross. We spent a few minutes explaining to the custody sergeant why we were there, and James Porter and Sasha Lovell reluctantly furnished their details. The custody sergeant filled up all the forms that were necessary and, at my request, placed them in separate interview rooms.

Porter was still demanding a lawyer, and the custody sergeant undertook to call out one of the duty solicitors.

During the journey from Battersea to Charing Cross, I had phoned Kate Ebdon and asked her to meet us at the police station.

'What've we got, guv?' she asked when she arrived.

'What we've got is Sasha Lovell and James Porter,' I said, and quickly brought Kate up to speed on what we'd learned of the Porters so far.

'Have you nicked them both?'

'Not yet, Kate, but Porter's running close to it.'

'D'you want me to have a go at the sheila, then, guv?' asked Kate.

'Yes, but only when I've had a few words with her. Then I'll have a chat to Porter. I'm sure he's not telling us the truth. In fact, I don't think anyone is.'

Leaving Dave to get a cup of tea in the canteen, Kate and I entered the interview room where Sasha was sitting. She was now dressed in jeans, a loose sweater and high-heeled mules.

Kate dismissed the woman police officer escort, switched on the tape recorder and told it who was present.

'I don't know why you had to bring me all the way up here,' Sasha began.

'In your own interests this interview is being recorded,' I said. 'Now, you told me earlier that you disappeared because you were afraid that the letting agency would come after you for the arrears of rent.'

'That's right.'

'But you weren't the official tenant, so they wouldn't have had any claim over you.'

'I didn't know that, did I?'

'Are you living with James Porter?'

'Yes. What of it?'

'How long have you been having an affair with him?'

'About a year and a half, I suppose.'

'Quite some time before he was divorced from Kerry, then?'

'Yes.'

'How did you meet him? Did he turn up one day to collect Kerry from her Italian classes? The Italian classes where you and she first met?'

Sasha laughed. 'There were no Italian classes. Certainly not for her, and I only went a few times. I tried to learn Italian, but I gave it up. It was a story we made up for Jamie's benefit. I know she probably told you that she and Jamie went to Italy for their holidays, but that was balls. She's never been there in her life.'

'So where did she go when she told her husband that she was learning Italian?'

Sasha laughed again. 'She came round to our place every Tuesday and got laid by Jack.'

'And you didn't object to that?'

'Of course not. I was doing the same with Dominic.' After a moment's pause, Sasha added, 'And then with Jamie. Well, with both actually.'

'But you were also having an affair with Jack.'

'So what? Variety's the spice of life, so they say.'

'How long have you known Dominic Finch?' I knew what she'd said before, but I do like checking.

'Five or six years.'

'So you knew him before your marriage to Georges Gaillard,' said Dave.

Sasha's eyes opened wide in surprise. 'How did you know about that?'

'I'm a detective,' said Dave.

'It was a mistake marrying that bastard. He beat me up.'

'Why? Because you continued to pose for Finch?'

'Something like that.'

'Well, he won't bother you any more.'

'I'm divorced from him.'

'He's dead,' said Dave.

'Dead? What happened to him? Someone murder him, did they?'

'Possibly,' said Dave. 'He was hit on the head by a golf ball and died instantly. Apparently he had a thinner skull than usual. The French police are satisfied that it was an accident.'

'I shan't be shedding any tears over that bastard,' said Sasha. 'He gave me one hell of a time.'

'Did Kerry Porter ever tell you what she did for a living, Miss Lovell?' I asked.

'Of course she did. She took part in blue movies. Or blue DVDs, I s'pose they call them now.'

'So how did you two little whores really meet up, mate?' Kate's coarse question in her hammed-up Australian accent cut through what had, until then, been quite a civilized exchange.

Sasha looked startled at the blunt question, and a brief expression of fear flitted across her face. 'I can't really remember,' she said.

'Try again, love,' said Kate, leaning across the table so that her face was much closer to the girl's.

'All right,' said Sasha, with an air of resignation. 'We're both in the same game.'

'In the same game, or *on* the game?' demanded Kate.

'I'm not a prostitute, if that's what you're thinking,' Sasha responded spiritedly. 'I take part in the same sort of DVDs as Kerry.'

'Oh, there's a difference, is there?' asked Kate. 'As I see it, porn actresses and toms both get paid for getting screwed. So you tell me the difference.'

'It's not like that,' protested Sasha. 'What we do is a form of art.'

Kate scoffed and leaned back in her chair. 'And where d'you make these films?'

'Chelsea.'

'That reckons. Where in Chelsea?'

Sasha Lovell spent a couple of seconds

plucking a cotton thread from her jeans before looking up. 'Dominic's place,' she said.

'So he makes pornographic films as well as taking photographs for adult magazines, does he?' I asked. Once again, I was attempting to confirm what we'd already heard from Kerry Porter.

'Yes, and he's very good at it.'

'And that's where you met Kerry, is it?' asked Kate.

'Yes.'

'But how did you meet James Porter?' Again I asked the question that Sasha had not answered before.

'It was like you said. Just before I gave up the Italian classes, he turned up one evening to collect Kerry. But, of course, she wasn't there and never had been. It gave me a hell of a fright – and Kerry too when she found out – because he'd never done that before.'

'How did you talk your way out of that?'

'I told him she'd already left. And then I rushed into the ladies' room and called her on my mobile. I knew she'd be at Jack's. She asked me if I could delay Jamie while she got dressed and raced home.'

'And did you delay him?' Kate was determined to get to the bottom of this fascinating tale.

'I told him I fancied a drink, but didn't like going into a pub on my own, and I asked him if he'd like to join me. He jumped at it, and when we parted – an hour or so later – he suggested I should skip next Tuesday's classes, and go round to his flat in World's End while Kerry was learning Italian.' Sasha gave a hollow laugh at the recollection. 'Ironic, isn't it?'

'And that's when you gave up learning Italian, was it?'

'Got it in one,' said Sasha, with an arch smile. 'It was the ideal arrangement. Every Tuesday after that, I went round to see Jamie, and Kerry went to Jack's place.'

'Did Kerry know that's where you were going?'

'Of course. I told her.'

'And she didn't mind?'

'No. In fact, she said it suited her fine that I was having it off with Jamie.'

'And this continued after Kerry's divorce?'

'That didn't make any difference. Jamie and I still kept up our affair. And Kerry moved in to Badajos Street, and carried on her affair with Jack.'

'Did James Porter ever meet Jack Harding?' I asked.

'Not as far as I know. That would've been asking for trouble.'

'But you can't be certain.'

'No, of course not.'

'Where were you the Saturday night that Jack disappeared?' I knew what she'd said, but I do like to check.

'I told you that. I was in bed with Dominic.'

'And you didn't leave him all night? Or he you?'

'No, of course not.'

'Why were you taking Italian classes, Miss Lovell?' asked Kate.

'I had an Italian boyfriend at the time, and I thought it'd be nice to be able to speak his language. But I just couldn't seem to get the hang of it.'

'And who was this boyfriend?' I asked.

There was a moment's hesitation, and then, 'His name is Giovanni Maroni, but we split.'

'When?'

'Just before I started seeing Jamie.'

'And where does this Giovanni Maroni live, Miss Lovell?'

'Why d'you want to know that?' Sasha looked quite fearful at our asking.

'Because I intend to speak to him.'

'What about?'

'About Jack Harding.'

'He doesn't know him.'

'Mr Maroni's address, please, Miss Lovell.'

Reluctantly, Sasha gave us an address. It was in Docklands.

'One other thing,' I said. 'I've heard that two men called on Miss Maitland, your upstairs neighbour at Badajos Street, enquiring after you. They implied that they were from some sort of debt collecting agency. D'you know anything about that?'

Sasha shrugged. 'Nothing to do with me. I don't know anything about it. They were probably after Jack. He owed money all over the place.'

'Very well, Miss Lovell,' I said. 'You may go.'

'But how do I get back to Battersea?' wailed Sasha, a plaintive note in her voice.

'Try hailing a taxi,' said Kate.

And there we left it. For the time being.

James Porter was in earnest conversation with a young bespectacled fellow who, I presumed, was the duty solicitor. And he confirmed it by introducing himself.

'My client is at a loss to know why he's been detained here, Chief Inspector,' he began.

Kate Ebdon had returned to Curtis Green, and I'd prised Dave out of the canteen to join me in interviewing Porter.

I waited until Dave had done the necessary with the recording machine before replying to the solicitor's question.

'Your client, as you call him, has not been detained. I asked him to come to this station to answer some questions regarding the murder of Jack Harding on or about the eighth of September.'

'Does that mean he's free to go at any time he wants?'

'Yes, it does.' What I didn't say was that if

he attempted to do so, he'd be arrested.

'My client has nothing to say,' announced the solicitor, with more gravitas than his youthfulness warranted.

'We'll see about that,' I said. 'Mr Porter, I have evidence that when you discovered your then-wife had been having an affair with Jack Harding, you threatened to kill Mr Harding.'

'Nonsense,' said Porter.

'This was around about the time you also discovered that your ex-wife had been taking part in pornographic films.'

From the look on the young solicitor's face, it was obvious that Porter had not told him about this part of Kerry Porter's chequered history.

'This is all rubbish,' said Porter, a little too lamely for it to be accepted as the truth.

'I also understand that you've been conducting an affair with Sasha Lovell for the past eighteen months.'

'Is that a crime now?' Porter sneered.

'When did you meet Jack Harding?'

'I never met him.'

'Where were you on the night of the seventh and eighth of September. That was a weekend.'

'I can't remember.'

'Try.'

'Probably in bed with Sasha.'

'Sasha claims that she was in bed with Dominic Finch that night, Mr Porter.'

'What? She can't have been.' James Porter shot forward in his chair. That his current girlfriend was two-timing him had clearly come as a shock. 'I don't believe it. You're trying to trap me.'

'Mr Finch confirms it, and your girlfriend freely admitted that she enjoys playing the field. But, being an actress who takes part in pornographic films, I suppose she has a different view on life and morals.'

That statement produced an even more shocked expression on Porter's face. 'She doesn't take part in those films,' he protested.

'I suggest you ask her,' said Dave. 'She seemed quite proud of it. In fact, that's where she said she met your ex-wife.'

James Porter stood up so hurriedly that his chair fell over with a crash. 'I'm not staying here to listen to any more of this damned nonsense,' he said.

'But you are, Mr Porter. I'm arresting you on suspicion of having murdered Jack Harding on or about the eighth of September.' I turned to Dave; he knew what to do, and he also knew that I could never remember the correct form of words.

'James Porter, you are not obliged to say anything, but it may harm...' And Dave rattled off the caution. From memory. I really must learn it one day.

'This is outrageous,' protested Porter, and turned to the duty solicitor. 'Can they do this?' he demanded.

'Yes,' said the solicitor. 'But only if they have sufficient evidence.' He turned to me. 'And have you?'

'No, but I have sufficient suspicion to warrant Mr Porter's arrest,' I said.

'Right, that's it,' said the young solicitor, clearly out of his depth. 'It's obvious that you haven't been entirely honest with me, Mr Porter, and, in the circumstances, I can no longer represent you.' And with that, he picked up his briefcase and made for the door. I got the impression that anything beyond a simple shoplifting would be far too testing for him.

'I shall now arrange for your fingerprints to be taken, Mr Porter,' I said.

'What the hell for?' demanded Porter.

'In order to confirm or disprove your involvement in Harding's murder. You see, Mr Porter, some fingerprints were found in Harding's flat that we've not yet been able to identify.'

In the absence of the duty solicitor, Porter had no one to turn to. Reluctantly, he yielded to having his fingerprints taken.

We then returned to the interview room.

'I must remind you that you are still under caution, Mr Porter,' I said. 'Now, can you remember where you were on the night of the seventh and eighth of September?'

'Yes, of course I can,' said Porter churlishly. 'I was in bed with a girl.'

'Her name?'

Porter let out a sigh. 'She's Liz Blair, and she lives in the flat above mine at Battersea.'

'I presume she's unmarried,' said Dave.

'Well, you presume wrong,' said Porter with a sneer. 'Her husband's away in Dubai or some such place. He's an engineer, so Liz says.'

I was on the point of releasing Porter to police bail when the results of his fingerprint search came through. This modern technology is wonderful. In the old days we'd wait for weeks before we got a match. Or didn't get one.

A detective sergeant from Charing Cross CID entered the interview room and handed me a sheet of paper. Porter's fingerprints had been found in the basement flat at Five Badajos Street. But, more to the point, they were identical to the print found inside the packaging of the explosive device that had been sent to Dominic Finch.

Well and good. Although Porter would have some explaining to do about the exploding package, I was far from being able to prove he'd killed Jack Harding.

I left Porter in Dave's care and telephoned the DI at Chelsea to tell him the glad news.

'Nice one, guv,' said the DI.

'What d'you want me to do with him?' I asked.

'Lock him up there, please, guv, and I'll send an escort to pick him up ASAP.'

Back in the interview room I told Porter that he was being detained for further enquiries by the Chelsea police.

'What for? What have the Chelsea police got to do with it?'

'I don't know,' I lied. But I didn't want to tell him that he would, in all probability, be charged with arson, because that would preclude my colleagues from asking him any questions. In any event, I'd no doubt that the Crown Prosecution Service would come up with something more complicated than that. On the other hand, they might decide there was insufficient evidence to take him to court. Believe me, the CPS works in mysterious ways.

Ten

That area of London known as Docklands lies to the east of the capital. During the Second World War it was largely devastated by German bombers, and very efficient they were at destroying vast acres of it. But nowhere as efficiently as the trade unions. After the war, and seeing no further than the ends of their noses, militant dockers succeeded in destroying a once thriving port far more effectively than the *Luftwaffe*.

Today it is covered by huge office buildings and blocks of expensive apartments. It was in one of these blocks that we eventually found the penthouse flat that Sasha Lovell said was occupied by her ex-boyfriend Giovanni Maroni.

Inside the vast marbled entrance hall an elderly man was seated behind a desk. On this desk was a small brass plaque bearing the single word 'Concierge'.

'Can I help you, sir?' asked this functionary politely.

'We're police officers, and we're looking for Mr Maroni,' I said.

'Well, sir, I'm afraid you won't find him here.' The concierge opened a loose-leaf file, and ran his finger down the page of entries. 'He moved out two weeks ago last Monday, sir.'

'Did he indeed?' It was interesting, but probably irrelevant, that Maroni had departed a week before the discovery of Jack Harding's body on Ham Common. 'Is there anyone occupying the flat now?'

This time the concierge had no need to examine his file. 'Yes, sir, a single gentleman called Bowyer. Only a young chap – about twenty-five, I should think – *and* he drives a Porsche.' He seemed to attach much importance to this last piece of information.

'What does this Mr Bowyer do for a living?' Dave always collected information about people with whom he came into contact, no matter how immaterial.

'I think it's something to do with...' The concierge paused. 'I think he said the futures market, whatever that is. Does that make sense to you?'

'Not at all,' said Dave, 'but I do know it makes a lot of money for some people.'

'D'you know if Mr Bowyer's in?' I asked.

'I do believe so, sir. He doesn't seem to go out much before lunchtime. Take the lift and press the button marked "Penthouse".'

The concierge was on the phone the moment we started crossing the entrance hall towards the lift. I've no doubt that taking such care of his residents ensured that he was similarly cared for around Christmas. The amount of whisky he received probably saw him comfortably through to next Yuletide.

The entrance to what had once been Maroni's penthouse suite was on the far side of a broad, carpeted lobby. The occupant – wearing a checked shirt, chinos and loafers – was standing in the open doorway. As I thought, the concierge had alerted him to our impending arrival.

'Mr Bowyer?'

'Yes, I'm Tom Bowyer.'

'We're police officers, Mr Bowyer. May we come in?'

'Yeah, sure.' Bowyer led the way into a spacious, airy room with a balcony that overlooked the river.

'Nice place you've got here,' said Dave, looking around at the expensive, if somewhat bizarre, furnishings.

'I like it,' said Bowyer. 'Have a seat, guys, and tell me what I can do for you. This is Suzy, by the way.' He indicated a slender Asian girl with very long black hair. She was wearing a black Lycra catsuit and lounging on a black leather settee. The effect was to make her almost invisible.

'Hi!' said the girl. 'I'm going to take a shower, Tom.' She stood up and walked casually out of the room.

'The porter tells us,' began Dave, obviously having no truck with this 'concierge' business, 'that you only moved in recently.'

'Yeah, about a fortnight ago. I reckon I was lucky to get this place.'

'And the porter told us you drive a Porsche.'

Bowyer laughed. 'I wish,' he said. 'I've only borrowed it from a mate of mine. Got to give it back when he comes home from Barbados.'

'Did you happen to meet the previous tenant, a Mr Giovanni Maroni?' I asked.

'Only briefly, on the day he moved out and I moved in.'

'Have you any idea where he went?'

'No, I haven't. I still keep getting the occasional letter for him. He obviously didn't put in one of those redirection things at the post office. Bit of a nuisance really.'

'What d'you do with those letters?' asked Dave.

'I give them to Cyril. I imagine he marks them "Gone Away", and sticks 'em back in the postbox.'

'Who's Cyril?' Dave knew damned well who Cyril was, but he never makes assumptions.

'He's the concierge. The chap you met on the way in.'

'How d'you know we met him on the way in?' Dave posed the question impishly.

'Because he phoned me and told me you were on your way up,' said Bowyer with a grin. 'That's why I was waiting with the door open.'

'What did this Maroni look like?' I asked.

'About five-nine, I suppose, black hair and a thin moustache.'

'Age?'

'I should think he was about thirty-five,' said Bowyer. 'Possibly forty.' It suddenly seemed to occur to him to query why we were in his flat asking questions about the previous tenant. 'Is this Maroni guy in some sort of trouble?'

'No,' I said. 'We just need to talk to him. Incidentally, was there a woman with him when you met him?'

'No, he was alone.'

'Did he drive a Volvo, by any chance?' Dave was obviously thinking about the man who'd bought the wooden box from Ted Middle-

152

ton, the Tooting carpenter.

'I've no idea what he drove, but I'm sure Cyril will know.'

I concluded that Cyril was likely to be a more useful source of information than our futures trader. We thanked Bowyer for his time and descended to the ground floor.

'Mr Bowyer tells me you're called Cyril,' I said.

'That's me, sir.' The concierge folded his copy of the *Daily Mirror* and looked up. 'Get what you wanted, gents?'

'Yes and no,' said Dave. 'This Maroni guy, what car did he drive?'

'A Bentley. Beautiful green job it was. Sometimes he'd ask me to park it in the underground garage for him.' Cyril's face adopted a dreamy expression. 'I wouldn't have minded giving that a run up the M1, I can tell you.'

'Was that the only car he had?'

'As far as I know, yes. I mean, he might have had others, but if he did, he didn't park them here.'

'Didn't have a black Volvo estate, I suppose?'

'Not to my knowledge, guv'nor, no.'

'Have you any idea where he moved to when he left here?' I asked.

'No, sir,' said Cyril. 'A bit of a dark horse was our Mr Maroni. Mr Bowyer still gets letters for him from time to time. I've got one here that arrived this morning.'

'We'll drop that in the box for you,' said Dave, and took the letter from Cyril. He, like me, was hoping it might shed some light on Maroni and his activities.

'Very kind of you, guv'nor. Thanks.'

'This one's marked "NKATA".' Dave pronounced it 'en-carter'. 'Sounds like an African name,' he said with a straight face. He was a great wind-up merchant. 'Was this Maroni African, then?'

For a moment Cyril looked mystified. 'Oh, no, guv'nor, Mr Maroni was Italian. "NKATA" stands for "Not known at this address".'

'D'you happen to have any more of these letters, Cyril?' I asked.

'No, sir. The last one turned up on Saturday, but they're getting less and less. I s'pose by now Mr Maroni's told everyone that he's moved. P'raps he's gone back to Italy,' he added helpfully.

'I suppose you don't happen to remember the index mark of this Bentley of Maroni's, do you?' asked Dave hopefully.

'Yes, guv'nor,' said Cyril. 'We keep a record of all the residents' vehicles in case there's a fire or something in the underground car park.' He took yet another of his folders from a drawer in his desk, and thumbed through the pages. Turning it so that Dave could read the appropriate entry, he pointed to it.

'Thanks, Cyril,' said Dave, scribbling the details in his pocketbook. 'Did anyone live with him?'

The concierge ran a hand round his chin. 'Yes, there was a young lady who was more or less permanent, but she left about a year ago. Since then there have been girls who stayed for a week or two.' He looked around as though afraid of being overheard. 'He picked some good-looking girls, did Mr Maroni.'

'D'you remember the name of the woman who left a year ago?'

'No, I'm afraid not. In fact, gents, I never knew her name.' Cyril looked somewhat crestfallen that we'd come up with a question that he was unable to answer.

'Never mind, Cyril,' said Dave, 'you've been a great help.'

'We aim to please, guv'nor,' said the concierge.

As we left Maroni's last known address, Dave ripped open the envelope of the letter he'd offered to post, and read the contents. 'Wonderful,' he said. 'This is junk mail from a company that sells conservatories. They're offering him one at a discount.' He laughed. 'They'd have a job building that on to a penthouse.'

We now had a name, an approximate age, and a description that could have fitted thousands of men. We also knew Maroni drove a green Bentley, and we had its index mark. The one important piece of information we didn't have was where he was now.

Back at Curtis Green, I instructed Colin Wilberforce to feed these scant details into the Police National Computer to see what came up. What came up was nothing. And it still showed the Docklands address for the Bentley's owner. Finally, I told Colin to put the details of the Bentley on to the PNC with instructions that the driver should be stopped and detained, and that I should be informed immediately. Whoever said that a detective's life was exciting and romantic had never tried to find someone who apparently didn't want to be found.

I decided to interview Sasha Lovell again, to see if she could shed any more light on the mysterious Giovanni Maroni.

'What have you done with Jamie?' Sasha's opening question was aggressive.

'Mr Porter's been detained by the Chelsea police in connection with an incident at Dominic Finch's studio,' I said.

'Incident? What incident?'

'I'm not at liberty to discuss that, Miss Lovell.'

'What are you here for, then?'

'We've been attempting to interview Mr Maroni, Miss Lovell,' said Dave. 'But he's no longer at the address in Docklands you gave us.'

'I've not seen him for a year, so I can't help you.' Sasha tried to sound indifferent, but I got the impression that his apparent disappearance worried her.

'What exactly was your relationship with him?' Dave asked.

'What's that got to do with you?' Sasha reached across to take a cigarette from a packet on a side table.

'Miss Lovell,' I said, 'I'm investigating the murder of Jack Harding, your boyfriend. Or should I say one of your boyfriends. I therefore need to speak to anyone I think might be of assistance to me in that enquiry.'

Sasha let out a sigh of resignation. 'And if I don't tell you?' she demanded.

'Then I'll start to think that you played some active part in Mr Harding's death.'

'That's nonsense. Why should I have wanted to kill Jack? Anyway, I was in bed with Dom that night.'

'Well, someone wanted him dead, and I intend to find out who that someone was.'

'Gio and I had a fling.' Sasha was sitting bunched up on a settee, puffing furiously at her cigarette.

. 'How did you meet him?'

'I was an exotic dancer at one of the clubs he owned in the West End.'

'You mean you slithered round a pole stark naked,' said Dave, always one to get to the nub of things.

'Yes.' Sasha shot Dave a death-dealing glance. 'Gio was always at one or other of his clubs, and one night he invited me to have dinner with him.'

'Just dinner?'

'Yes, just dinner.' Sasha was clearly annoyed at Dave's intrusive question, accurate
though its implication probably was.

'What happened next?'

'We went out together quite regularly after
that, and a few weeks later he invited me to
move in with him at his penthouse in Docklands.'

'When did all this start?'

'About three years ago. I lived with him for
a couple of years.'

'So why did you split up?'

Sasha stubbed out her cigarette and remained silent for a while. But eventually she
said, 'Gio's one of those men who loves to
control people. And he tried to control me.
All he really wanted was a woman who'd be
available to hop into bed with him whenever
he wanted. And someone he could take out
and show off, like he was saying, "Look at
me, I've got this good-looking woman, and
she's all mine." He made me give up my job
as a dancer, and dictated my every move,
and what I wore.' She smiled. 'Or didn't
wear. But after two years of it, I began to feel
suffocated.'

'So you left him?'

'Too bloody right I left him.'

'And that's when you moved in with Jack
Harding, was it?'

'Not directly. I went back to Dom.'

158

'Dominic Finch?'

'Yes. He and I are old friends. I've known Dom for about five or six years, ever since I started modelling for him.'

'But during that time,' I said, 'you got married to Georges Gaillard, the golf professional from Le Touquet.'

'Yes, but that was a mistake. He was very like Gio. Just wanted a trophy wife to parade around. Frenchmen are like that, you know.'

'You don't seem to have had much luck with men,' commented Dave. 'What was Maroni's reaction to you moving out of his apartment?'

'He was bloody furious. He hates not getting his own way. Usually he was able to buy anything he wanted, but it didn't work with me.'

'And that was it, was it? You just walked out of his life, and you've heard nothing from him since. Seems strange that he would have given up that easily, if he was the sort of man you say he was.'

There was a long pause before Sasha spoke again. 'He has tried to contact me from time to time. He found out I was living with Jack, and he called there once when I was out. Jack said he was quite nasty about me, and said that he wanted me back, and wasn't going to take no for an answer.'

'Was Maroni ever violent towards you, Miss Lovell?' I asked.

Again there was a pause. 'He often forced

me to have sex with him when I didn't really want to.'

'You mean he raped you?'

'I suppose that's one way of putting it, yes.'

'I can't think of another way of putting it.'

'It was one of the reasons that I left him.'

'And you've really no idea where he is now?' It was obvious that I needed to have a word with Giovanni Maroni, and urgently at that. If he'd been violent towards Sasha Lovell, there was no reason to think that he wouldn't have offered violence to Jack Harding. 'D'you think he might have returned to Italy?'

'I don't know, but I'd like to think so.'

'You remember that I mentioned a couple of men who called on Davina Maitland looking for you. Is it possible that they might have been working for Maroni?'

'They could've been, I suppose. I certainly don't owe anyone any money, and I can't think of any other reason why they should have been looking for me unless Gio had sent them.'

'Is that why you left in a hurry?'

'Partly. I thought that when Jack was killed, it might've been something to do with Gio.' Sasha stared at me with a pathetic look. 'And now that Jamie's not here, I'm quite worried that he might track me down.'

'Did he ever own a black Volvo estate, Miss Lovell?' asked Dave.

'Not that I know of, but he did have a

friend who did.'

'D'you know who this friend was?'

'No, except to say that he was Italian too.'

'You met him, then?'

'Not exactly. We were leaving the apartment one day when this guy turned up just as we were getting into the Bentley. Gio steered him away from me and spoke to him.'

'Did you hear what they were saying?'

'I heard, but I didn't understand. They were speaking in Italian. But whatever it was that Gio was saying, he certainly sounded annoyed about something.'

'What did this man look like?'

'Tall, thin, and he had a thin moustache like Gio's. And he wore sunglasses.'

'And you've no idea who he was.'

'No. I said I didn't know.'

'Did Maroni have any other business interests?' I asked.

'Not as far as I know. He never went out to work, not a regular sort of job. Most of the day he was in the apartment, and spent a lot of time on the phone, and on his computer.'

'Have you any idea what he was doing on this computer of his?' Dave asked.

'No. I went into his study once, but he hit a key and the screen went blank. Then he told me never to go into the study again. He was very annoyed that I'd gone in there.'

'I propose to put a woman police officer in here with you for the time being, Miss

161

Lovell.' I hadn't come to that conclusion lightly. With the current obsession about budgets that prevails in the Metropolitan Police, it was not a decision to be taken without careful consideration. And without worrying what our beloved commander would have to say about it.

'What for? Won't Jamie be home soon?'

'I wouldn't bank on it,' said Dave crushingly.

'D'you think I'm in some sort of danger, then?' asked Sasha. There was an expression of alarm on her face, and it was clear that my offer of protection had had a disturbing effect on her.

'Not necessarily, but I think it would be a wise precaution,' I said. 'Now, about this club of Maroni's where you worked as a dancer...'

'What about it?'

'Where is it?'

Sasha gave a Soho address.

Dave called the incident room on his mobile, and asked DI Kate Ebdon to make the necessary arrangements for the protection of Sasha Lovell. It was a damned nuisance, and it would mean taking two operational officers away from their normal duties, at least until I could make other arrangements.

Half an hour later, DCs Sheila Armitage and Nicola Chance arrived. They were not happy. 'Babysitting' is not a detective's favourite chore.

I briefed the two women officers about Maroni, and his Italian mate, and told them that I would have them relieved as soon as possible.

Once outside Sasha's flat, I called Davina Maitland on my cellphone. Last time we had seen her, she had been thoughtful enough to give us her mobile number.

'I'm sorry to bother you, Miss Maitland, but you may recall telling us about two men who called enquiring after Sasha Maitland.'

'Yes, I do.'

'I know you gave us a rough description of what they looked like, but I was wondering if you could expand on it.'

Although Davina Maitland did her best, the descriptions were predictably commonplace, and she repeated that the one who'd spoken to her sounded foreign, and he was of medium height and had what she described as 'a mean little moustache'. And, she added, he was wearing sunglasses.

'You don't happen to know what sort of car they arrived in, do you, Miss Maitland?' I asked hopefully.

'No, sorry.'

Back at Curtis Green, I sought out the commander.

'Ah, Mr Brock.' The commander swept off his half-moon glasses and stared at me. 'Progress in the Harding homicide?'

There were two things about the commander that irritated me. Firstly, he always called me 'Mr Brock' rather than 'Harry', presumably for fear that I might use his first name in return – something he couldn't have coped with – and secondly he always referred to felonious deaths as homicides, rather than murders. Just in case the jury returned a verdict of manslaughter, I suppose. Me, I just called them toppings, but then I'm a real detective.

'I've authorized the employment of two detectives to guard Miss Sasha Lovell on a round-the-clock basis, sir,' I said.

'What?' The commander was clearly appalled at my exercise of corporate profligacy. 'D'you realize the cost of that, Mr Brock?'

'Oh, indeed I do, sir.' *And I don't care*, I thought.

'There'd better be a good reason. For a start, who is this … what did you say her name was?

'Sasha Lovell, sir.' I summarized what we had learned of the Harding murder so far, a summary that caused the commander to blink several times; especially the bits about porn actresses, nude models and mysterious Italians. I then went on to explain, as briefly and as simply as possible, where Giovanni Maroni featured in all this, and his alleged reputation as a man of violence. 'I think we have to consider the possibility that Maroni topped Harding, sir.'

The commander wrinkled his nose. He didn't care for slang expressions like 'topped', and, as I've mentioned before, laboured under the delusion that any police officer promoted to the rank of inspector and above automatically became a gentleman.

The commander dithered. 'I'm not sure that the deputy assistant commissioner will look upon this favourably, Mr Brock.'

That was predictable. I'd presented our beloved chief with a crisis. On the one hand, he could probably see the sense of what I'd done, but on the other he was fearful that the DAC might hold him personally responsible for wasting money.

I tried to help him out, but probably only made things worse.

'The problem is this, sir,' I began. 'If Maroni was responsible for Harding's death, he might just be tempted to silence Sasha Lovell. Frankly, I don't think she's told us the truth about her relationship with Maroni. And bearing in mind the sort of criticism that's been levelled at the Metropolitan Police in recent years, I think that not to protect Miss Lovell might be seen as gross negligence.'

'Yes, yes, I do see that, Mr Brock.' The commander played briefly with a letter opener, spinning it on his desk. It stopped with the point directed straight at me. Not a good omen. 'I'll see if I can clear it with the DAC.'

'Ideally, sir, it would relieve my two detectives if the Uniform Branch could be persuaded to provide protection. Say someone from CO19.'

'I'm not sure that Firearms Department would be prepared to provide officers for that sort of duty.'

'Perhaps not, sir,' I said, secure in the knowledge that the ball was now firmly in the commander's court. I'd done my bit, and the rest was up to him.

'Leave it with me, Mr Brock,' was all the commander said.

And I did leave it with him, unhappy though the thought of his impending conversation with the DAC made him.

Eleven

The DAC obviously shared my view of the possible danger to which Sasha Lovell might be exposed, and authorized a 24-hour guard on her. The commander, when he gave me this glad news, appeared relieved, particularly as the DAC had persuaded the Uniform Branch to provide the coverage.

I also heard from the DI at Chelsea that James Porter had been charged with sending an explosive device to Dominic Finch, and had been remanded in custody. Apparently the district judge at West London magistrates' court seemed to think he was some sort of terrorist.

On Wednesday morning, I came to the conclusion that another interview with Dominic Finch might throw up some more information. One of the things that interested me was why James Porter should have targeted the Chelsea photographer with his pathetic letter bomb. I was also curious to learn the full story behind Finch's relationship with Sasha Lovell, who'd returned to him after her failed marriage to Georges Gaillard, and again after she'd left Maroni.

Finch himself answered the door of his studio on this occasion.

'What is it about you coppers? Can't you resist the sight of bare female flesh?'

I didn't dignify that comment with a response. I knew of some policemen who, in order to gather evidence, had been given the task of viewing porn films, or conducting observations on strip joints. After a week or two, they'd begged to be relieved, because, they claimed, it had taken the magic out of their sex lives.

'I want to talk to you about Sasha Lovell, Mr Finch.'

'I've told you all I know, but I suppose you'd better come in. As luck would have it, we're having a break from filming.'

In the big studio at the back of the house two men and two women were sitting around smoking and drinking coffee. All of them were clad in dressing gowns. One of them was Kerry Porter; she looked away, clearly not wanting to acknowledge me. This morning, Finch had a woman with him who was assisting in the filming. I somehow doubted that she shared Finch's bed; from the look of her, I thought she probably fancied some of the actresses.

Finch led us out of the studio and into the small kitchen where the letter bomb, allegedly sent by Porter, had exploded. He closed the door. 'Well?'

'We've located Miss Lovell,' I began.

'Really? Where is she?'

'I'm not at liberty to disclose that information, Mr Finch, but what interests me more is why James Porter should've sent you an explosive device.'

'It was Porter, was it?' Finch didn't seem surprised.

'It's only an allegation at this stage – not that I think there's much doubt – but you'll have to wait for his trial to confirm it.'

'That guy's a bloody nutcase.'

'Maybe, but why?'

'He found out that his wife Kerry was working for me, making blue flicks, and he didn't like it. He came round here on one occasion threatening me, and saying he wanted his wife to give up her acting, and go back to him.'

'When we asked you previously whether anyone had threatened you, you said no one had. What you actually said was that you couldn't think of anyone offhand.'

Finch shrugged, but said nothing.

'So, when was this?' asked Dave.

'The first time was about a year ago,' said Finch, 'but after that he kept phoning me up, or coming round, shouting the odds about reporting me to you lot. I don't know whether he did, but I know the law, and I know I'm on the right side of it ... just. He struck me as belonging to the holier-than-thou lobby who hold up their hands in horror at what I do, but half of 'em aren't above drooling over the results.'

'What did you do about Porter? Did you take out a restraining order?' I asked.

Finch laughed scornfully. 'What difference would that have made? Come on, Chief Inspector, you know the score, and you know damned well that people like Porter wouldn't take any notice of a bit of paper handed down by a magistrate. Do yobboes take any notice when they're given an ASBO?'

'You're probably right about that,' I said. Most of the young tearaways who received anti-social behaviour orders regarded them almost as a badge of honour, something to boast to their mates about.

'Anyway, the last time Porter turned up

here, I told him that if I ever saw him again, I'd give him such a hiding that his private health insurance wouldn't be able to cover it.'

'And did he come round again?'

'No, he took the hint. Or I thought he had. But now you tell me he was the bastard sent me that letter bomb or whatever it was. It could've killed Michelle. I'll tell you this much: if I ever see him again, I'll bloody kill *him*.'

'Making a threat to murder is an offence,' said Dave mildly.

'So's trying to kill one of my birds,' said Finch, quite unperturbed by Dave's comment.

'Sasha Lovell told us that she'd known you for five of six years,' I said.

'That's right. So?'

'That means that she knew you before she married Georges Gaillard, the French golf professional.'

'Yeah, that's right. Look, what the hell is this all about?'

'But she came back to you after she left him.'

'Yes. According to Sasha, Gaillard was a tosser.'

'But then she went off with Giovanni Maroni.'

'Is that the Italian guy?'

'Yes. And then she came back to you again, after she'd split with him.'

'It's my irresistible sex-appeal,' said Finch.

'Didn't you mind that she kept going off with other men, and then returning?'

'Why should I? It's a free country, so they tell me. Anyway, she's good in the sack, man. And she's good at what she does for me.' Finch laughed. 'Mind you, I don't exactly see her getting a best-actress Oscar for it.'

'Did you ever meet this Italian called Maroni?'

'No. In fact I never knew his name. Why? Did he have something to do with Jack's murder?'

'That's what I'm trying to find out.'

'Is that it, then?' asked Finch.

'For the time being,' I said.

We walked out through the studio. Finch's camerawoman was filming an animated pair coupling on a bed, one of whom was Kerry Porter.

Colin Wilberforce greeted us with the sad news that a check with the Driver and Vehicle Licensing Agency at Swansea showed that Giovanni Maroni's Bentley was still registered at the Docklands apartment we'd visited yesterday.

'Well, at least we can do him for failing to notify a change of address,' said Dave mournfully. 'And knowing our luck, that's about all we'll be able to do him for.'

It was a week since I'd taken Gail out for a

meal, and as there was a lull in the enquiry into Harding's murder, I decided to make it up to her.

I rang her home phone number, but there was no answer. Just her mellifluous tones on the answering machine, inviting me to leave a message. I tried her mobile.

'Hello?'

'Where are you?' I asked.

'At the Granville Theatre,' she replied.

'What are you doing there?'

'Auditioning for a part, darling.'

'You didn't tell me anything about that,' I said.

'I never see you for long enough to tell you anything that I'm doing,' said Gail, a note of censure in her voice.

'What part is this? More chorus line stuff?'

'Certainly not. It's a musical about Gipsy Rose Lee, a striptease artiste, and I'm after the principal part.'

'*What?*' I nearly dropped the phone.

'Only kidding,' said Gail. 'It's a Noël Coward revival called *Design for Living*.'

'Never heard of it,' I said.

'It's all about a successful *ménage-à-trois*,' Gail said, determined not to let me down lightly.

'And which part are you after?' I didn't like the sound of this.

'Well, it's not the man's part, darling. Anyway, I'm about to go on. What did you want?'

'How about dinner tonight?'

'Good idea. I'll cook. You bring the wine, and it'd better include a bottle of champagne, just in case I get the part.'

This was good news, especially as I'm frequently exposed to the delights of the police canteen. Gail is an excellent cook, and her meals are a banquet.

I arrived at Gail's Kingston townhouse at half past seven.

'I got it!' Gail was ecstatic about her return to the theatre, and well she should be.

'You've finally broken the barrier, then,' I said. Gail had been married to a theatre director called Gerald Andrews, but it ended in divorce. She had returned home unexpectedly from the theatre where she'd been performing, and found her husband in bed with a nude dancer. Well, she was nude at the time. In fact, they both were. Unfortunately for Gail's career, Gerald Andrews had quite unfairly harboured a grudge – even though he was the guilty party – and she was sure that he'd blocked her attempts to get back to acting. As a result, she'd been forced to take parts as a chorus girl, and that's how I met her, when she was in a production called *Scatterbrain*, curiously enough at the Granville Theatre where she'd been auditioning that afternoon.

'Yes, and it could be in for a long run. I hope you brought some champagne.'

173

'Right here,' I said, holding up a super-market bag. 'It's not chilled, but I'll stick it in the freezer for ten minutes.'

'Sacrilege,' murmured Gail.

I was not too happy about this business of my girlfriend returning to the theatre, not that I begrudged her success. It meant that she would be working every evening – Monday to Saturday – with matinees on Wednesdays and Saturdays. It was not as if she *had* to work; her father, George, a property developer who lived in Nottingham, provided her with a substantial allowance. I'd met George – and his wife Sally, a former dancer – on several occasions. George's only vice was his incessant talk about Formula One motor racing, and the land-speed record.

We saw off the champagne, and I toasted Gail on her triumph in securing the part. The dinner she'd prepared came up to my expectations, and afterwards we settled in her sitting room on the first floor. The weather was good enough to have the French doors open, and we sat there at peace with the world.

Until my mobile rang.

'Oh no!' Gail exclaimed. 'Don't they ever leave you alone?'

'I was at a studio this morning watching them make pornographic films,' I said, determined to pay Gail back for her earlier comments about appearing as a striptease

174

artiste in a play. 'I expect it's something to do with that.' I opened my cellphone before she could reply.

'It's Gavin Creasey, sir.'

'What is it, Gavin?'

'Giovanni Maroni, sir. He's been detained.'

'Where?'

'On West End Central's ground, sir. He's being held at the nick now. The Black Rats pulled him for jumping a red light, and then gave him some fanny about the address his car was registered at not being the same as the one he gave the officers.'

'Excellent. Sounds like they used a bit of initiative. I'll be there ASAP. Give Dave Poole a ring and tell him to meet me there.'

This suited me. I had intended to visit Maroni at his club, the address of which Sasha Lovell had given us, but I prefer to interview suspects on my territory rather than theirs.

Gail groaned as I closed my mobile phone. 'You're off, then?'

'I'm afraid so, darling,' I said. 'I'm not going to risk a traffic patrol car again.' Traffic division drivers, although extremely competent, scared the hell out of me. 'I'll get the train. It'll be just as quick.'

'I've no doubt you'll have pleased Madeleine, too,' said Gail. Madeleine was Dave's ballet-dancer wife.

'She's working tonight, so Dave'll be at a loose end. By the way, when do you start at the Granville?'

'On Monday, with rehearsals,' said Gail.

'Mr Maroni?'

'*Si!*' Maroni was olive-skinned with a thin moustache, and was wearing sunglasses, even though it was nearly ten o'clock at night and he was indoors. His suit, essentially Italian in cut, must have cost a small fortune. 'I am *Signor* Giovanni Maroni. Why have I been arrested, eh?' He pushed his sunglasses up to the top of his head.

'You haven't been arrested, Mr Maroni, but I understand from the officers who asked you to come to the police station that they weren't satisfied about the ownership of the car you were driving.'

'This is nonsense. Of course I own it.'

'But you don't live at the Docklands address at which that car is registered. And why don't you sit down?'

'I prefer to stand.' A shifty individual, Maroni's eyes darted everywhere as though he feared someone would creep up and hit him behind the ear. Every few minutes he would take the coins from his pocket, carefully arrange them in size order, and then, just as carefully, replace them in his pocket. He seemed the sort of man who should have had a purse, and I wondered why he hadn't got one. 'So, I forgot to change it. It is not so important, eh?'

'Where do you live now?' asked Dave.

176

Maroni sat down on one of the hard-back-ed chairs in the interview room and took out a gold cigarette case.

'We do not allow smoking here,' I said.

'Pah! Ridiculous.' Maroni returned the case to his pocket.

'You were about to give me your present address,' Dave said, in a way that brooked no refusal.

Maroni produced a visiting card and toss-ed it on to the table. It showed that he lived in a flat in Curzon Street.

'Can I go now, or do you want to send half a dozen policemen to my apartment to make enquiries?' Maroni's question was larded with sarcasm. 'I'm surprised that you take so much trouble about my Bentley when there are people running about all over London killing each other.'

'Sasha Lovell,' I said.

Maroni's jaw dropped, and an expression of shock crossed his face. But a moment later he recovered. 'As I am not under arrest, I shall leave now.'

'No you won't. Giovanni Maroni, I'm arresting you on suspicion of having murder-ed one Jack Harding on or about the seventh or eighth of September.'

'This is outrageous,' protested Maroni. 'I have never heard of this person.'

'But you do know Sasha Lovell.' It was a statement, not a question.

'Of course. She's a lovely *signorina*.'

177

'And she lived with you for some time, did she not?'

'Is that a crime?' asked Maroni haughtily.

Dave glanced at me with a raised eyebrow. I knew what he was thinking: that I should caution Maroni. But I knew that I didn't need to until I was satisfied that he had committed the crime of which I suspected him.

'I have evidence that on one occasion you called on Jack Harding and threatened him.' Unfortunately, I didn't have a written statement to that effect, but I was sure that if I were ever in a position to charge Maroni, Sasha Lovell would be prepared to make one once her erstwhile lover was locked up.

'Nonsense,' said Maroni, with a dismissive wave of a well-manicured hand.

'I put it to you that you were so incensed at Sasha Lovell's departure that you determined to get her back, no matter what it took. Even if it meant killing Harding.'

'It is true that I was upset when she went, but Sasha is a free spirit. She must do what she wants.'

'Some time ago, a man who drives a Volvo purchased a wooden box. That box has been identified as the one in which Jack Harding's body was found at Ham Common on the morning of Sunday the eighth of September.'

'All this talk of boxes. Are you mad? What do I know of boxes? What has that to do with me?'

'That man, and that car, fits the description of a man who was known to have called on you at your Docklands apartment.' I was going out on a limb with that allegation; there was no proof at all that they were one and the same. And Maroni obviously guessed that to be the case.

'I've never heard of such a man.'

I was surprised that Maroni had not asked for a solicitor, but I'd formed the impression that he was so self-confident that he didn't see the need for one. And I was forced to agree: he seemed to be doing quite well on his own.

'Do you deny that such a man called on you, on a day when you and Sasha Lovell were about to leave in your Bentley?'

I wasn't worried about disclosing my source. If Maroni now attempted to 'silence' Sasha Lovell, he would be met by armed police.

'I repeat, I've never heard of this man. Whoever told you this is lying.'

'I understand that you own a club in the West End of London.' I tried another tack.

'I own two clubs, but I can assure you that they are both properly regulated. We have had frequent visits from your Clubs and Vice Branch, and they found nothing to complain about.'

'Where were you on Saturday and Sunday, the seventh and eighth of September?'

Maroni placed the tips of his fingers together and stared at the ceiling. After a short period of introspection, he looked at me again. 'I can't remember,' he said.

This interview was going nowhere, and I decided that much more evidence would have to be garnered before I could lay a charge against this arrogant Italian.

'Very well, Mr Maroni.' I stood up. 'I shall admit you to bail to return to this police station in one month's time. Should we not require you to attend, you will be notified.'

'You will be hearing from my solicitor.' Maroni stood up too, and drew himself up to his full height. 'There is such a thing as wrongful arrest in English law, I believe.'

'Well, that was a blow-out, Dave,' I said, as we made our way down Burlington Street.

'Cocky bastard, isn't he?' commented Dave. 'So what do we do now, guv?'

We reached Regent Street and I peered up and down for a cab. But, like policemen, there's never one about when you want one.

'We've got Maroni's Curzon Street address, Dave,' I said, finally spotting a taxi and waving furiously at it. 'I can see no alternative but to mount an observation on it. I'm bloody sure that this mysterious Volvo driver will make a meet with Maroni at some time or another.'

'That should make you popular with the commander, guv,' said Dave.

The taxi ignored my frantic gestures and
180

settled for a quartet whose dress implied that it consisted of well-heeled American tourists.

It was clearly not my day.

Twelve

I decided to use some of our own people to mount the surveillance on Giovanni Maroni, hoping that it wouldn't last too long. On Thursday morning, I sent for DI Kate Ebdon, and asked her to arrange it. For the early shift, she nominated DS Charles Flynn – a recent arrival in HSCC from the Fraud Squad – and DC Sheila Armitage; DS Tom Challis and DC Nicola Chance were tasked to take over at three o'clock.

Colin Wilberforce had checked with Clubs and Vice Branch, and confirmed that Maroni was registered as the owner of two clubs in the West End.

I briefed the four surveillance officers about Maroni, mentioning that I was particularly interested in any contact he might have with the elusive Volvo owner. The Challis and Chance team took up the observation at three o'clock that afternoon, and all we had to do now was sit and wait.

* * *

By Saturday morning, I was beginning to think that I was wasting our slender resources. Flynn and Armitage had kept observation on Maroni's flat during the mornings, but he hadn't left there during their tour of duty. That didn't surprise me: Sasha Lovell had said that he rarely ventured out before the evening.

The evenings, however, were different. At eight o'clock on Thursday, Tom Challis and Nicola Chance had followed Maroni from his Curzon Street flat to one of his West End clubs. They reported that he was treated with great deference by the staff, but appeared not to meet anyone of significance. That is if you discounted a half-naked bimbo who sat on his lap for ten minutes before the pair of them disappeared to a private room. A similar excursion occurred on Friday evening, but to his other club. The reaction of the staff there, Challis reported, was similar to that of the previous evening, even to the extent of providing Maroni with the services of a 'friendly' young woman.

On the Saturday evening, however, things began to happen. At just after ten o'clock, Maroni left the club he was at, and drove to Putney in south-west London. He called at a house in Bloxwich Road, stayed for about twenty minutes, and then returned to Curzon Street.

The house, Challis reported, was a detached property, probably worth three-quarters of a million. It had a garage, but he was unable to tell whether it contained a black Volvo estate without showing out.

I decided to switch the surveillance from Maroni's flat to the Bloxwich Road address in the hope that we might learn something that would lead us to Harding's killer.

I recalled Dave's throwaway comment when Ted Middleton, the carpenter, was describing the man who had bought the wooden crate that was almost certainly the one in which Jack Harding's body had been found. Dave had said it looked like the work of a Mafioso. And given that Sasha Lovell had told us that Giovanni Maroni had visited Harding, and made threats, I was beginning to wonder whether Maroni had any mafia connections.

That thought was strengthened when we learned that the occupant of the Bloxwich Road address was called Vincenzo Camilleri. The manner of Harding's murder certainly smacked of the mafia's style of demonstrative killings.

The Flynn and Armitage team took up the observation on Camilleri's house at seven o'clock on the Sunday morning. There was no movement, and no signs of life. The late-turn team of Challis and Chance took over at three o'clock, and when they booked off at eleven that evening they also reported that no movement had occurred.

On Monday morning, I decided that we couldn't afford to waste any more time. Summoning Dave, we drove to Putney.

I walked over to the nondescript observation van from which the surveillance team were keeping watch.

'Any movement, Charlie?' I asked Flynn.

'Nothing, guv. Quiet as a grave.'

Dave and I crossed to the house and rang the bell. There was no reply.

'We'll have a look round the back, Dave,' I said, pushing open a wrought-iron gate at the side of the property.

The back garden was large, and laid mainly to lawn. A teak table and half a dozen chairs stood on a deep patio that ran the full width of the house.

I peered through the windows of the conservatory and saw just what I didn't want to see. A man's body lay sprawled on the floor, a large patch of red staining the front of his white shirt.

'At a guess, guv,' said Dave, 'I'd say we've just found *Signor* Vincenzo Camilleri.' He paused before adding, 'Well, Charlie Flynn said it was as quiet as a grave.'

I had a nasty feeling about this. Not because we'd found a dead body, but because we'd found it in Putney, within the London borough of Wandsworth. And Wandsworth was in the area covered by Homicide and Serious Crime Command *South*. But I knew instinctively that the commander would give it to me, and I was right. I rang him on my mobile and explained the situation.

'I think it would be as well for you to investigate this suspicious death, Mr Brock, as it seems to be connected to the Harding homicide.'

I suppose it was my own fault. I'd been foolish enough to mention Maroni and Harding in the same breath when I'd briefed the commander. Harding had been killed between Fulham and Ham Common, and here we had an Italian living in an expensive house in Putney. The only tenuous link was Giovanni Maroni. And, boy, they don't come any more tenuous than that.

While I'd been talking to the commander, Dave had been busy on his mobile. Twenty minutes later, two PCs arrived from Wandsworth nick, and smashed in the front door with their custom-built ramming device.

We walked through to the conservatory and examined the body. There was no doubting that our man was indeed dead.

While we waited for the scientific teams and the pathologist to arrive, Dave and I took the opportunity to have a look round.

The house was immaculate, and expensively furnished. Original paintings adorned the walls of the living rooms, and the bathroom – about the size of a double garage – contained a jacuzzi as well as an ordinary bath and a shower area. The master bedroom was dominated by a bed that must have been at least six feet wide, but curiously there was no evidence of a woman's presence anywhere in the house. Certainly none of the battery of built-in wardrobes contained any female clothing.

'Bit of a hedonist, this guy,' said Dave.

'If you say so, Dave,' I said. There had been no expense spared in creating a luxury home. Whatever Camilleri did for a living must have paid well, but I had the feeling that whatever it was would be illegal.

Just as we finished our tour of inspection, Dr Henry Mortlock arrived, muttering about the inconvenience of having to turn out on a Monday morning, and generally complaining about the traffic. Henry's arrival was followed by that of Linda Mitchell and her team of forensic practitioners.

Meanwhile, Dave had set Flynn and Armitage the task of calling at neighbouring houses to enquire if they had seen or heard anything out of the ordinary.

'What d'you think, Henry?' I asked Mortlock when he'd finished his cursory examination.

Unusually for Henry, he offered an opinion, something he was normally loath to do until he'd conducted the post-mortem examination. 'At a rough guess, Harry,' he said, waving a rectal thermometer at the body, 'this man's been dead between twenty and twenty-four hours. Subject, of course, to what I find at the post-mortem.'

186

'Of course,' I murmured. And that fitted in very neatly with Maroni's visit to the house. Surely it couldn't be that easy.

We went through the internal door to the garage. And there, to no one's surprise, was a black Volvo estate.

I sent for Linda Mitchell.

'I want this vehicle taken to Lambeth, Linda, and gone over with a fine-tooth comb. Anything you find could be useful.'

'And perhaps you'd let us know if the headlights don't come on when you turn on the ignition,' said Dave, thinking back to what Ted Middleton had said about the car in which the box was taken away.

Linda appeared mystified by this request, but Dave obviously decided that it would take too long to explain.

DS Flynn returned. 'We've spoken to those householders who were at home, guv. Nobody heard or saw anything.'

'That reckons,' I said. Nobody ever hears or sees anything when you want them to.

'We tried the three houses either side of this one. But we got no answer at two of them. I'll try again later, but it'll probably be this evening if the residents are at work.'

Dave and I went through the house, looking for anything that might indicate who had killed Camilleri. Unusually, we found no correspondence of any description, apart from an Italian passport that showed Camilleri to be forty-three years of age. Dave suggested that he kept anything of interest on his computer, but that it would probably need a password to gain entry. There were, however, a number of CDs alongside the computer, of the type used to record information. Well, that's what Dave said. Personally I know very little about computers, and don't want to know.

Dave played about with the telephone in the study.

'There are quite a few numbers recorded on here, guv,' he said. 'The last thirty calls that Camilleri received. And there's a fairly lengthy directory.'

Near the computer we found a mobile phone. That too revealed numbers recently called and received.

'We'll take that lot with us, Dave,' I said, indicating the phones, the computer and the CDs. 'You never know, they might tell us something.'

'Someone needs to tell us something, that's for sure,' muttered Dave.

Detective Sergeant 'Shiner' Wright arrived from the laboratory. His task was to take custody of Camilleri's body and maintain the continuity of evidence.

After three hours, we handed over responsibility for the security of the house to the local police. They arranged to have the front door repaired, and posted a PC on the property to prevent anyone interfering with our crime scene.

Back at Curtis Green, Kate Ebdon's legwork team set about tracing the subscribers to the telephone numbers that had been found on Camilleri's two phones. The computer and CDs were sent over to the Metropolitan Forensic Science Laboratory in the hope that they might be able to retrieve something of interest from them.

Throughout the day, results began to come in, but none of them was very helpful, except that Linda reported that the headlights on the Volvo did not come on automatically when the engine was started. That meant that Camilleri's Volvo was the one used to collect the box from Ted Middleton's workshop in Tooting. Probably.

Charlie Flynn reported back that the two householders he had been unable to see this morning had been contacted. They had neither seen nor heard anything. Well, there's a surprise.

The outcome of the laboratory's examination of Camilleri's computer was disappointing. Both that and the CDs indicated that Camilleri had been involved in an apparently legitimate import and export business dealing mainly in electrical goods from the Far East. That was something that would have to be looked into; it was not unknown for drug barons and others engaged in some villainous enterprise to disguise their accounts so that they appeared to be

189

perfectly legal.

The telephone numbers were meaningless, at least for the moment. Each of them would have to be checked out and the subscribers' names put through the Police National Computer. One of the numbers, however, needed no such investigation: it was the number on Giovanni Maroni's visiting card. But there was nothing startling about that.

'I'm amazed that Camilleri left all this stuff on his phones, Dave,' I said.

'Perhaps he wasn't expecting to be murdered, guv,' was Dave's laconic reply.

Henry Mortlock's report confirmed his original estimate that Camilleri had been dead between twenty and twenty-four hours when we found him. The report also stated that Camilleri had been killed with two nine-millimetre rounds to the chest, one of which had penetrated the aorta.

Giovanni Maroni was now firmly in the frame.

The district judge at the City of Westminster magistrates' court needed no persuading to grant me a search warrant in respect of Maroni's flat in Curzon Street. That Maroni was known to have visited Camilleri at about the time of his death was sufficient to convince him of the justification.

We went straight from the court to Maroni's flat, but I didn't intend telling him that I had a warrant until I'd asked him a few questions.

'Mr Maroni, I'm investigating the murder of Vincenzo Camilleri.'

'Vincenzo has been murdered?' Maroni, attired in a colourful silk dressing gown, contrived a convincing expression of shock. 'This is terrible news. He is an old friend of mine.'

'When did you last visit Mr Camilleri?' I asked, as Maroni led the way into his sumptuously furnished living room.

'On Saturday evening.'

'For what purpose?'

'We had some business to discuss.'

'What sort of business?'

'He was wanting to invest some money in my clubs, and I wanted to invest in his import and export business. It would have given me great pleasure to have him as a partner.'

'What time did you arrive at Bloxwich Road, Mr Maroni?'

Maroni thought about that before replying. 'It must have been around eleven o'clock, I suppose.'

'And at what time did you leave there?'

'It was only a short meeting. Perhaps about half an hour later. But why these questions?' Maroni still managed to maintain an urbane demeanour, almost as if he was anxious to assist us in discovering his friend's murderer.

'How was Mr Camilleri when you left him?' asked Dave.

Maroni smiled. 'A little drunk, but apart from that, in good health.'

'The pathologist puts the time of Mr Camilleri's death at about the time you were with him.'

'Then I can only suggest that your pathologist has made a mistake. A genuine mistake, of course.'

It became clear that there was no way Maroni was going to hold up his hands to Camilleri's murder. If, as seemed likely, he was the killer, he'd have made damned sure that there was no incriminating evidence anywhere in his flat. We certainly wouldn't find the gun with which Camilleri had been killed.

I decided not to execute the search warrant, but to wait until we had more proof of Maroni's involvement. But where we were going to get that was, for the moment, a mystery.

I toyed with the idea of reinstating the surveillance on Maroni, but decided that he was not going to do anything suspicious, and that he was unlikely to do a runner. He owned two nightclubs, and was so supremely confident of himself that I was sure he thought he could talk his way out of anything.

DI Kate Ebdon had some interesting news for us when we returned to Curtis Green.

'We've been through the numbers found

on Camilleri's two phones, guv, and we obtained copies of his phone bill. There are some interesting tie-ups with what the lab found on his computer.'

'I think I'd better sit down for all this, Kate.'

◦ 'On the twentieth of August,' Kate began once she, Dave and I were settled in my office, 'there was a call from Maroni to Camilleri. Two days later, Camilleri rang a number that goes out to a Terry Foster. Now, Foster's an interesting character. Fifteen years ago, he was charged with the murder of Sammy Gold, but was found not guilty. The story was that Gold, who ran a team in the East End, encroached on Foster's territory and did a heist that netted eight grand. Foster was heard to swear vengeance, and, lo and behold, a few days later Gold's body was found in an alley in Bermondsey with his throat cut. But there was a wall of silence, and no charge was brought.'

This was not an unfamiliar problem for the CID. Most detectives had heard about the methods the Kray twins had employed to silence anyone who might've thought about informing on them. And I was in no doubt that it still went on.

'And presumably, he's still at it,' said Dave.

'Very much so,' Kate continued. 'Criminal Intelligence Branch has got quite a thick file on Foster. Ten years ago he was sent down for seven years for armed robbery, but was paroled after three and a half. Since then he's done a bit of bird for various offences like handling stolen property and burglary.'

'Does he have any other occupation, Kate?' I asked. 'Apart from being a professional villain.'

Kate laughed sarcastically. 'According to his criminal record, he's a scrap-metal dealer.'

'Well, there's a surprise,' I said. 'Who does he run with?'

'According to his docket, he's been involved with an Albert Goodwin. Goodwin's got form as long as your arm.'

'It looks very much as though we'll have to have a word with Messrs Foster and Goodwin.'

'It gets better, guv,' said Kate. 'On the twenty-eighth of August there was a phone all from Camilleri to Maroni. But now we turn to Camilleri's computer. It took the lab a while to hack into it, but when they did they found that he kept all his personal finances on it. Two days after Camilleri rang Maroni, Camilleri's bank account showed that he paid in ten grand that he was daft enough to show he'd received from Maroni. And on the weekend of the seventh–eighth of September, Harding was murdered. Then, on the day following the discovery of Harding's body, Camilleri gets another ten grand from Maroni.'

'It's beginning to come together, Kate,' I

said, but was careful not to get too enthusiastic. I'd gathered evidence before that was seemingly as strong as that, only to find it all went pear-shaped at the trial. 'Maroni said that he and Camilleri were discussing business the night that Camilleri died.'

'That's quite right. He said that Camilleri wanted to invest in Maroni's clubs, and that Maroni wanted to invest in Camilleri's import and export business. But why should he have paid him anything, unless Maroni was investing more in Camilleri's business than Camilleri was putting into Maroni's, and the twenty grand was the balance? Anyway, the day after the cash was paid into Camilleri's account, Camilleri rang Foster, and the next day Camilleri drew eight grand in cash.'

'If I read this aright, the phone call was probably to arrange a meet so that Camilleri could pay Foster. And somehow I don't think Camilleri was buying scrap metal.'

'Nor do I, guv. But that's not all. When the Volvo was examined, Foster's fingerprints were found on the steering wheel, and on the tailgate.'

'Very careless of him,' commented Dave. 'Either that or he's getting cocky.'

'He obviously thought that a Volvo in a garage in Putney wasn't going to be tied in to an East End villain and a murder that finished up on Ham Common,' said Kate.

'And he obviously didn't reckon on Camilleri getting topped,' Dave said.

'In that case, I think it's time we pointed out the error of his ways,' I said. 'Have we got an address for him, Kate?'

'Flat Five, Ramsay MacDonald House, which is on the Horsfall Estate in Bermondsey, guv. But if you're thinking what I think you're thinking, it's no good for an obo. I had a word with the local CID, and they said that any attempt at surveillance anywhere near Foster's drum would be a definite no-no. It seems that Foster has got his own little intelligence set-up there, and anything foreign in the neighbourhood is reported to him immediately.'

'Could ring him up and ask him to call at the Yard, I suppose,' said Dave phlegmatically.

'It might come to that,' I said. 'What about Goodwin, Kate? Have we got an address for him?'

'Burbush Road, Stepney, guv.'

'I think the plan is to hit both addresses mob-handed and nick the pair of them before they get their second wind. Kate and Dave, you'll both come with me, and Tom Challis can take a team to Stepney and lift Goodwin.'

'When d'you propose to do that, guv?' Dave asked.

'How does five o'clock tomorrow morning strike you, Dave?'

'D'you know, guv, I had a nasty feeling you were going to say something like that.'

Thirteen

At exactly five o'clock on Wednesday morning, Dave Poole, Kate Ebdon and I arrived at the Horsfall Estate in Bermondsey. Ramsay MacDonald House was one of several equally depressing 1950s blocks of flats that surrounded a paved area littered with detritus. A burnt-out car reposed in the centre, but I somehow doubted that this was an attempt by the local council to introduce pop art to the residents. It almost goes without saying that the denuded flower beds contained the usual quantity of used condoms and discarded hypodermic needles.

We were followed on to the estate by a full complement of the Territorial Support Group comprising an inspector, two sergeants and twenty PCs. The inspector had been enthusiastic about the task, claiming that it was time his unit showed itself there again. Just to watch the residents running about like a disturbed ants' nest, he said. Minutes later, Linda Mitchell and her crew arrived in their white vans.

I sent half a dozen officers to the rear of the block containing Terry Foster's ground-floor flat, just in case he decided to make a quick exit by way of a window.

Two constables accompanied Kate, Dave and me to the front door.

'In you go,' I said.

'Shouldn't you try ringing the bell first, sir?' asked a young PC.

'The guv'nor just did,' said Dave. 'Didn't you see him?'

With a grin and a look of relish on his face, one of the PCs levelled his battering ram at the door and smashed it in, shouting 'Police' as he did so.

The TSG officers quickly fanned out through the flat, and eventually one of them gave a cry of triumph when he reached the bedroom.

'In here, guv,' he shouted.

There were two people in the room. A shaven-headed man wearing dirty Y-fronts was standing up and had adopted an aggressive pose. In bed was a young woman, all but her face hidden beneath the covers.

'We're police officers,' I announced, in case there was any doubt.

'Well, you do surprise me,' said the shaven-headed one.

'Are you Terry Foster?'

'Yeah. What the bloody hell's this all about? Have you done my front door in?'

'I'm arresting you on suspicion of murdering Jack Harding on or about the eighth of September.' I wasn't concerned about the front door; no doubt the council would end up repairing it. But whether they would pay for it was another matter altogether. Already I could visualize the protracted correspondence that would pass between the borough council and the Receiver for the Metropolitan Police District, the Job's finance manager, before liability for the damage was finally admitted. But whatever the outcome, the taxpayer would end up footing the bill one way or the other.

'Do what?'

'You heard my guv'nor,' said Dave. 'Get dressed.'

'This is a diabolical bloody liberty,' protested Foster. 'I ain't never heard of no one called Harding.'

Dave winced at Foster's liberal use of negatives. 'Who's the bird, Terry?' he asked.

'That's Cheryl. She lives with me.'

'Cheryl who?'

'Cheryl Green, not that it's any of your bleedin' business.'

'Leave him alone, you bastards,' shouted Cheryl, at last taking a part in the proceedings. 'Like he said, he ain't done nothing wrong.'

Kate Ebdon stepped up to the bed. 'Just shut your racket unless you want nicking as well,' she said.

'I ain't scared of no fucking dyke.'

'Right, that's it.' Kate took hold of the duvet and pulled it off, leaving Cheryl naked. 'Now, are you going to shut it, or d'you want trouble?'

Cheryl snatched the duvet back and pulled it up around her neck. 'What you lot bloody staring at?' she screeched at the PCs who were enjoying this little sideshow.

'And what do you do for a living?' asked Kate.

'I'm a dancer, ain't I?'

While this pantomime was going on, Foster had pulled on a pair of jeans and a tee shirt. 'I want my solicitor,' he said.

'I'm sure you do,' I replied. 'We'll arrange that once we get to the nick. But not before we've searched this place.'

'You gotta warrant, then?'

Dave took a pace closer to Foster. 'We don't need one, but I'd have thought you'd have known that with all the experience of the criminal law you've amassed over the years.'

Foster puffed himself up with indignation. 'I'm going to write to my MP and tell him I've got a complaint,' he said.

'Don't worry about that,' said Dave. 'We'll get the divisional surgeon to take a look at you at the nick.'

'It's a bloody liberty,' said Foster, not for the first time. He was clearly a man with a limited vocabulary.

But Dave was too busy answering his mobile to respond to Foster's last outburst. When he'd finished, he drew me to one side.

'Just had a call from Tom Challis, guv. Albert Goodwin has been nicked.'

'Excellent. Tell Tom to take him to Charing Cross nick. We'll meet him there.'

'Can you give me some fags before you go, Tel?' wailed Cheryl from beneath the duvet.

'I thought you was s'posed to have a job, you stupid cow. I ain't made of money.' Nevertheless, Foster pulled out a packet of cigarettes and tossed it on to the bed.

It was at this point that Linda came into the bedroom. 'We found this under the bath, Mr Brock.' She displayed a pistol contained in a clear plastic evidence bag. 'It's a Beretta Modello eight-four. An Italian job.'

'Italian, eh? Well, well.' I didn't have to tell Linda to have it checked for fingerprints. That's routine. But I was interested that we had discovered yet another Italian connection to Harding's murder.

Foster's face became suffused with rage at Linda's dramatic announcement. 'I ain't never seen that before,' he yelled. 'It's a bleedin' stitch-up. You bloody planted it.' He took a lunge at Linda, but was intercepted by Dave who promptly twisted Foster's arm into a classic hammer-lock-and-bar hold. Within seconds of this smart manoeuvre he had the prisoner handcuffed and bent face down on the bed. 'This is police brutality,' protested Foster, his voice muffled by the duvet.

'You haven't seen anything yet,' Dave

responded.

'Put him in the van, Dave,' I said, tiring of this charade.

The arrival of the TSG had not been what the police are pleased to call a silent approach. In fact, the drivers of the two carriers had given a couple of yelps on their sirens just for the hell of it. As a consequence – despite it being not yet six o'clock – interested parties were leaning over the balconies of Ramsay MacDonald House and the surrounding buildings, watching the unfolding drama of Terry Foster being placed in a police van.

'You wanna lock that toe-rag up for life.' A woman with arms like legs of mutton, and her hair in curlers, shouted the advice from the safety of the second floor of Aneurin Bevan House, the block opposite Ramsay MacDonald House.

'Go fuck yourself, you old bag,' responded Foster.

'Up yours,' replied the woman.

We left DI Kate Ebdon at Foster's flat to supervise a thorough search of the premises. The traffic was light at that time of the morning, and we arrived at Charing Cross police station at twenty-five minutes to seven.

'Yes, sir?' queried the custody sergeant when we produced our prisoner.

'Terry Foster, arrested on suspicion of

murder,' I said.

'Blimey,' said the sergeant, 'that's the second one nicked for murder since I came on duty less than half an hour ago, and I haven't even had my breakfast yet.'

Thanks to a government obsessed with data and statistics, it took the sergeant about twenty minutes to complete all the necessary forms, but finally we were able to adjourn to an interview room.

Now that Foster was in police custody, there was no further need for a display of machismo to impress the woman he'd been sleeping with, and he became more conciliatory. Linking his fingers together, he leaned across the table, an earnest expression on his face.

'Look, guv'nor,' he said, 'I know I've got a lot of form, and if you've got me bang to rights, well, that's the way the cookie crumbles. Know what I mean? But I swear on my mother's grave, I've never seen that shooter before. I don't know how it got there, but it's nothing to do with me.'

'Well, it finished up under your bath, in your bathroom, in your flat, Terry. Got any suggestions?' I was always sceptical about villains who swore on their mother's grave. It usually meant that they were about to tell you a pack of lies.

'I've no idea, Mr Brock, as God's my witness.'

And that was the other preamble to the

trotting out of untruths. Nevertheless, I was beginning to have doubts. It was true that Foster was a hardened criminal, and, as his record showed, he'd done a fair bit of bird. Although I'd not had dealings with him before, I got the impression that he would shrug and accept the inevitable if, in fact, he was guilty of the crime for which he'd been arrested.

'We'll have to see if your fingerprints are on it, then, won't we, Terry?'

Foster emitted a throaty chuckle. 'Leave it out, Mr Brock, I'm a professional. If I'd handled that shooter, I'd've wiped it clean. So you won't find my dabs on it.'

'Well, we'll have to see, won't we?' I said, and promptly changed tactics. 'How well d'you know Giovanni Maroni?'

'I've never heard of him.'

'Or Vincenzo Camilleri?'

'Don't know him neither.'

'If that's the case, how d'you explain your fingerprints being on the steering wheel of Mr Camilleri's car?'

'What car?' Foster had the worried expression of a man who was about to be fitted up by the Old Bill.

'A black Volvo estate.'

'With headlights that don't come on when you switch on the ignition,' put in Dave.

'The only black Volvo I've driven belongs to a guy who lives at Putney,' said Foster.

'What was his name?'

'Vince Cameron.'

'And where does he live in Putney?' I asked. The coincidences were building up much too conveniently for my liking. It was interesting too that Vince Cameron sounded very much like an anglicized version of Vincenzo Camilleri.

'Bloxwich Road. Number ten if memory serves me right.'

I produced a photograph of Camilleri that had been taken just before Henry Mortlock opened him up. 'Is that your Vince Cameron, Terry?'

'Yeah, that's the geezer. He don't look too healthy though.'

'That's probably because he's dead,' said Dave.

Foster started back in alarm. 'I don't know nothing about that, guv'nor, and that's the God's honest truth. I hope you're not going to try putting that murder on me.'

'Who said he'd been murdered, Terry?'

'Well, he had to have been, otherwise you wouldn't be toting that picture of him about.'

It was evident that Foster was a bit sharper than I'd originally given him credit for.

'Was this Vince Cameron an Englishman, Terry?' asked Dave.

'I dunno, but he spoke with a foreign accent. P'raps he was a Scotsman.'

'This man – Camilleri or Cameron – telephoned you on the twenty-second of August, and again on the tenth of September. What was that about?'

Foster's face assumed a foxy expression. 'Bit of business.'

'You'll have to do better than that, Terry,' said Dave, 'otherwise my guv'nor will likely put you on the sheet for murder.'

Foster turned to me in the fallacious hope that I might be sympathetic. 'Look, Mr Brock, I swear I never had nothing to do with no murder. Not Cameron's nor this bloke Harding.'

'So what was this bit of business?' I sat back and waited. The problem facing villains of Terry Foster's calibre is that often their alibi for one crime is that they were committing another crime somewhere else at the time. It was what Joseph Heller called a Catch-22 situation.

'All right, we was casing a joint,' said Foster with a deep sigh.

'Where was this?' asked Dave.

'A betting shop down Fulham, but it never come off. Vince decided it was too dicey, what with the traffic and that, so he kicked it into touch.'

'And that was what the phone calls were about, is it?'

'Yeah. See, I drove over to his drum in Putney, and then drove his car to Fulham, so's I could get the feel of it like. On account of it being better suited for a quick getaway. That's how you come to find my dabs on the steering wheel.'

I laughed. 'Are you telling me that this Camilleri or Cameron, whatever his name may be, was prepared to use a car registered in his own name to pull a betting-shop heist?'

'Leave it out. Vince was a cunning bastard. He was going to report it stolen the day before the heist, and then the Old Bill would think it'd been nicked special for the job, like.'

'D'you know how many villains have come up with that ploy, Terry?' I glanced at Dave. 'How many, Sergeant?'

'Four thousand, three hundred and seventy was the latest figure Stats Branch had, sir,' said Dave with a perfectly straight face.

'It's true, Mr Brock, I swear,' said Foster plaintively.

The trouble here was that the tale Foster was telling might just be true. Generally speaking, villains are not noted for their high IQ, or their inventiveness when it came to planning a crime.

'But I suppose he still paid you the eight grand he drew from the bank the day after the phone call. Come on, Terry, that phone call was to arrange a meet so he could pay you for topping Jack Harding.'

Foster's jaw dropped in amazement. 'Eight grand? I should be so lucky.'

'Where does Albert Goodwin fit into all this, Terry?' I asked.

'Bert Goodwin? What's he got to do with it?'

'I just asked *you* that.'

'Nothing. He wasn't in on the betting-shop job, if that's what you mean.'

'No, it wasn't what I meant. I'm talking about the murder of Jack Harding, whose body was found in a box on Ham Common. And whoever left it there had set fire to it in a lame attempt to destroy the evidence.'

'For the last time, guv'nor, I tell you I don't know nothing about no murder. I don't even know where this Ham Common is. I read about it in the *Sun*, of course, and I thought to myself that whoever done that job must be a bloody amateur.'

'A better idea would have been to cut his throat and leave him in an alley somewhere in Bermondsey, I suppose.'

'That job wasn't down to me,' protested Foster vehemently, 'and I was never charged. You ask anyone. In fact, you can ask Bert Goodwin. He was with me the night that topping was pulled.'

'Oh, I will, Terry. I've got Goodwin locked up next door. But I'm not interested in the topping of Sammy Gold, the man you *didn't* murder.'

'What you got Bert banged up for?'

'Because he runs with you, and I thought he might have had something to do with this murder I'm talking about. You see, Terry, I'm in a bit of a predicament. Here we have a

Volvo with your fingerprints on the steering wheel and it was a Volvo that was used to collect the box in which our friend Harding was found. Dead. On Ham Common.'

'Bert wouldn't have had nothing to do with no murder, Mr Brock, any more than what I would. I'll hold me hands up to the occasional robbery.' Foster gave me a crooked grin. 'Well, I can't deny it, can I? After all, you've got a big fat file on me up the Yard. But the sort of topping you're on about ain't worth the grief. That'd score thirty years minimum at the going rate.'

'Tell me where you were on the night of the seventh and eighth of September. That was a weekend.'

Foster ran a hand round his stubbly chin. 'Not sure, Mr Brock. I think I spent a couple of hours down the Crooked Crow – that's a boozer – and then I went back to my place and spent the night in bed with Cheryl.'

'And she'll verify that, will she?'

'She better had or I'll give her a smacking.'

We left Foster to the tender mercies of the jailer at the nick, and went next door to interview Albert Goodwin.

'What's all this about me getting nicked for murder?' demanded Goodwin, the moment we appeared in the interview room.

'Because you run with Terry Foster, and he's just been nicked for murder,' said Dave, and turned to deal with the recording machine.

'I never had anything to do with no murder,' protested Goodwin. 'Who's been topped?'

'Jack Harding. His body was found in a box in the middle of Ham Common, and someone had set fire to it.'

Goodwin let out a coarse guffaw of derision. 'You're having a laugh, guv'nor. Me and Tel's professional robbers, and we wouldn't have had nothing to do with some half-baked job like that.'

I asked Goodwin the same question that I'd posed to Foster regarding his whereabouts on the weekend of Harding's murder. And got a surprising answer.

'I spent the night in Southwark nick,' said Goodwin, with a smug expression of satisfaction.

'What was that about?'

'Some toffee-nosed git and his mates come in the boozer we was in and started throwing their weight about. Someone called this geezer a fat poof, and, well, the up and down of it was a bleedin' great punch-up. Bottles was thrown, tables got smashed up, and some bloke got his face chivved with a broken beer glass. The landlord called the Old Bill, and the next thing I know is the boozer's full of coppers and we're all down the nick being charged with making an affray and GBH an' all that sort of caper. Never got bailed till Sunday morning.'

Dave disappeared to ring the custody

sergeant at Southwark police station. Moments later, he returned with a mournful look on his face.

'It's confirmed, sir.'

'Well, that lets you off the hook, Albert,' I said. 'Now you can tell me where you were last Sunday night.'

'Last Sunday? Sorry, guv'nor, I can't remember.'

'Chuck him out, Dave,' I said, but I wasn't going to leave it that. Last Sunday was when Vincenzo Camilleri was murdered, and it was just possible that Goodwin had something to do with it.

'What about Foster, guv?'

'We'll let him stew for a bit, Dave, until we've had a word with his bird Cheryl. If she backs his story, then we've got to start all over again. Get hold of DI Ebdon. If she's still at Foster's flat, she can check his alibi with Cheryl.'

Ten minutes later, Kate rang back.

'It's a blow-out, guv,' said Dave, when he'd finished his conversation. 'Cheryl Green denies having spent that weekend with Foster. In fact, she reckoned she could produce a witness who'd swear she spent the night with him, not Foster.'

All I needed now – despite what Foster had said – was to find his fingerprints on the pistol that had been found beneath his bath.

I got Dave to telephone Linda Mitchell to see if they'd got a result yet.

211

They had, and the result was encouraging. Sort of.

'The only dabs on that weapon belonged to Cheryl Green, guv.'

'How did they know that so quickly?'

'Because she's got a conviction for theft.' Dave gave me an owlish grin. 'And at the time of her arrest she was working at one of Giovanni Maroni's nightclubs.'

I rang Kate Ebdon on my mobile. 'Where are you, Kate?'

'Still at Foster's place, guv.'

'Is Cheryl there?'

'Yes, she is.'

'Good. Nick her for being concerned in the murder of Jack Harding, and bring her to Charing Cross.'

'It'll be a pleasure, guv.'

I opened the door of Foster's cell. 'I've got bad news for you, Terry,' I said. 'Cheryl Green denies spending the night of the seventh of September with you.'

'The lying little cow,' yelled Foster. 'You wait till I get my hands on her.'

Fourteen

'I don't bloody believe it,' said the custody sergeant at Charing Cross police station. 'Three in for murder in one day. That's got to be some sort of record.' He scratched his head and pondered that remarkable occurrence for a few seconds. Finally, he stared at the flame-haired young woman in jeans and a man's white shirt who was standing beside the prisoner. 'And who might you be, lass?'

'Detective Inspector Ebdon,' snapped Kate. 'And when you've quite finished preparing your submission for the *Guinness Book of Records*, perhaps you'd find time to process my prisoner ... *Sergeant*.'

'Ah, yes, ma'am. Sorry, ma'am.' The custody sergeant hurriedly adopted an air of contrition, searched feverishly for his pen, and then pointed it at the prisoner. 'Name?'

'Cheryl Green, and I wanna make a complaint.'

'Yes, they all do,' said the sergeant, with a world-weary expression on his face that implied that every prisoner made the same demand. He took a form from one of the many stationery drawers behind him, and held it out. 'That tells you all about making a complaint,' he said. 'I s'pose you do speak English?' he queried, as an afterthought. 'If not, we've got 'em in Hindi, Farsi, Russian, Lithuanian, Gujarati, Chinese, Japanese and stand-at-ease.'

The plethora of paperwork was eventually completed, and the prisoner escorted into an interview room.

I decided to let Kate begin the interrogation, and sat back to see what Cheryl had to say.

'The pistol that was found under the bath at Terry Foster's place...' Kate began.

'What about it?'

'It's got your fingerprints all over it, but none of Terry's. Now, how d'you explain that?'

'I dunno nothing about it. You must've made a mistake. They must be someone else's prints.'

'The chances of that happening are sixty-four billion to one.' Kate's casual reply was one that CID officers were often obliged to quote to doubting villains, and prosecuting counsel to doubting jurors. 'But let me put it to you this way, you dumb sheila: our finding a gun with your prints on it, at the place where you were shacked up, ties you directly into the murder of Jack Harding. You've already told me that you weren't with Terry Foster the night Harding was killed, so I reckon it's down to you.' This, of course, was all flimflam; Harding had been stabbed, not shot, but Kate was obviously trying to trap Cheryl into making an admission that would indicate that she had some connection with the Camilleri murder. It was a classic ploy: imbue the prisoner with a false sense of optimism that she was in the clear with regard to one crime, and she might just inadvertently make a give-away statement concerning another.

The colour drained from Cheryl Green's face as she realized the significance of failing to furnish Foster with an alibi. 'I never had nothing to do with no murder!' she exclaimed. 'Honest I never.'

'Where d'you work, Cheryl? You said earlier that you were a dancer.' Kate had learned from Cheryl's criminal record that, at the time of her arrest, she had worked as a dancer at one of Giovanni Maroni's clubs, but she wanted to make sure that she was still there.

'At Gio's club, the one in Soho.'

'And how long have you been there?'

'About a year.'

'So you were there when you were convicted of the theft of a client's wallet containing about two hundred and fifty pounds and a number of credit cards.'

'That was a mistake. He'd left it on one of the tables and I was looking after it till he come back for it.'

'I don't think so,' said Kate, reading from

Cheryl Green's criminal record. 'According to this, it was stolen from his jacket pocket while he was in a private room with you. And a day or two later you attempted to use one of his credit cards to buy a television,' added Kate. 'And that's how you came to get nicked.'

'He could afford it,' said Cheryl. 'Anyway, he owed me.'

'What for?'

'I ain't saying.'

'No need to,' said Kate. 'I can guess.' She turned to me. 'I think we might as well put her on the sheet for murder, guv, don't you?'

But before I could answer, there was the anticipated outburst from Cheryl.

'I ain't taking the rap for what he done.'

'For what who did?' I asked.

'Gio, of course.'

'Well, don't leave it at that,' I said. 'Explain.'

'I was shacked up with Gio till about the beginning of September.'

'Was this at Docklands?'

Cheryl raised her eyebrows in surprise. 'How d'you know that, then?'

'I know a lot of things, Cheryl. But do go on with this fanciful tale.'

'Well, one night about then, a mate of Gio's come in the club—'

'What was his name?' Kate interrupted.

'I don't rightly remember, except it was foreign.'

'How about Vincenzo Camilleri?' I suggested.

'Yeah, it was something like that. Anyway, he brought a guest with him, and that was Terry Foster. Gio asked me to put on one of my special shows for him in one of the private booths, see.'

'What does one of your "special shows" amount to?' asked Kate.

Instead of looking at Kate when she answered, Cheryl fixed me with a defiant stare. 'A complete strip,' she said, 'and then ten minutes wrapping meself round the pole, all suggestive and sexy like.'

'And then what happened?'

'Gio had given me a grand to talk Tel into spending the night with me. Well, he never needed no persuading, not after I'd finished me strip and the other stuff, and sat on his lap cosying up to him. So Gio sends the pair of us down Tel's place in the Bentley.'

'Where does the gun fit into all this?' I asked.

'Well, about a week later, Gio gives me the gun. He says if I'd go down Tel's place and hide it, he'd give me another grand. And on top of that, if I stayed with Tel, he'd let me off dancing *and* he'd pay me a monkey a week.'

'By a monkey, I take it you mean five hundred pounds?' I knew what a monkey was, but I wasn't sure that the jury would know when it listened to the tape recording.

Cheryl looked surprised. 'Of course I do.' There was a pause, and then, 'Oh, my Gawd!'

'What?'

'He told me I mustn't tell no one.'

'Bit late for that, Cheryl. Now then, let's go back to the weekend of the seventh and eighth of September. Was Terry Foster with you that night?'

'Yeah, he was.'

'Then why did you say he wasn't when I asked you this morning?' queried Kate.

'I was getting back at him, weren't I? He's a right horny bastard is Tel, three times a day minimum he wanted it, and that pad he's got down Bermondsey is a bleedin' tip.'

'Not what you're accustomed to, I suppose,' said Kate, with an edge of sarcasm.

'Nah! I was brought up in a proper house, I was.'

'And where was that?'

'Down Billericay. That's in Essex.'

'Now,' I said, appearing to go off on a different tack altogether, 'what about last Sunday night?'

'What about it?'

'Where were you?'

'I was in bed with Tel, the rat bag. Getting screwed as usual. Why?'

'Just another line I was pursuing, Cheryl.' I decided not to mention the murder of Vincenzo Camilleri. At least, not yet.

And that was as far as we could go. All

218

sorts of charges sprang to mind, but that would be a matter for the Crown Prosecution Service. Although I was a little doubtful about Cheryl's story, I didn't think she had the brains to make it up. Particularly when it could be checked. It did, however, throw up one or two other useful bits of information. From what the girl had said, Giovanni Maroni was guilty of allowing his premises to be used as a brothel, and of procuring a woman for sexual intercourse. There was no doubt in my mind that Cheryl had no alternative but to go with Foster – payment apart – and that amounted to a threat.

I wondered why girls of Cheryl's type got involved in this sort of unsavoury business. They surely didn't enjoy it. But, come to think of it, I didn't enjoy my job very much.

'Right, you'll now make a statement to Inspector Ebdon here, and we'll see what happens next,' I said, hoping that she would not exercise her right to refuse. And she didn't.

One of the advantages of taking a statement is that it gives us a chance to compare what has been said with what has been written.

But in Cheryl Green's case it was exactly the same.

One of the problems with the Police and Criminal Evidence Act is that it gets in the way of police work. Consequently it was some two hours later – after Cheryl's statement had been transposed into written form – that we were in a position to interview Terry Foster again.

I went through the rigmarole of telling him he was entitled to legal representation, but he declined. In fact, he commented that the last time he'd been up for robbery, the best his counsel could do was a plea in mitigation. And Foster had worked out that it had cost the taxpayer five pounds a word.

'You are entitled to have a copy of a statement made by Cheryl Green earlier today, Terry,' I said, handing him the three pages of what she had said.

'The conniving little bitch.' Having read through the statement, Foster chucked it on the table with an exclamation of disgust. 'I wondered what that was all about,' he said. 'It's not every day some geezer takes you up West and pours Scotch into you. And if that wasn't enough, he conjures up a dolly bird who not only does a striptease, but then comes on to me so strong that I finish up in bed with her.'

'Who was this man who took you to the nightclub, Terry?'

'Vince Cameron.'

'Otherwise known as Vincenzo Camilleri.'

'So what? I knew him as Vince.'

'Where were you on the night of last Sunday, the twenty-second of September, Terry?'

'In bed with Cheryl, and if she tells you different, she's a lying little bitch. Anyway what happened then, that you're so interested?'

'That was when your friend Vincenzo Camilleri was murdered in his house at Putney.'

'Yeah, you told me that. Who done him, then?'

. 'I was hoping you'd tell me,' I said.

So far, it looked as though Foster, Goodwin and Cheryl were rowed out of the murders of Jack Harding and Vincenzo Camilleri. The one thing I now needed to know was whether the two rounds taken from Camilleri's body came from the Beretta found underneath Foster's bath. Although Foster and Cheryl had given each other an alibi for the night of that murder, it wasn't worth a light. And Goodwin couldn't remember what he'd been doing last Sunday, only three days ago. Clearly there was much to be done.

We admitted Cheryl Green to police bail, and got back to Curtis Green at exactly five minutes past six. The timing was quite deliberate because our beloved commander is a strict by-the-clock man: in at ten, out at six. The consensus among the troops is that Mrs Commander nags him. Be that as it may, the last thing I wanted was to start explaining the details of my two murders to the boss. I knew that he would pose un-answerable questions, and having risen at three thirty that morning, I could do without that sort of ill-informed interrogation.

'The ballistics report has arrived, sir,' said Colin Wilberforce. 'The Beretta found at Foster's place was the weapon used to murder Camilleri.'

'So all we've got to do now is to have a word with Giovanni Maroni,' I said.

'What's the betting he's done a runner, guv?' said Dave, rooting around in his excuse for a briefcase, and producing one of the oranges that his wife Madeleine had said were so good for him.

'What, and leave two profitable nightclubs behind? I doubt it, Dave.'

'No, perhaps you're right, guv,' agreed Dave, peeling his orange.

I sent for DC John Appleby. 'John, see if you can find any trace of Giovanni Maroni at the General Register Office in Southport. If he had been born here, it would've been about forty years ago. You'd better try the one in Edinburgh as well; there are a lot of Italian families in Scotland. And, John...'

'Sir?'

'Don't waste any time.'

And he didn't waste any time. Thirty min-utes later, Appleby returned to my office.

'No trace of Maroni's birth in England and Wales, or in Scotland, sir.'

The next step was to contact the Italian

police. As usual, Colin Wilberforce was a mine of information when it came to finding his way around foreign police forces.

'The *Carabinieri* has responsibility for criminal investigation, sir, and they're the guys to talk to if Maroni had anything to do with the mafia.'

'Good,' I said, 'so talk to them, Colin.'

It was not until the following morning that we received a reply from the *Carabinieri*. And that, for the Italians, I thought, was remarkably quick.

'It seems that Giovanni Maroni is well known to the *Carabinieri*, sir,' said Colin, reading from a lengthy email as he entered my office. 'He's a native of Palermo in Sicily, and he was indeed involved with the mafia.' He looked up and gave me a knowing grin. 'And he's wanted for murder.'

'Well, well. So, what's the SP, Colin?'

'Some five years ago, Maroni was implicated in the assassination of a provincial judge. The judge was heavily involved in hunting down the mafia, and had become something of a nuisance to the *Cosa Nostra*. So they eliminated him, and Maroni is the man who is alleged to have pulled the trigger.'

'Do they know that for sure?' I asked.

'According to this,' said Colin, flourishing the printout, 'one of their number turned supergrass and spilled the beans. But Maroni was only a foot soldier, not a capo.'

'What the hell does that mean?'

'A foot soldier is one of the mafia rank and file, sir, but a capo is a gang boss. It's all here.' And Colin flourished the email again.

'What did they send you, a book?'

'Very nearly, sir. It runs to four pages. However, after the assassination, Maroni disappeared and they'd no idea where he'd gone. They were very pleased to hear from us, and, as a direct result of our email, they are about to file an Interpol red-corner circular for his arrest.'

'Five years ago, and they've only just got around to logging his name with Interpol?' I was amazed at this lackadaisical approach to murder.

'Yes, but now they know he's here, sir, they're preparing extradition papers.'

'Good luck to them,' I said, 'but they're not laying hands on him until after he's appeared at the Old Bailey.'

Kate Ebdon came into the office. 'I've just read the ballistics report on the pistol found at Foster's place. So, what now?'

'Go and nick Cheryl Green again, Kate,' I said.

While I was waiting for Cheryl to be brought back to Charing Cross police station, I sent DS Tom Challis to Tooting with a photograph of Vincenzo Camilleri. I was hoping that Ted Middleton, the carpenter who made the box in which Jack Harding had been found, would be able to confirm that Camilleri was the man who'd made the purchase. Certainly Camilleri's ownership of a black Volvo estate – modified so that the lights didn't function when the engine was turned on – seemed to point to him being the buyer.

Challis rang back an hour or two later. Ted Middleton had looked at the photograph of Camilleri. He'd told Challis that it *might* have been the man who bought the box, but he wasn't sure. Well, nothing new there.

At two o'clock I received a phone call from Kate Ebdon to say that Cheryl was in custody.

'We're going to stop playing cat and mouse, Cheryl,' I said, and turned to Kate. 'Caution the prisoner, Inspector.'

Kate reeled off the words formulated by a government that had greater concern for the perpetrator than for the victim. I was pleased to see that it had a profound effect on Cheryl.

'I ain't done nothing wrong,' she protested, fear apparent on her face.

'Apart from being in unlawful possession of a firearm, and that's worth at least two years in chokey,' Kate said, gilding the lily outrageously. 'And I should think the lady screws up at Holloway have got all sorts of surprises in store for a sexy little girl like you.'

Cheryl now looked even more frightened. 'I ain't going down for something I ain't done,' she protested.

'On Monday of this week,' I said, 'I found the dead body of Vincenzo Camilleri at his house in Putney. He had been shot sometime between nine o'clock on the Sunday evening and nine o'clock Monday morning. The rounds taken from his body have been subjected to a ballistic examination, and they came from the Beretta pistol, which, on your own admission, you placed beneath the bath at Terry Foster's flat at Ramsay Mac-Donald House.' I sat back and waited.

'I told you I was in bed with Terry that night. You ask him.'

'I did, and he agrees with you.'

'Well, there you are, then.'

'How very convenient,' said Kate.

'What is?'

'You and Terry – both convicted criminals – giving each other an alibi.'

'Well, it's true.'

'And do you think a jury at the Old Bailey's going to believe it?' I asked. 'It's as simple as this, Cheryl: Camilleri was murdered, and you put the gun that killed him under the bath. I'll tell you what I think happened. You and Terry went out to Putney last Sunday night and one of you murdered Camilleri, and then you conveniently claim that you were each in bed with the other. It won't wash, my girl.'

In my experience, an allegation of that sort made against an innocent party will usually bring forth the truth. Whatever you might have heard to the contrary, there's no honour among thieves. Particularly when the chips are down.

'I never had nothing to do with it. I told you what happened. Gio give it me and told me to hide it somewhere in the flat.'

'Did he tell you why he wanted it hidden?'

'He said it was a joke.' But even Cheryl could see how unbelievable that suggestion was, and shrugged her shoulders. Her bra strap slipped so that it showed beneath the short sleeve of her tank top, but she ignored it.

I found difficulty in crediting this strip-tease artiste with the guts to commit a murder, although she might have been an accessory.

'So, it was Terry who committed the murder.'

'No, he never. I told you, we was in bed together. You ask him.'

If what Cheryl said was the truth, it left only one solution. Giovanni Maroni must have murdered Vincenzo Camilleri. Given that Maroni was a Mafioso wanted for murder in his native country, there might be a deeper motive for the killing. The 'men of honour', as the mafia likes to style its thugs, sometimes get murdered by other 'men of honour'.

The door of Maroni's Curzon Street flat was opened by a young woman. Probably no older than Sasha Lovell, the woman was wearing jeans and a sweater, both of which closely fitted her shapely body.

'Yes, what is it?'

'I wish to speak to Mr Maroni.'

'He's not here.'

'We're police officers. Can you tell me where he is?'

'He's at one of his clubs. It's the one just off Soho Square.'

'And who you are?' enquired Dave.

'Mandy Forsyth.'

'And are you a friend of his?'

'No, I'm his cleaning lady.'

'Yes. Of course,' I said, with a disbelieving smile. If only my cleaning lady, Gladys Gurney, looked anything like Mandy Forsyth, I'd double her wages.

We thanked the girl and went on our way.

Fifteen

It was seven o'clock when Dave and I strolled into the club where Mandy Forsyth had told us Giovanni Maroni would be. And he was.

'Gentlemen, how nice of you to patronize my little establishment.'

'We're not patronizing it; we're on duty, Mr Maroni.' Dave looked around at the glitzy decor, the overstocked and overpriced bar, and the chromium poles around which two or three nude dancers were slithering. 'It wouldn't have been worth the outrageous price you're charging.'

Maroni bridled at Dave's comment, but managed to keep his temper under control. 'So what can I do for you, gentlemen?'

'You can start by telling me why you gave a Beretta pistol to Cheryl Green,' I said.

'This is harassment,' exclaimed Maroni. 'I refuse to be cross-examined in one of my own clubs. I must ask you to leave.' He flicked his fingers imperiously at a bullet-headed moron bulging out of a badly cut dinner jacket. I imagined him to be the head bouncer.

'If we leave, you're coming with us, Mr Maroni,' I said quietly. 'To West End Central police station.'

The bouncer homed in rapidly, his hands revolving around each other oleaginously. 'Yes, Mr Maroni, sir?'

'Everything all right, Ricardo?'

'Yes, Mr Maroni.'

'Good. Perhaps you'd ask a waitress to bring me another Campari.'

'Yes, Mr Maroni,' said the bouncer, and oiled his way towards the bar.

'I didn't ask you to have a drink,' said Maroni sarcastically. 'I understand that policemen don't drink on duty.'

'Let's start again,' I said. 'Why did you give a Beretta pistol to Cheryl Green with instructions to hide it at Terry Foster's place?'

'I did no such thing,' said Maroni. A topless waitress placed a glass of Campari in front of her boss, but received no word of thanks. 'And anyone who tells you this is a liar. What is this girl trying to do to me?'

There was an element of bluster in Maroni's protestations, and I was sure that the interruption of the bouncer had been staged deliberately to give him time to think. There was no doubt in my mind that the Italian's prevarication was an attempt to stave off the inevitable, and he must have been wondering how much we knew about his background. On the other hand, he was so self-confident that he probably thought the

Carabinieri hadn't told us anything about the crime for which he was wanted in his native country. And that view was supported by the fact that if we hadn't asked the *Carabinieri* for that information they probably wouldn't have told us.

'So you categorically deny that you know anything of this weapon?'

'Of course I do. I am a successful business-man. Why should I have need of a gun?'

'Let me put it to you this way, Mr Maroni,' I said. 'The Beretta in question – it was found hidden at Foster's place in Bermond-sey – was the weapon with which Vincenzo Camilleri was murdered. And you, my friend, were at his house at around the time he was killed.'

Maroni nodded slowly, and took a sip of his Campari. 'I have to make a confession, Mr Brock,' he said. 'I did go to Vincenzo's house, that is true. But I told you that be-fore, and I don't deny it. But when I arrived, Vincenzo was already dead.'

'Is that so?' queried Dave sceptically. 'In that case, how did you get in?'

'I had a key, Sergeant Poole. Vincenzo had given me one for safe keeping, just in case there was an emergency. Normally I ring the doorbell, as I did on this occasion, but as there was no answer, I let myself in. Imagine my grief when I saw my dear friend lying there dead.'

'Why didn't you call the police, then?' I

asked. 'That's what any concerned law-abiding citizen would do.'

Maroni ran a finger down the side of his glass, drawing a little line in the condensation. And then he looked up. 'I was afraid you wouldn't believe me, Chief Inspector. You see, I am a Sicilian, and everyone thinks that that automatically makes me a member of the mafia.'

'But that, I assume, is untrue,' I suggested.

'Of course it's untrue.' Maroni forced a laugh. 'I am a respectable nightclub owner. I am not a gangster.'

'So you know nothing of the murder of Vincenzo Camilleri, is that what you're saying?'

'If I did, Mr Brock, I would have told you a long time ago. But, as you say this gun was found at this man's place – I've forgotten his name already – I suggest that he is the man you should be questioning.'

Dave and I stood up. 'Enjoy the rest of your evening, Mr Maroni,' I said.

'Yes, make the most of your free time,' Dave added. There was an element of the sinister in his comment, one that was not lost on Maroni.

'What did you make of that, Dave?' I asked as we made our way back to Curtis Green.

'A couple of violins in the background, guv'nor, and he'd have had me in tears. Or, to put it another way, Maroni's a lying bastard. But why should Cheryl Green have spun us that yarn about Maroni giving her the gun if it wasn't true? Frankly, I think she's too dim to have made up a complicated story like that.'

'So do I,' I agreed. 'But we'll have another go at Terry Foster. I think if we start charging one or two people, the truth will out.'

'So, another heavy-handed raid on Ramsay MacDonald House, guv?'

'No, Dave, I've got a better idea,' I said.

On the Friday morning, I telephoned Terry Foster and told him his bail had been rescinded, and that I wanted to see him at Charing Cross police station at ten o'clock sharp.

'I've got an appointment this morning, so I won't be able to make it,' said Foster.

'That would be most unwise, Terry,' I said, 'because if you don't show, I'll come looking for you. And so will the other twenty-eight thousand officers of the Metropolitan Police.'

'What the bloody hell's this all about now?' Foster demanded the moment he stepped over the threshold of Charing Cross police station.

I ignored his protest, and escorted him into the interview room.

'Well?' Foster was in one of his more combative moods, doubtless as a result of my peremptory summons.

'I'm not going to mess about, Terry,' I began. 'I'm charging you with the murder of Vincenzo Camilleri on or about the twenty-second of September this year.' I turned towards Dave, and nodded.

'You are not obliged to say anything, but it may harm your defence—' But that was as far as Dave got.

'That's not down to me,' yelled Foster. 'It's a bloody stitch-up.'

'I hope you're not suggesting that we've fabricated the evidence to support such a charge, Terry,' I said mildly. 'The murder weapon was found under the bath in your flat at Ramsay MacDonald House, and your girlfriend Cheryl, whose fingerprints were on it, has admitted putting it there.'

'Planting it there, more like. Anyway, I was in bed at the time screwing the arse off of the bitch.'

'So she said. But all that proves is that the pair of you decided to provide an alibi for each other. I really thought you could do better than that. I put it to you that the two of you acted together. That you both went to Putney and murdered Camilleri, and then you each conveniently stated that you were miles away and in bed with each other.'

'But why should I want to top Vince? It don't make sense.'

'Well, you'll have every opportunity to explain all that to a jury at the Old Bailey,

Terence, my son. And very soon.'

For a long time, Foster sat in deep contemplation. Eventually, he spoke. 'If I give you the SP, Mr Brock, will that go in my favour?'

'You know I can't promise anything, but if you volunteer valuable information the judge might be persuaded to impose a lesser sentence.'

'Yeah, well I ain't going down for murder, and that's a fact. I never had nothing to do with topping Vince. And I'll swear to that on a stack of Bibles.'

'So, what have you got to tell me?'

'It's about Jack Harding.'

'What d'you know about that job?'

'I know that Gio Maroni was behind it.'

'Why would Giovanni Maroni want Harding dead?'

'He'd got the right needle over some bird. Sasha something she was called. He was a nasty bastard if he didn't get his own way. See, that night I was up one of his clubs with Vince, he offered me a job as a bouncer, bleedin' sauce. But I'd seen the way he treated his staff. While we was there, he got hold of one his nude dancers and gave her a right bollocking for not dancing sexy enough, and then he sacked her. Poor little cow went off in tears, she did. So when he offered me a job I told him to stuff it up his arse. If Vince hadn't been there to smooth things down, I'd've given Maroni a bloody good smacking and no mistake.'

'This woman Sasha you mentioned, would that have been Sasha Lovell?'

'Sounds right, yeah.'

'Why had Maroni got the needle about her, then?'

'Apparently she was shacked up with him down Docklands somewhere. She'd been his bed mate for a year or so, he reckoned. But then she slung her hook. Now that don't suit Mr Bleedin' Maroni. He gets right pissed off if he don't get his own way. And a bird walking out on him really gets up his hooter. But apart from anything else, she saw him off for about thirty big ones, so he reckoned.'

'Yes, go on.' I wondered what Sasha Lovell had done with thirty thousand pounds, if, in fact, she'd had it in the first place. I had great difficulty in believing that; there was certainly no evidence of it when I started to investigate Harding's murder. Apart from anything else, Sasha and Harding appeared to have little or no money, and Sasha had admitted as much.

'I wondered why Vince Cameron had got in touch with me, but I soon found out.'

'How did he find you, Terry?'

'He'd put the word out that he wanted someone for a job. You know how it works, Mr Brock. Anyhow, I got a phone call from him asking for a meet at some boozer down Barnes way. So I done a bit of asking around, and no one had heard anything about this geezer Vince. Never seemed to have no form, if you know what I mean.'

'Nevertheless, you did meet him,' I suggested.

'Yeah, but not without a bit of back-up.'

'What sort of back-up are you talking about, Terry?' asked Dave.

'I took a couple of me mates down there with me. Not that I let on to Vince that they was with me. They sort of strolled into the boozer and hung about, just in case things went nasty. Quite handy with their dukes, them two. S'matter of fact, I thought it might be some of your lot trying to set me up. The Heavy Mob, like.' Foster gave me a crooked grin.

I somehow doubted that the Flying Squad would've gone to that much trouble. They've got plenty of customers without going out touting for business.

'Anyway,' Foster continued, 'this Vince said he was acting as a go-between for some rich Eyetie who wanted a job done. Well, I thought he was talking about a heist some place. I mean, that's me trade. But then you know that, Mr Brock.'

'But it wasn't a heist?'

'Nah! It was a bleedin' topping, wasn't it? But I never knew that when I went to his club for the meet. Well, topping ain't my scene at all. All Vince had said was that he wanted me to meet this geezer up West a couple of days later.'

'And it turned out to be Giovanni Maroni,

I suppose?' I said.

'Yeah. To cut a long story short, and after I'd told him what to do with his bouncer's job, he offered me twenty grand to top this Jack Harding. I asked Maroni what Harding had done to upset him, and he give me this spiel about Harding having taken his girl off of him, and that she'd had thirty grand of his spondulicks off of him what he reckoned this Harding had had away.'

'What did you say when this offer was made?'

'I said I'd give it a bit of thought. But to tell you the truth, Mr Brock, I wasn't too happy about doing business with Maroni. Like I said, he was a nasty bastard.'

'But you did get involved.'

'Yeah, more's the pity. Maroni said I was to let Vince know if I was prepared to take the job on, and that he never wanted us to meet again. He said it'd be too dodgy, like.'

'So what happened next?'

'I thought I could make a few sovs without getting me hands dirty. You know what I'm saying? So I had a word with Bert Goodwin, and told him about the job, and that it was worth eighteen grand. I reckon I was entitled to a couple of grand off the top for making the arrangements.'

'And did Albert Goodwin agree to take it on?'

'Yeah, he did.'

'You're telling me that Goodwin murdered

Jack Harding. Have I got that right?'

'Well, I give the job to Bert Goodwin, and Harding finished up getting topped. So what d'you reckon?'

'Then who murdered Vincenzo Camilleri?'

'I reckon that's down to Bert an' all.'

'Why? Why should Albert Goodwin have topped Camilleri?'

'It all went a bit pear-shaped when it come to settling up. The promise was twenty grand, but that was between me and Maroni with Vince acting as the middleman. But when it come to it, there was only ten grand in the pot. Leastways, that's what Vince come up with. He said that putting the geezer in a box and setting fire to him was asking for trouble, and that Maroni was pissed off with all the publicity.'

'I think he was probably right. Did you speak to Maroni again? Did he say he'd reduced the payment because of the way it'd been done?'

'Nah, I never saw him. Like I said, he'd told me not to contact him again, so I had to take Vince's word that Maroni had changed his mind. See, Vince had forgotten that Maroni said as how he wanted it done that way. When I met him up his club, he said something about teaching Harding a lesson and letting everyone else know that they don't fuck about with Giovanni Maroni.'

'What did Albert Goodwin say about this when you gave him the cash, Terry?'

'He did his nut, and swore that someone was going to get a smacking. And he reckoned he was going to start with me.'

'What did you say to that?'

'I told him straight that it wasn't down to me. So I give him the full SP.'

'How did he know how to find Camilleri, then?'

'Dunno, Mr Brock, 'cept I told him where I'd met Vince. Both two places like. Like I said, once in a boozer in Barnes, and the next time up one of Maroni's rub-a-dubs.'

'Even so, you took your two grand off the top, and paid Goodwin eight grand. Is that right?'

'That's it, guv'nor. Like I said, two grand for the arrangement seemed a fair cut for me to have for me trouble.'

'There's only one snag in this tale of yours, Terry. The murder of Jack Harding would've taken more than one man to carry out. I don't see Bert Goodwin kidnapping Harding, putting him in a wooden box, and then manhandling it out of a car on Ham Common all by himself, do you?'

'Shouldn't think so,' said Foster. 'But I never asked. It don't do to ask too many questions when a job like that's coming off. I s'pose Bert made his own arrangements, but I wasn't having nothing to do with it.'

'But you have, Terry. On your own admission you're guilty of conspiring to commit murder. That's worth ten years.'

'But I'm turning Queen's Evidence, Mr Brock.' There was an expression of shock on Foster's face. 'Have a heart.'

'Yes, that's all very well, but it's up to the Crown Prosecution Service. And they'll probably say that once you were aware of this conspiracy to murder Jack Harding, you should have informed the police. But you didn't, did you?'

'But I ain't a grass,' pleaded Foster.

I couldn't help laughing. 'Well, if what you've just told me isn't grassing, I'm the fairy on the Christmas tree.'

'Yeah, well, I s'pose you're right,' said Foster miserably. 'But d'you reckon you can do anything for me? I don't want to do no more bird, Mr Brock, and that's gospel. You don't get decent villains in stir these days. All young tearaways, the lot of 'em. I mean to say, half of 'em are bloody kids going around stabbing each other for no reason at all. You just don't know where you are.'

'Sergeant Poole will now take a statement from you, Terry, and you'll be required to give evidence at the Old Bailey. After you've stood trial for conspiracy to murder.'

'Bloody hell!' exclaimed Foster. 'That's a bleedin' turn-up and no mistake. Do I get protection?'

'We'll see about that, Terry. If Goodwin makes a confession and pleads guilty, that'll row you out of getting in the witness box. But in the meantime you can repeat your story to Sergeant Poole, and he'll write it down.'

It took about two hours for Dave to record Terry Foster's statement. If what he'd said was the truth, it meant that our next step would be to arrest Albert Goodwin and Giovanni Maroni, and charge them with murder and conspiracy to murder respectively. With any luck, the extradition papers for Maroni would arrive in time for me to arrest him on the charge of the murder he was alleged to have committed in Sicily. And that would keep him banged up until his trial or extradition hearing, whichever came first.

However, I was doubtful about the part of Foster's statement that claimed that Maroni had ordered the mafia-style 'execution' of Jack Harding for no better reason than he'd stolen Maroni's girlfriend. And that meant that we'd have to speak to Sasha Lovell once more to enquire about the thirty thousand pounds she was alleged to have stolen from Maroni.

But the one aspect of Foster's 'confession' that didn't hold water was the suggestion that Albert Goodwin had committed the murder of Jack Harding. Goodwin had told us that he'd spent that Saturday night in Southwark police station, and Dave had confirmed it with the custody sergeant.

'Dave, when Goodwin was arrested last Wednesday, was he photographed?'

'Yes, guv.'

'Good. Get a copy and take it down to Southwark police station. Speak to the custody sergeant who processed him when he was arrested on Saturday the seventh of September, and show it to him. I want to be certain that it was our Albert Goodwin who was nicked.'

As luck would have it, the sergeant concerned was on duty when Dave got to Southwark. As a result he was back within the hour.

'It wasn't our Albert Goodwin, guv,' said Dave triumphantly.

'Well, who the hell was it?'

'I don't know yet, but apparently the guy who gave his name as Albert Goodwin was the guy who started the fight in the boozer, and made sure he got nicked when the Old Bill arrived. Looks like a set-up to me.'

'But surely they checked his identity before he was bailed on the Sunday morning, didn't they?'

'Sort of,' said Dave. 'By a curious co-incidence, the Goodwin in custody was carrying an old gas bill with him. It showed him to be Albert Goodwin of Seven Burbush Road, Stepney. And the custody sergeant telephoned Goodwin's wife before Goodwin was bailed. She confirmed that Albert Goodwin lived there, but said that she hadn't seen him since seven o'clock the previous evening when he went out for a drink with his mates.'

'I think you're right, Dave. The saucy bastard set it up,' I said. 'I wonder if his wife knew what he was up to. If she did, she's a party to the conspiracy as well.'

'A pound to a pinch, she'll have known nothing about it, guv,' said Dave.

I hoped he was right. I'd got enough on my plate without complications of that sort.

Sixteen

We left Terry Foster locked up in Charing Cross police station pending his appearance at court the next day. I had charged him with conspiring with others, deceased or not in custody, to murder Jack Harding. Whether that's what the CPS would arraign him for was another matter altogether.

It was about eight o'clock that evening by the time we arrived at Albert Goodwin's place in Burbush Road, Stepney. Although Dave and I intended to carry out Goodwin's arrest quietly – if possible – I had arranged to have a half serial of the Territorial Support Group on standby at the end of the street in case there was trouble. Knowing how involved Goodwin was with local villains who might be tempted to come to his aid, I considered it a sensible precaution.

Burbush Road comprised a row of terraced council houses. They were uninspired, flat-fronted buildings, their doors and windows giving straight on to the street. Tawdry curtains hung at some of the windows; others had no curtains at all.

'Blimey!' said Dave, 'they're just like the houses in Vallance Road. Which comes as no surprise.'

The Kray twins, notorious gangsters of the 1960s, had run their so-called 'Firm' of villainy from Vallance Road in Bethnal Green, an area of London whence Dave had originated, and which was but a stone's throw from Stepney.

It was a fine evening, and some of the Burbush Road residents – mainly women – were outside, chatting to each other while their offspring played football in the street. But the game ceased abruptly at the sound of an ice-cream van's strident chimes.

Our arrival sparked interest. The chatting stopped, but started again almost immediately. Whatever else they lacked, these people were skilled at detecting the arrival of the Old Bill.

There was some delay before a woman opened the door of number seven.

'What is it?'

'Mrs Goodwin?'

'Might be.' The woman looked beyond me to the groups of sightseers, their eyes all focused on the Goodwin residence.

245

'Is Mr Goodwin at home?'

'Who wants to know?'

I suspected that the question was a ploy to give Albert Goodwin time to flee. It was only afterwards we discovered that there was no easy escape route; these were back-to-back houses.

'Police.'

'Oh, not again,' said the woman. 'You'd better come in.' She glared across the street. 'Had yer bleedin' eyeful, you lot?' she yelled at the group of idlers. I got the impression that the arrival of the police at her front door was a fairly frequent occurrence, and came as no surprise either to her or her neighbours.

Albert Goodwin appeared in the hallway of his house. He was dressed in a pair of ragged jeans, and a singlet that afforded us the doubtful privilege of admiring his tattoos. 'What d'you bloody lot want now?' he demanded.

'You,' said Dave.

'I'm arresting you on suspicion of conspiring with others to murder one Jack Harding on or about the eighth of September last,' I said, just to make the matter clear.

'You what?' Goodwin let out a bellow of laughter. 'What are you talking about?' He turned to his wife. 'Did you hear that, Shirl?' And he laughed again.

'You can either do this the easy way or the hard way,' said Dave. 'But if you want to make a party of it, half the Territorial Support Group is at the end of the road.'

'You'd better go quietly, Bert,' cautioned his wife. 'I'm sure they've got it all wrong.' Shirley Goodwin obviously didn't want to give the neighbours any more to talk about than they had already. The prospect of having about eleven uniformed policemen overseeing her husband's arrest clearly alarmed her. She faced me again. 'My Bert never murdered no one,' she announced. 'He was in the nick that night.'

But the alibi came a little too readily for it to have been other than carefully rehearsed.

It was getting on for nine thirty by the time we got Goodwin back to Charing Cross, and he'd been processed by the late-turn custody sergeant.

'Are you going to start talking to him now, guv?' asked Dave.

'We'll see if we can get a quick cough, Dave,' I said. 'If not we'll put him down for the night and start again in the morning.'

'But that'll take at least twelve hours out of the twenty-four we're allowed to keep him here, guv,' said Dave, as ever worrying about the strictures of the Police and Criminal Evidence Act.

'That's all right, Dave,' I said. 'He'll have all night to think about it, and if he doesn't cough by nine o'clock tomorrow evening, then he's not going to confess at all.'

And that is just how it panned out. Goodwin demanded a solicitor, and refused to say anything until he arrived. And Goodwin's mouthpiece told the custody sergeant that there was no chance of him arriving before nine o'clock tomorrow morning. All of which was a damned nuisance, and probably a ploy on the solicitor's part to reduce the time we had available to us. It also meant that I would have to send Kate Ebdon to court with Terry Foster the next morning to plead for a remand in custody.

The solicitor looked more of a villain than Goodwin, but in a more refined way. Dave's view of him was that he wouldn't trust him as far as he could throw a grand piano. But then that was Dave's view of most solicitors.

Regrettably the law required me to furnish Goodwin with a copy of the statement made by Terry Foster. Of course, Foster didn't know that was going to happen, despite what I'd told him to the contrary, otherwise he wouldn't have said anything. Maybe. But then coppers can be devious at times. Foster had already admitted being a party to the conspiracy to murder Harding, but he didn't know that the Beretta pistol had played no part in the killing. However, I had a strong suspicion that it had been provided by Maroni in case it was needed. In the event, there was no evidence that Harding had been shot. Dr Henry Mortlock's view was that the victim had been overpowered, bludgeoned and then stabbed to death, but perhaps the pistol had played some initial part in coercing him.

Goodwin's solicitor scanned the statement and tossed it to one side.

'The evidence of one co-conspirator against another...' he began.

'Yes, I know all about that,' I responded.

'I have advised my client not to answer any questions,' continued the solicitor unabashed.

'That doesn't prevent me from asking them, though,' I said. When I was a very young detective a wise old sergeant had given me some advice about interrogation. Prepare your questions in advance, and don't accept a blanket refusal to answer, he'd told me; just keep asking them. When you get to court, you can trot out all the questions you asked, and each time you can say that the accused declined to answer. And let the jury draw what inference they will from that. But if you don't ask them, you can't put them in evidence.

The solicitor drew a large legal pad from his briefcase and made a great show of getting out his pen and adjusting his rimless spectacles. He didn't know that almost every shyster lawyer I'd come into contact with tried the same tricks in an attempt to dissuade me from carrying on. Makes life interesting, but achieves very little else.

'Where were you over the weekend of the seventh and eighth of September?' I asked, just to see if he came up with the same story, even though we'd proved it to be untrue.

'I told you before, I got nicked for being in a fight, and I was in Southwark bloody nick all night. All bloody bollocks, of course.'

Well, that bit was certainly true.

'Enquiries have been made of the police at Southwark, and I'm satisfied that you were not arrested that weekend. But someone assumed your identity, presumably at your behest. Who was it?'

'No comment,' said Goodwin.

'You were approached by Terry Foster sometime before that date, and on behalf of Giovanni Maroni were offered eighteen thousand pounds to murder Jack Harding. That murder was carried out by you and an accomplice during the weekend in question. Who was that accomplice?'

'No comment,' said Goodwin, and laughed.

I got the impression that Goodwin was enjoying himself.

'To that end, you were provided with a Beretta pistol. That pistol was later used to kill Vincenzo Camilleri, otherwise known as Vince Cameron, at his house at Ten Bloxwich Road, Putney, sometime prior to Monday the twenty-third of September. You later returned that pistol to Maroni. What d'you have to say to that?'

'Don't know anyone called Macaroni,' said Goodwin derisively, causing his solicitor to place a staying hand on his client's arm.

'I suggest that you were also responsible for the murder of Camilleri, and that you did so because he welshed on the deal, inasmuch as he only paid you eight thousand pounds instead of the eighteen you were originally promised.'

'No comment,' said Goodwin.

The solicitor now decided to put in his twopenny-worth. 'I suggest to you, Chief Inspector, that you don't have a shred of evidence, and I demand that you release my client immediately.'

'Interview suspended,' I said, and stood up. For the benefit of the tape-recorder, I added, 'Detective Chief Inspector Brock and Mr Goodwin's solicitor are now leaving the room.' I crooked a finger at the lawyer and led the way into the corridor outside the interview room.

'If you're about to try to make a deal—' the solicitor began, but I cut him short.

'I don't make deals,' I said, 'but I do have some useful advice that you might care to pass on to your client.'

'Really?' The lawyer smirked.

'I am satisfied that Giovanni Maroni is the man behind all this. I'm also satisfied that your client was responsible for the murder of Jack Harding.'

'There is no admission to that—'

'Will you just shut up for a moment?' I said. 'Although I accused your client of the murder of Vincenzo Camilleri, I actually think that Giovanni Maroni murdered him, and I'll tell you why. Maroni is wanted on an international arrest warrant by the Italian police. They also told us that Maroni is a Mafioso who, it is alleged, murdered a judge in Sicily some five years ago. They seem to think he's got a hate campaign against lawyers,' I added, garnishing the truth somewhat.

Whether or not that statement had the necessary effect, I don't know, but the solicitor blanched and, taking off his glasses, began to polish them.

'Now, I suggest that you tell your client about this,' I continued, 'because Maroni isn't the sort of man to establish guilt "beyond all reasonable doubt" before he takes action. I'm pretty sure that he's ruthless enough to eliminate everyone who took part in this conspiracy so that the spotlight isn't turned on him by a grassing accomplice. And he started with Camilleri. D'you get the message?'

'Why hasn't this Maroni been arrested?' asked the solicitor.

'We can't find him,' I said, fairly certain that Maroni might have done a disappearing trick by the time we looked for him again, 'but I don't doubt that he'll find your client. And right now, the safest place for him is to be banged up in stir.'

'How do I know this is true?' The solicitor obviously thought that I was trying to beat him at his own game.

'Read it for yourself,' I said, and gave him the email we'd received from the Italian police.

Goodwin's solicitor spent several minutes reading the information about Maroni.

'Give me quarter of an hour to consult with my client.'

'Take your time,' I said. 'Perhaps you'd send Sergeant Poole out.'

Fifteen minutes later, the solicitor re-appeared. 'If my client makes a full statement, what do you think the sentence will be, Chief Inspector?'

I laughed at such contrived naivety. 'You know perfectly well that I can't predict the length of sentence the judge will impose,' I said, 'but you also know from your experience that he might look favourably on an accused who has cooperated with the police.'

'What can you do to safeguard my client's life? The witness protection programme, for example.'

'Nothing. Your client needn't think he's going to get away scot-free with this murder, and it'll be up to the prison authorities to arrange protection. Rule Forty-three, most likely.'

'Very well. My client is prepared to answer

questions.'

Albert Goodwin wasn't nearly so truculent when we resumed our interview.

'I'm not going through all those questions again,' I said. 'Just tell me about it.'

'You were right about me not being nicked that weekend. I got me brother-in-law to stand in for me. He went down the boozer and deliberately started a punch-up so's the law would get called. And after about ten minutes they turned up with their sticks out.'

'You were bloody lucky they turned up at all,' commented Dave. 'Usually, the only way to get instant police action these days is to park on a double yellow line. Or put a black golliwog in your window.'

I had to laugh at that last comment; only a black policeman could've got away with it.

'What's the name of your brother-in-law?' I asked.

'Charlie Gibbons. He's me wife's brother,' Goodwin explained.

'And what's his occupation?'

'Same as me, market trader.'

'And where does he live?'

'Twenty-seven Manster Road, just round the corner from me.'

'And did he know why you asked him to stand in for you that night?'

Goodwin gave a crooked smile. 'Sort of,' he said.

That amused me. Goodwin obviously

didn't realize that he'd just made his brother-in-law part of the conspiracy. Not that I thought the CPS would be much interested in pursuing that.

'Go on, then.'

'Well, it's pretty much what that toe-rag Terry Foster said in that.' Goodwin gestured at the copy of Foster's statement that was still lying on the table. 'Terry come down my place about a week before and told me about this job that Maroni wanted doing, and that eighteen grand was on offer.'

'But you didn't do this job on your own, Albert, did you?' I asked.

'Course not, Mr Brock.'

'So who helped you?'

There was a long pause while Goodwin 'considered his position' as politicians say when they're in deep shtuck.

'Terry Foster.'

That came as no surprise, although it might have been a case of Goodwin putting in the poison for Foster because he'd grassed.

'But Foster claims that he was in bed with Cheryl Green at the time.'

'Well, he would say that, wouldn't he?'

'Where did the box come from?'

'What box?'

'The one we found Harding's body in.'

'Oh, that one. Camilleri got hold of it. We picked it up from his drum about three days beforehand.'

'Where did he get it from?'

'I never asked. Didn't matter, did it?'

'When I spoke to you previously about this murder you said that you wouldn't have anything to do with a half-baked job like that.'

Goodwin laughed. 'Well, it was, wasn't it, but according to Terry Foster that's the way Maroni wanted it. Anyway I wasn't going to hold me hands up to that job because I reckoned you hadn't got no evidence, on account of me being in Southwark nick that night.'

'Except that you weren't, were you?' said Dave.

'Well, I had to spin a fanny, didn't I? And I reckoned that being banged up in the nick was the best alibi I could have.'

'How did you go about this job?' I asked.

'We kept obo on Harding's place at Badajos Street – that's in Fulham – and when we saw his bird leaving, we went straight in and grabbed Harding.'

'What time was this?'

Goodwin thought about that. 'About three o'clock, give or take. Anyway, Harding put up a bit of a fight, but Terry put the knife in a few times. Croaked him straight off. Then we got him out to Camilleri's Volvo and shoved him in the box. We'd already picked up a jerry can of petrol from the Tesco filling station, and that was it, basically.'

'You mean you carried his body out to the

car in broad daylight?' I was astounded at this brazen act of foolhardiness.

'Yeah, why not? Never any coppers about these days.'

'What time did you get to Ham Common?'

'Where?' Goodwin appeared genuinely mystified by the question.

'Ham Common. It's where you dumped the box,' Dave said.

'I never knew where it was. We didn't want to go down our neck of the woods, so we just drove out of London until we found a quiet bit of grass. There weren't nobody about, so we dumped the box, poured a bit more petrol over it, and set it alight. That must've been about seven o'clock. In the morning, like. Then we buggered off a bit sharpish, drove to Putney and gave Camilleri his car back.'

'Where did you keep Harding's body between killing him and dumping him on Ham Common?' I asked.

'Nowhere. We bunged it in the box in the back of the Volvo, and left it in the council car park about a hundred yards from where Terry lives.'

I have ceased to be amazed at what some villains will do in the course of committing crime, but this had to be a first.

'What would've happened if the police had taken an interest in it, Albert?'

'Nothing to do with us, was it, guv? It would've been down to Camilleri, and I reckon he's got a bit of form, so he'd've had a hard job talking his way out of that.' Goodwin laughed, presumably at the thought of Camilleri trying to explain why his car had been found in Stepney with a dead body in it.

'Did you speak to Camilleri when you took his car back?'

'No, we just dumped it outside his place, and took off.'

'How did you get back to Stepney, then?'

'Got a cab, didn't we?' Goodwin stared at me as though this course of action was the obvious thing to do.

It took another three hours to get Goodwin's story down on paper in a form that would be acceptable to the CPS. That afternoon we set out to pay a visit to Cheryl Green who, we hoped, would still be at Terry Foster's flat in Bermondsey.

There was a look of concern on Cheryl's face when we arrived at Ramsay MacDonald House, and I imagined that she'd guessed that something wasn't quite right.

'What d'you want now?' she demanded.

'I want to talk to you about the weekend of the seventh and eighth of September, Cheryl.'

She said nothing, and with a resigned look on her face, turned and walked into the sitting room.

'I told you, I was in bed with Terry that

258

night.' Cheryl flopped into an armchair, her legs sticking out in an ungainly fashion.

'Terry's changed his story,' said Dave. 'He now says he wasn't with you that night.'

'I wish he'd make up his mind *what* he wanted me to say,' protested Cheryl. She took a packet of cigarettes from the coffee table, and lit one.

'So you now agree that he wasn't here.'

'If that's what he says, then yes.'

'Who was it who gave you the Beretta pistol that you hid under the bath? Was it Bert Goodwin?'

'No, it was Gio Maroni, the bastard. I dunno why Terry had to get himself mixed up in all this.'

We didn't really need to take a statement setting out her change of story, but we did anyway. The more bits of paper we can give the CPS, the more they like it.

Then we drove from Bermondsey to Battersea.

Seventeen

I was mildly surprised that a strange woman, dressed in a black trouser suit, answered the door of James Porter's flat.

'Who are you?' I asked.

'More to the point, who are you?' demanded the woman, holding up her warrant card for me to see.

'Detective Chief Inspector Brock,' I replied, and produced my own warrant card. I'd momentarily forgotten that we'd placed a twenty-four-hour guard on Sasha Lovell. 'And this is DS Poole.'

'I'm PC Sandra Roberts, sir. All correct.'

'That's a relief,' I said lightly. This custom of saying 'All correct' was the prescribed way of reporting to a senior officer, whether things were all correct or not. 'Are you armed?'

'Yes, sir.' Sandra Roberts pulled back the skirt of her jacket to reveal a holstered pistol on her left hip.

'Why d'you wear it on that side?' I asked, more out of interest than anything else.

'I'm left-handed, sir,' said Roberts with a smile.

'Any visitors?'

'No, sir.'

'Where's Sasha Lovell?'

'Taking a shower at the moment, sir.'

'I hope she hasn't seen *Psycho*,' muttered Dave quietly.

Fifteen minutes later, during which time we had been treated to a cup of Sandra Roberts' tea, the door to the sitting room opened.

'Oh God! It's you.' Sasha's surprise was at seeing us, not that she was attired in just a towel. After all, she was a porn actress. 'What d'you want?' She sat down in the armchair nearest the window.

'I wouldn't sit there, Miss Lovell,' cautioned Roberts. 'I keep telling you it's not safe.'

With a cluck of annoyance, Sasha moved to another chair. 'Oh, is there a sniper on the roof opposite that I haven't spotted?' she asked sarcastically.

'I've been hearing some funny stories, Sasha,' I began.

'You and me both,' said Sasha scornfully.

'I've learned that when you left Giovanni Maroni, you took with you some thirty thousand pounds that you then gave to Jack Harding.'

'How much?' Sasha sounded genuinely surprised.

'Thirty grand.'

Sasha scoffed. 'I'd've been lucky to get out of there with a fifty-pence piece.'

'Are you saying that Maroni is lying?'

'Of course I am.'

'Why was he so annoyed, then?'

'He was more than annoyed. He was hopping bloody mad. What really got up his nose was that I'd left him for another man. Gio was a really conceited bastard, and he couldn't bear to think that any woman would turn him down. But I told him that he couldn't buy me with all the clothes he got me, and the expensive restaurants he took me to. I told him I was sick and tired of his bullying, him wanting to be always in control, and the fact that he used me as his own personal prostitute. He wouldn't let me wear anything at all when I was in the flat, you know.'

'What did he do about you running away, then?'

'You name it, he did it,' Sasha said. 'First of all, he got someone to find out where I was living.'

'Would they be the pair that turned up at Davina Maitland's flat asking questions about Jack?'

'Probably. Anyway, not long after I'd skipped, Gio turned up one day, pleading with me to go back to him. He apologized for his behaviour, and promised he would change his ways.'

'And you told him to get lost, I suppose.'

'Too right I did. Once I'd told him that a leopard didn't change its spots, and that I

262

was fed up with him and the way he sodding treated me.'

'What was his reaction?'

'He did his bleedin' nut, didn't he? He ranted and raved, and called me a common tart – in Italian. It's what he used to call the girls who worked with me at his clubs. One of them spoke quite good Italian, and I remember asking her what it meant.'

'Did you see him again?'

'No, but he said I hadn't heard the last of it. He went all Italian on me, thumping himself on the chest, and said that no one turned their back on Giovanni Maroni. Then he went. But he came back one day when I wasn't there, and threatened Jack. He told Jack that if he knew what was good for him, he'd send me back to Docklands.'

'What did Jack do?'

'Apparently he just laughed, and told him that he might get away with that sort of attitude in Italy, but in England, women did what they liked, and men respected them for it. I bet he hated that. He didn't like anyone taking the piss out of his nationality. But then Jack told me that whenever he went out, a couple of heavies would follow him, making remarks and threats.'

'Sounds like the two who called on Davina, but why on earth didn't you, or Jack, report it to the police?'

'To be perfectly honest, we didn't take it seriously.' Sasha paused, a sad expression on her face. 'I never thought it would finish up with Jack getting murdered though.'

'And you think that Maroni was responsible?'

Sasha stared at me with a look of incredulity on her face. 'Well, if it wasn't him, who the hell was it?'

And with that, of course, I was bound to agree.

'Has he ever been in touch with you here?'

'No, never.' Sasha paused as a thought occurred to her. 'What's happening to Jamie?'

'His case is nothing to do with me,' I said, 'but I do know that he's been remanded to stand trial at the Old Bailey on charges under the Explosive Substances Act.'

'Is that serious?'

I thought it a rather naive question. 'He could go to prison for life,' I said.

'Good God!' Sasha blanched quite noticeably. 'He never meant to hurt anyone,' she said.

'I somehow doubt that a judge will share your view, Sasha.'

It was now getting on for seven o'clock on the Saturday evening. I wasn't going to arrest Maroni at one of his clubs because I didn't want to give him the opportunity of putting on a show in front of all the punters who patronized his establishment. Nor, for that matter, did I want to get involved in a ruck with his army of bouncers. I decided to

264

leave it until Monday morning when we would, with any luck, find him at his flat in Curzon Street.

I got home at about eight o'clock, and decided to give Gail a call.

'Sorry I'm so late,' I began, 'but things are stacking up.'

'It doesn't matter,' said Gail. 'Come round and I'll get you some supper.'

I walked through to my kitchen, somewhere I hadn't visited since yesterday morning. And all I'd done then was to have a quick cup of tea.

Neatly arranged on the worktop was a bra, and beside it, another of Gladys Gurney's charming little notes.

Dear Mr Brock
Your young lady left this on the bedroom floor.

I give it a good wash, and perhaps you'll give it back to her.

Yours faithfully
Gladys Gurney (Mrs)

I put the bra and the note in my pocket, and made my way round to Gail's house.

When I presented her with Gladys's bit of personal laundry, she collapsed with laughter.

'I think your Mrs Gurney knows about us, darling,' she said.

'She'd be hard put not to,' I said, 'if you insist on leaving your underwear all over the place.'

'I'll leave a G-string next time,' said Gail. 'That should get her going.'

'Somehow I doubt that anything would faze my Mrs Gurney,' I said.

We spent most of Sunday morning in bed, and then we drove out to a country pub beyond Esher for lunch.

'How are your rehearsals going?' I asked.

Gail smiled. 'I thought you'd forgotten all about that,' she said. 'They're going well. You'll have to come and see the show one evening.'

'When does it start?'

'Tomorrow week.'

'You know, I might even get an evening off by then,' I said. 'But I've forgotten what the play's called.'

'Oh, men!' muttered Gail. 'It's Noël Coward's *Design for Living*.' She paused for a moment. 'It's all about a *ménage à trois*.'

'Oh yes,' I said, giving her a sly smile, 'so it is. I hope it doesn't give you any ideas.'

'Or you,' Gail rejoined.

On Monday morning, I left Kate Ebdon with the task of taking Albert Goodwin to the City of Westminster magistrates' court, and asking for a remand in custody, so that Dave and I would be free to arrest Maroni.

It was a beautiful late-September day and,

266

much to Dave's displeasure, I decided that we would walk to Curzon Street. I'm not much taken with what passes for public transport in London, and there was no point in taking a police car; there would be nowhere to park it.

There were, however, still quite a few tourists in London, drawn like magnets to the Horse Guards' change of guard in Whitehall.

'Excuse me, sir.' A rather fat, jolly man, speaking in heavily accented English, approached me and raised his green Tyrolean hat. His equally fat, jolly wife stood silently beside him, also wearing a green hat, but with a bigger feather.

'Yes?'

'I am tourist from Austria,' said the man, raising his hat once more.

'I see,' I said, deciding not to reveal that I spoke German; I'd have been there all day.

'These soldiers in the tin bodices, sir...' The man waved a telescopic umbrella at the two mounted troopers in their sentry boxes. 'Is one of them your Prince William? I'm told he is officer in the Guards.'

'Yes,' said Dave, 'and the other one is Prince Harry.'

We left a somewhat bemused Austrian tourist taking photographs, and carried on. But to avoid any further interruptions or inane questions, I gave up and hailed a taxi.

We waited at the entrance to Maroni's block of flats. Dave had arranged for a van to be sent from Charing Cross police station in order that Maroni could be conveyed there once we'd arrested him. Two minutes later it arrived.

'Mr Brock, sir?' asked the PC driver.

'That's me.'

'Got the meat wagon here, guv. Just the one prisoner, is it?'

'Yes, just the one,' I said. 'So far.'

We climbed the stairs to Maroni's first-floor flat and rang the bell.

The door was answered by Mandy Forsyth, Maroni's so-called 'cleaning lady'. She was wearing a satin robe, and her hair was somewhat dishevelled.

'Oh!' she said, and gathered her robe more firmly around herself.

'Been working in the bedroom?' enquired Dave.

Mandy ignored that remark. 'Are you wanting Mr Maroni?' she asked.

'That's the general idea,' Dave said.

'He's in bed at the moment,' said Mandy.

'Perhaps you'd ask him to come out, then.'

Muzz Forsyth disappeared, and I heard a whispered conversation emanating from what I presumed was the bedroom.

Moments later, Giovanni Maroni appeared in the narrow hallway of his flat. He too was attired in a robe, but far more colourful – and doubtless more expensive – than that of his 'cleaning lady'.

'What d'you want?' he demanded.

I'd decided to let Dave do it; there's no point in giving the Maronis of this world an inflated sense of their importance.

'I'm arresting you on suspicion of having conspired with others to murder Jack Harding,' said Dave.

'This is preposterous,' protested Maroni loudly, and began to wave his arms about. I was glad that I'd decided against arresting him at one of his clubs.

'I suggest you go and get dressed,' I said. 'Unless you want to go to the police station wearing that.' I waved at his robe.

'I refuse to be taken away like a common criminal.' The more Maroni protested the louder became his voice. 'I will come when I'm ready. Maybe this afternoon.'

'I take it you do want to go to the station dressed like that, then.' Dave took out a pair of handcuffs and waved them gently in front of Maroni's nose.

Without a word, Maroni turned on his heel.

'You'd better go with him, Dave.'

'He's not likely to do a runner from the first floor, is he, guv?'

'It's happened before,' I said. I recalled a similar occasion when, years ago, a pyjama-clad man with many previous convictions had been arrested in a second-floor apartment by a young detective constable. The prisoner was sent off to get dressed, but after a while, the officer realized that no sound was coming from the bedroom. Rushing through, he discovered that his quarry had climbed out of the window, and was shinning down the drainpipe. But the drainpipe gave way, and the prisoner described an arc before hitting the hardstanding at the rear of the block of flats. The officer's only contribution to this unfolding drama was to yell 'Geronimo' as the prisoner hit the ground, breaking both his legs. As a result, the detective spent one hell of a long time writing reports. How do I know this? Simple. That detective constable was me.

Eventually, Maroni declared himself ready, but was still shouting the odds about suing the police for wrongful arrest, false imprisonment, slander, deprivation of his civil rights, and anything else he could think of.

'Shut up,' said Dave, finally tiring of this diatribe.

Dave decided that Maroni was likely to attempt an escape once we had him in the street, and promptly handcuffed him. Predictably this brought forth further protests.

For a few moments, the custody sergeant sat patiently as Maroni harangued him in Italian, and then gave him a form – written in Italian – telling him how to complain against the police. But finally the paperwork was completed, and we took Maroni into an interview room.

'I demand to have my solicitor here.'

'Why?'

'I am entitled to have my legal representative present when you ask me questions, even though I will not answer them. You see, I know all about English law.'

'Oh, very well.' It was damned annoying, but there was nothing I could do about it. As Maroni had said, that was the law. To my astonishment, however, the custody sergeant knocked on the door, announced his arrival, and then informed me that Mr Maroni's solicitor had arrived.

'Blimey!' said Dave. 'Has he got second sight or something?'

'I arranged for my cleaner to telephone him before you dragged me from my apartment,' said Maroni, a sneer on his face.

'Oh yes, your cleaner,' said Dave, and smirked.

The solicitor bustled into the room, introduced himself, and sat down. He could have been a carbon copy of the mouthpiece that Goodwin had conjured up from somewhere.

'My client is an upright member of London's business community, and he has a complete answer to whatever you are accusing him of,' announced the solicitor, 'and he refuses to answer any questions.' With that, he sat back in his chair, a smug smile on his face.

Oh yes, this guy knew how to deal with the Old Bill all right.

'I'm not going to ask your client any

questions,' I said, 'because I am going to charge him with conspiring with Vincenzo Camilleri, Terry Foster and Albert Goodwin to murder Jack Harding.'

'This is outrageous!' protested Maroni.

'Be quiet, Mr Maroni,' said the solicitor.

'I will not be quiet!' yelled Maroni. 'I have heard these stories about these people from Scotland Yard, making up evidence about innocent people, and getting them sent to prison for something they did not do.' By now he was red in the face, and looked as though he was heading for a cardiac arrest as well as the criminal one we'd already placed him under. I decided that the sooner we charged him, the sooner he would cease to be my responsibility. The death of a prisoner in custody is very time-consuming in terms of report writing, a coroner's inquest, and – if you're very unlucky – a discipline board.

I signalled Dave to switch off the recording machine. 'There is just one other thing, Mr Maroni,' I said, 'and it may help you if you give me a truthful answer.'

'I said that my client is not answering any questions,' protested the solicitor.

'And what is that?' Maroni lifted his head and stared at me down his nose.

'Cheryl Green, one of your dancers, has stated that you gave her the Beretta pistol to hide somewhere in Foster's flat.'

'I deny it.'

'You're not helping yourself,' I cautioned.

272

'What I want to know is, when did Terry Foster return the pistol to you?'

There was a long pause, during which Maroni glanced at the tape-recorder, and then at his solicitor. The solicitor nodded. I rather thought he'd given up on his client.

'Well?' I said.

'It was Tuesday, the twenty-fourth of September.'

'Thank you, Mr Maroni,' I said. 'You've been most helpful, and on reflection,' I continued, addressing both Maroni and his solicitor, 'I don't think there is enough evidence to charge you.' The solicitor shot me a look of triumph. 'But I shall admit you to police bail to return to this police station one month hence.'

Maroni nodded slowly, as though he'd known this all along.

'That was interesting, Dave,' I said, once Maroni and his legal adviser had left. 'According to Maroni the pistol was returned to him *after* the murder of Vincenzo Camilleri. If he was telling the truth, he couldn't have used it to commit that murder. But was he telling the truth?'

'"Ay, there's the rub" as Hamlet said ... *sir*.'

Eighteen

Despite the inherent risks of encountering more tourists – and fielding their daft questions – I decided to walk from the police station down Whitehall to Curtis Green. Fortunately, the change of guard at Buckingham Palace, at the far end of The Mall, had attracted most of those rubberneckers who were still in the capital.

Suddenly Dave stopped and drove the fist of one hand into the palm of the other. 'It's just dawned on me,' he said.

'What has?' I stopped too.

'Suzy.'

'Who?'

'D'you remember when we called at Maroni's old flat at Docklands, and saw a young guy called Tom Bowyer, guv?'

'Yes.'

'And d'you remember the girl who was there?'

'What are you getting at, Dave?' I asked.

'I've seen her since. I knew it rang a bell, but I couldn't place her.'

I sighed. 'Are you going to get to the crux of this, Dave?'

274

'D'you remember the night we went to Maroni's Soho club?'

'Yes, it was last Thursday.'

'Well, guv, she was there. She was one of the nude dancers wrapping herself round a pole.'

I mulled over this latest twist as we walked the last few yards to the office.

'A coincidence, or what?' I said as Dave and I settled in my office.

'It throws up a connection between Maroni and Bowyer, guv, other than the fact that he let or sold his flat to Bowyer. If you remember, Bowyer said he'd only met Maroni once, and that was the day he moved in.'

'Maybe it does, maybe it doesn't,' I said as I pondered what we should do about it. But then I decided. 'We'll catch her one night when she's leaving the club, and have a few words with her.'

'Could be two o'clock in the morning, guv,' said Dave, unhappy at the thought that he would probably be the one lumbered with doing the catching.

I telephoned Sasha Lovell.

PC Sandra Roberts answered my call, reported that everything was 'all correct', and called Sasha to the phone.

'Have you any idea what time the dancers at Maroni's Soho club finish work, Sasha?' I asked.

There was silence for a moment, and then,

'I think they work in two shifts, Mr Brock. The first shift comes on at about two in the afternoon, and goes off at about eight. The later shift takes over then until about two. Why?'

'On the occasions you went to this club with Maroni did you recall seeing a Chinese girl among the dancers?'

'Yes, I do. She was the only Asian girl working there. I remarked on her to Gio and he said her name was Suzy Ho.'

'What time was that?'

There was another pause, and then, 'About half past seven, I think. Is this girl in trouble?'

'Possibly,' I said, and thanked her.

'A bit of night duty, guv?' asked Dave.

'I don't think so. If we're near the club at just before two in the afternoon, we might be lucky enough to catch her going in. If Sasha got the time wrong, it'll be an evening stint.'

'Let's hope she starts at two, then,' said Dave.

I glanced at my watch. 'If we skip lunch,' I said, we could be there just in time.'

Dave groaned. 'I knew there'd be a catch in it somewhere,' he said.

'Ah, Mr Brock.' Just as we were about to leave, the commander appeared.

'Yes, sir?'

'Come into my office for a moment, will you.'

I followed the commander into his paper empire, waited while he sat down behind his desk, and shuffled his way through a pile of files.

'A Mr Frank Harding made a complaint against you, namely that you failed to inform him of the death of his son Jack Harding as soon as possible.'

'Yes, sir, but the——'

The commander held up his hand. 'I know what you're going to say, Mr Brock, and I have to tell you that the DAC has marked the file "No case to answer". He's examined the relevant paperwork and is quite satisfied that you acted with all due expedition in the matter.' He scribbled a few words on the minute sheet, and closed the file. Somewhat reluctantly, I thought.

The Chinese girl named Suzy Ho alighted from a taxi outside Maroni's club at a quarter to two.

'Miss Ho?' I said as we drew closer to the girl. 'We're police officers.'

'What d'you want?' Suzy backed away, a frightened look on her face. I could only assume that the police wherever she came from struck terror into anyone they spoke to.

'We want to have a few words with you.'

'I don't have my papers with me.'

This conversation was taking a curious twist; I wondered why she thought we'd want to see her 'papers', whatever that meant. Perhaps that was a preamble to any conversation with the police in her native country. But it prompted me to follow it up with an enquiry as to where that was.

'Where d'you come from?'

'Hong Kong,' said Suzy, but she replied hesitantly.

Dave's mind was obviously working along the same lines as mine. 'D'you have a Hong Kong passport, Miss Ho?' he asked.

'No.'

'Then how did you get here?' I asked.

The girl turned away and started to run, but she was no match for Dave. He caught up with her and held her by the arm.

'I've done nothing wrong,' protested Suzy, her back now against the wall of the club.

'Then you've nothing to worry about,' said Dave.

I decided to let Dave carry on with the questioning.

'Why did you try to run away, Miss Ho?' he asked.

'Because you want to send me home.'

'And where is your home?'

'Tianin,' said Suzy.

'That's not in Hong Kong, it's in China,' said Dave, much to my surprise. 'It's south-east of Beijing. So why did you say you came from Hong Kong?'

'I thought it sounded better.'

'What are you doing in this country?'

'I came as a student to learn English.'

'You seem to have done pretty well,' said Dave, 'but why are you now working as a dancer?'

'I didn't go home. China is an awful place to be.'

'Do you have a work permit?'

'No.' The girl looked up and down the street, as though seeking an escape route.

'So, you're working here illegally.'

I was pleased that Dave knew so much about immigration and work permits, and the like.

'Yes,' said Suzy. 'I suppose you'll send me back there now.'

Given the number of illegal immigrants there were in the country, I didn't think one more would make that much difference. And at least this one was working rather than living off the taxpayer. Anyway, I had learned over the years that the Home Office couldn't care less, and I wasn't going to waste my time writing a report for them.

'No,' I said, taking back the questioning, 'but I think you might be able to help us. How long have you worked for Giovanni Maroni?'

'A year.'

'And how long have you known Tom Bowyer?'

'How d'you know I know him?'

'If you remember, Miss Ho, you were at the flat in Docklands when we called there.'

'Oh yes, I remember.' Suzy seemed to relax

as she realized that, having spoken to her at Bowyer's apartment, we were unlikely to be concerned about her immigrant status now.

'Well, how long have you known him?'

'Two months.'

'And how did you meet?' Dave asked.

'At the club. He often comes there.'

'Does he know Mr Maroni?'

'Oh yes. I think they are quite good friends.'

'Very well, Miss Ho,' I said, 'you can go.'

Suzy Ho looked up in surprise. 'You mean you are not going to send me home?'

'No, but if I was you, I'd arrange to get a work permit as soon as possible.' What I didn't say was that she probably stood little or no chance of obtaining one. But no one would care.

'I shall be late for work now. What shall I tell Mr Maroni?'

I thought about that for a moment. The last thing I wanted was for Suzy Ho to tell Maroni that the police had been interrogating her about Tom Bowyer. Not that I thought she realized that was the purpose behind our questions. In any case, I didn't think that Maroni would be in the club this early in the day.

'If he's there, tell him that you couldn't get a taxi, and that when you did, you were held up in traffic. It happens all the time in London.'

'Thank you,' said the girl, and hurried into

280

the club.

I rang Information Room and, against my better judgement, asked for the services of a traffic car to get Dave and me to Docklands as quickly as possible.

It was just possible that Suzy Ho was sharper than I'd given her credit for, and she might, at this very moment, be on the phone to Tom Bowyer. And if he had something to hide, I didn't want him disappearing before we'd had a chance to speak to him.

As usual, Cyril, the concierge, was at his post in the entrance hall. I wondered whether he kept a sleeping bag somewhere so that he could kip down on the job.

'Afternoon, gents.' Cyril looked up in some surprise. I suppose he thought that his tenants were above receiving regular visits from the police.

'Is Mr Bowyer at home, Cyril?' asked Dave.

'As far as I know, guv'nor.' The concierge reached for the telephone, but Dave placed a staying hand on the instrument.

'Don't tell him we're on our way up, Cyril. We'd like it to be a nice surprise.' But the way Dave said it left the concierge in no doubt that he was not to be defied.

We rode the lift to the penthouse, and rang the bell.

There was a momentary look of puzzlement on Bowyer's face until he recognized us.

'The police again. Come in, and tell me how I can help you.'

'Your girlfriend not here today?' Dave asked, in a casual sort of way.

'No, she's at work,' said Bowyer, indicating that we should sit down.

'What does she do?'

'She's a croupier in a gaming club in the West End,' said Bowyer, taking a seat on the black leather sofa opposite us.

'Oh really? I thought she was a dancer at one of Giovanni Maroni's clubs.'

'Look, what is it you guys want?' Bowyer tried to sound flippant about the conversation, but it was probably because he thought we were making a fairly unsubtle enquiry about Suzy Ho's employment.

'When we called here last, Mr Bowyer – nearly a fortnight ago – you said the only occasion you'd met Mr Maroni was on the day you moved in here, and he moved out.'

'That's true.' Bowyer spoke the lie confidently, but he was now very much on edge. 'What's this about? Have you got something on Maroni?'

'We may have,' I said, joining in for the first time, 'but nothing that need concern you. How well do you know Maroni?'

'I've been to his club a few times.'

'You said previously that you'd only met Maroni the day you moved in to your flat.'

Bowyer shrugged, but said nothing.

'And presumably it was at his club that you

282

met Miss Ho.'

'If it's anything to do with you, yes.' Bowyer's face suddenly lightened. 'Is this about her work permit?'

'She doesn't have one,' said Dave. 'She's working illegally as a dancer.'

'That's no big deal, is it?' By now, Bowyer's eyes had started darting about the room, fixing on anything but the two of us.

'Probably not. So why did you deny knowing Maroni?' Dave kept probing.

'Did I?' Bowyer reached across to a table close to the sofa on which he was sitting, and picked up a glass of water. He drained it before looking at us again.

'Yes, Mr Bowyer, you did. And I'm wondering why you should have done that. I mean to say, there's nothing wrong in knowing a reputable businessman like Mr Maroni, is there?'

By now, Bowyer was sweating profusely. 'Look, I'd like to help you, but I do have an appointment,' he said, glancing at the watch on his left wrist. His other hand was playing an incessant tattoo on the arm of the sofa.

I wondered why Dave was playing this cat-and-mouse game with Bowyer. It was unlike him not to move on quickly in an interrogation, and an interrogation was how this visit was shaping up. But I suddenly realized why when Dave played his trump card.

'How long have you been dependent on heroin, Mr Bowyer?'

'I don't know what you mean.' Bowyer was beginning to sound aggressive now, and glanced again at his watch.

'Time for a fix, is it?'

'For God's sake leave me alone,' protested Bowyer angrily. His hands had begun to shake quite noticeably.

'OK. As soon as you tell me what I want to know.'

Bowyer was fidgeting constantly now, and he kept crossing and uncrossing his legs. He was clearly in need of the drug. But Dave had played him well, pushing him until he started to sweat and get anxious. And it was this relentless questioning that had brought on Bowyer's need for more heroin. Dave, who some years ago had spent a tour of duty on the Drugs Squad, knew exactly what he was doing.

'I don't know anything,' said Bowyer, his tone now becoming anguished. 'I don't take drugs.'

'I only have to look at you to see that you're a habitual user,' responded Dave calmly, 'so there's no point in denying it.'

'All right, so I do. So what?' Bowyer finally capitulated, but it was an aggressive response. 'You going to nick me for it?'

'Who's your supplier?'

'I don't know his name, but I meet him from time to time in Dean Street, or maybe Gerrard Street. It's usually around Soho somewhere. He rings me and tells me where he's at.'

'Try again, Mr Bowyer. Are you really expecting me to believe that you've got a regular supplier, but you don't know his name? And frankly, I'm not taken in by all this fanny about sudden phone calls and covert meetings in various parts of Soho.' Dave sat back and waited, knowing that the longer he kept Bowyer away from his heroin, the quicker would come the answer.

'I'm not answering any more questions, and I want you to leave.' Bowyer was getting angrier by the second.

'We're not leaving until we've got the answer.' Dave sat back and folded his hands in his lap. But then he shot forward again, an earnest expression on his face. 'You're a user, Tom,' he said, 'and that's your bad luck, but I want to know who your supplier is. It's him we'll be arresting, not you. You're the victim here.'

When Tom Bowyer eventually answered, his reply came softly. 'It's a guy called Dominic Finch. He's a photographer in Chelsea.'

Then came Dave's crippler, the question I suspect he'd been leading up to all the time.

'Where does the money come from to feed your habit, Tom? And don't tell me you've made a killing on the futures markets, because I know you haven't.' The last statement must've been a guess, unless Dave had been keeping something from me. But Bowyer's admission, the last time we were here, that he didn't own the Porsche that Cyril had raved about, indicated that Bowyer wasn't a financial success. If he were, the first thing he would have bought would've been a Porsche or something like it.

There was a long pause, punctuated only by Bowyer's constant fidgeting. 'Giovanni Maroni,' he said eventually.

'I see. Tell me, Tom, how did you come to meet Dominic Finch?'

Bowyer's fingers were tightly interlocked, and he stared at Dave with a venomous look on his face. 'Suzy used to work for him. Well, still does.'

'Taking part in pornographic videos?'

'Yes.'

'I imagine she's quite good at getting screwed by the studs who work there,' said Dave, smiling at the man opposite.

'You leave Suzy out of this,' responded Bowyer angrily.

'I wish we could,' said Dave mildly. He glanced at me, signalling that I should take over the questioning.

'This Mr Maroni sounds a very charitable sort of individual,' I began, and waited.

'Is he hell!' snapped Bowyer.

'So what did you have to do for all this money he gives you? Heroin doesn't come cheap.'

'I do jobs for him,' mumbled Bowyer.

'What sort of jobs?'

'This and that.'

'Where were you on the weekend of the seventh and eighth of this month, Mr Bowyer?'

'I can't remember.'

'You'll have to do better than that,' I said.

The Tom Bowyer we had first met, full of confidence, the typical young entrepreneur, had degenerated into a sweating, shaking mess of a man from whom the carapace had been stripped away. He looked up at me, the tears running unchecked down his face, his lower lip quivering. He knew, just as I knew, that the game was up.

'All right, damn you, I did it.'

'What did you do, Tom?' asked Dave gently.

'I was there when he was killed.'

'When who was killed?'

'Jack Harding.'

'Who else was there? Who were you helping?'

'Finch, the bastard.'

Dave Poole knew a thing or two about drug addicts who'd been deprived of their 'fix'. He knew they could become violent, and aggressive, and he was taking no chances. He handcuffed him.

While he was doing that, I rang the local nick and asked them to send a unit to secure the penthouse until I could get more officers down there to conduct a search. And to send a van to take Bowyer, and us, to Charing Cross police station.

The difficulty we were now facing was that Bowyer was in his own home when he had confessed to murder, and it had not, therefore, been recorded. Her Majesty's judges don't greatly care for that; they always seem to think that we've invented any confessions that are made away from a police station. What we needed now was for Bowyer to say it all again in the interview room of Charing Cross police station. I just hoped to God that he would.

However, the one factor in our favour was that he was still in desperate need of a 'fix', but there was no way we would allow him to inject himself with heroin in our presence. For all we knew, he might inject a lethal dose, and that wouldn't go down at all well. As I've already mentioned, the Metropolitan Police gets terribly sniffy about prisoners dying in custody.

The first thing that would happen at the station would be for the divisional surgeon to take a look at him, and probably prescribe something like methadone before certifying him fit for interview.

We rode the lift to the ground floor.

Cyril looked up in surprise. 'Is there a problem, Mr Bowyer?' he asked.

It seemed a pointless question, seeing that Bowyer was handcuffed, and escorted by two police officers, one on either side of him.

'Mr Bowyer's helping us with our enquiries, Cyril,' said Dave.

Nineteen

By the time we got Tom Bowyer to Charing Cross police station he was almost a gibbering wreck. The divisional surgeon – who has probably got a more exotic title now – briefly examined him, gave him an oral dose of methadone, and certified that he was fit to be interviewed.

If we were to avoid nasty allegations, it was essential that we got Bowyer's confession on tape. Dave took him into the interview room, switched on the recorder, and cautioned him.

'You are entitled to have a solicitor present, Mr Bowyer,' I said. 'Do you want one?'

'No.'

'You are not obliged to answer any questions unless you wish to do so.'

'Just get on with it.'

I later learned that the methadone the divisional surgeon had given Bowyer was just enough to get him through the interview, and he'd promised him another dose once it was over. The outcome was that Bowyer was obviously in one hell of a hurry to get the interview done with. Had defence counsel learned of it, he would probably have demanded that the statement be excluded on the grounds that it was made under duress. As it happened, Bowyer didn't mention it to his counsel, and I saw no reason to do so either.

'Now, Mr Bowyer, I want you tell me again what you told me at your apartment earlier today. And begin by telling me where you got the box.'

'I collected it from Vincenzo Camilleri in a hired van.'

'What time was that?' I asked.

'About three o'clock on the Sunday morning.'

'And what happened next?'

'I drove from Putney straight to Chelsea, and picked up Dominic Finch from his studio. We went from there to Badajos Street and let ourselves into the basement flat.'

'You had a key?'

'I hadn't, but Finch had. Jack Harding was asleep in bed. We dragged him out to his studio on the front of the house, but he was fighting all the way. He and Finch were yelling, and I was terrified that someone in the house would hear us. Then, to my horror, Finch took out a knife and stabbed him. That's when I really began to panic. The plan was never to kill him. When Harding fell down, Finch dragged him up again, but it left blood on the carpet in the studio, and on the front door where he grabbed it as we dragged him out to the van. But by the time we got him into the box I could see he was dead.'

'Was Harding wearing anything?' I asked.

'No, he was in bed, naked.'

'Where did you go from there, Mr Bowyer?'

'We stopped off at an all-night filling station somewhere, and Finch filled a jerry can with petrol. He poured some over Harding's body, and locked the box. I don't know why; Harding was dead, but Finch said we had to destroy the evidence. Anyway, we weren't supposed to lock it. The idea was to leave Harding in the box naked, just to teach him a lesson, not to kill him. But it looked as though Finch had meant to kill him all along. When we arrived at Ham Common, we pulled the box out of the van, and Finch poured petrol over it and set fire to it. Then we got into the van and drove back.'

'What did you do with the van?'

Bowyer stared at me as though I'd asked a stupid question. 'I took it back to the hire company, of course. On Monday.'

I've dealt with a few murders over the years, but I couldn't believe how easy Bowyer had made it sound. The unfortunate aspect was that, even if we traced the van, the likelihood of it yielding fingerprints after this lapse of time was remote, to say the least. Not that it really mattered.

'Why did Maroni want Harding dead? Did he tell you that?'

'He didn't. He just wanted him scared. He said that Harding had been to Rome to study art or something. But while he was there, he met a girl called Sofia Maroni – Gio Maroni's sister – and they lived together for a few months. She told Harding that her brother had gone to London because the Italian police were after him for a murder near Palermo. It seems that Sofia knew where her brother was, and asked Harding to look him up when he went home. But Harding, who was always short of money, decided there was a profit to be made out of that situation, and threatened to expose Maroni to the authorities if he didn't pay up. Well, Maroni's a nasty bastard, and wasn't having any. He sent a couple of his strong-arm men to see Harding and tell him to keep his mouth shut or it would be shut for him permanently.'

That explained the letter, signed Sofia, which we'd found in Harding's flat.

'But he didn't take it seriously, I imagine.'

'According to Maroni, he laughed and said that things like that didn't happen in Eng-land.'

Which just goes to show how little Jack Harding had known about crime in London.

'How does Finch fit into all this?' I asked.

'According to Gio, Finch was making porn DVDs, but not doing very well at it, probably because the stuff from Holland and Scandinavia was much better quality, and cheaper. Finch was in debt up to his eyebrows, so Gio said.'

'Did you know Finch before this plot to murder Harding?' asked Dave.

'Yes. I told you he supplied me with heroin. Anyway, Gio told me to contact Finch, and said that he was going to help out.'

Going to help out! Bowyer made it sound like the pair of them were running a stall at a village fête, rather than carrying out a horrific murder.

'So, you clearly understood that you were to take part in a murder.'

'No. I told you that Gio just wanted Harding scared. He wanted it to be a demonstration of what happened to people who crossed him.'

'But you needed the money to buy heroin,' suggested Dave.

Bowyer said nothing, but he had started sweating again, and that was answer enough. Anyway, I thought that he wouldn't be able to carry on for much longer. But it didn't matter; we had all we needed. But there was one thing that still puzzled me.

'How much did you pay Giovanni Maroni for the penthouse flat you're living in, Mr Bowyer?' I asked.

'I didn't buy it. Gio's lent it to me. He said that I could stay there as long as I liked.'

That, to me, sounded like an extremely uncharacteristic stance for Maroni to have taken. Maybe he'd hoped that Bowyer would spend the rest of his life in prison. What Maroni hadn't anticipated was that Bowyer would tell us everything.

It was gone half past seven by the time we'd finished with Bowyer, and we now had to act quickly. If Maroni and Finch learned that Bowyer had been arrested, they would disappear like mist in the morning sun. The one weak link was Cyril, the concierge at Bowyer's Docklands apartment. It was possible that he might just be tempted – for a suitable reward – to telephone Maroni and tell him of the arrest. But on that possibility we had to take a chance. After all, Cyril had said he didn't know where Maroni had gone; that's why he was returning his letters to the post office.

However, I didn't want to have Maroni and Finch arrested this late at night; the regulations demanded that they could only be questioned at a civilized hour. If we felt their collars now, a good twelve hours would have elapsed before we could start interrogating them.

I got busy on my cellphone. I spoke to DI Kate Ebdon, and summarized what had happened at Bowyer's penthouse and at the police station. 'Organize two teams, Kate, one to rearrest Maroni, and another to pick up Dominic Finch. At six o'clock tomorrow morning. And make it low key – sergeants at the most – I don't want either of these people to think they're important.'

'That'll be right, guv,' said Kate. 'By the way, there wasn't a problem getting Albert Goodwin remanded in custody this morning.'

'In view of what we know now, Kate,' I said, 'it looks as though we might have to let him out.'

Kate laughed. 'If I think what's happened, has happened, we can do him for wasting police time.'

And that about summed it up. It was now apparent that Foster and Goodwin, and to a lesser extent, Cheryl Green, had come up with a credible tale to throw us off the scent. Had it not been for Dave recognizing Suzy Ho, we might never have found Harding's killer. Or Foster and Goodwin would've gone down for it. But, I later learned, there was no chance of that.

The following morning, Detective Sergeants Tom Challis and Charlie Flynn, and their teams, hit the two addresses concerned. Challis went to Curzon Street and rearrested Maroni, while Flynn went to Chelsea and took Dominic Finch into custody.

Dave and I arrived at Charing Cross police station at nine o'clock. I spoke to DS Flynn first.

'Any trouble with Finch, Charlie?'

Flynn chuckled. 'No, guv, apart from him saying that he'd done nothing wrong.'

'They all say that,' I said.

'I think he was more upset at being interrupted.'

'What was he doing, then?'

Flynn laughed. 'He was in bed with a smashing bird.'

I next spoke to Tom Challis, and he too reported that he'd had no trouble making the arrest of Maroni.

'Apart from him threatening all sorts of legal action, guv, like wrongful arrest and false imprisonment,' he said.

'They all say that,' I said, for the second time that morning.

I decided to interview Finch first.

'What the bloody hell are you lot playing at?' Finch demanded, the moment we stepped into the interview room.

'You have been arrested on suspicion of murdering Jack Harding,' I said, once the tape recorder had been switched on.

Finch laughed. 'Why the hell should I want to kill Jack?'

'For money,' I suggested. 'Your business is going down the pan, and you were in debt up to your eyes.'

'I don't know who told you that,' said Finch. But there was now less of the bombast that we'd encountered on our previous interviews with him. I think he was worrying about how much we knew. He didn't have long to wait.

'You're entitled to the services of a solicitor, Mr Finch,' I said. 'You can either nominate one, or one will be provided for you.'

'What do I need a solicitor for?' Finch waved a hand, as if dismissing the idea. 'I've done nothing wrong.'

'You are entitled to a copy of the statement made yesterday by Tom Bowyer, who is in custody at this police station, charged with murder.'

The expression on Finch's face showed quite plainly that he had no idea Bowyer had been arrested, let alone that he'd told us everything. He took the statement and read through it slowly.

'Is this guy off his rocker? This is all fiction.'

'Do you have anything to say in response to what Bowyer has said?' I asked.

'Too bloody right, I do. It's all balls.'

'It looks as though Giovanni Maroni's going to get away with it, then,' I said, in an aside to Dave.

Finch tensed, and looked as though he was about to say something, but then thought better of it.

'We'll leave you to mull over what we've been talking about, Mr Finch, and then we'll come back and have another chat.'

Finch didn't respond to that either.

★ ★ ★

By the time we got to Maroni, his sharp-suited solicitor had already arrived and was closeted with him.

'My client has nothing to say, and demands to know why he's been arrested.'

'He was told why by the arresting officer,' I said. 'I have here a copy of a confession made by Tom Bowyer which implicates your client in a conspiracy to murder.'

The solicitor took the statement and read through it. 'My client has nothing to say in response—'

'I suggest you let your client be the judge of that,' I interrupted, 'unless you wish to be excluded from the interview.'

'You have no power—'

'Oh, but I do, as you well know,' I replied, not that I had any grounds so far for doing so. But it had the effect of warning the solicitor that I was not to be messed about.

He took the hint, and handed Bowyer's statement to Maroni.

Maroni spent some time reading the document, but his face portrayed no sign of what must have been going through his mind. Eventually he put the statement on the table, took a deep breath, and leaned back in his chair.

'It is all because I am a wealthy foreigner,' Maroni said eventually. 'I don't know what it is about you English, but you resent anyone who is successful in your country.' He gestured towards the statement. 'This is merely an attempt to blacken my good name.'

'It seems rather strange, Mr Maroni, that Terry Foster, Albert Goodwin, Cheryl Green and Tom Bowyer have all made statements implicating you in the murder of Jack Harding.'

Maroni scoffed. 'They are conspiring against me,' he said. 'But I can tell you this, Mr Policeman: I had nothing whatever to do with this man Harding's death. As a matter of fact, I was at a party on the Saturday night before you found the body on ... where was it? My good friend Vincenzo Camilleri was there too. And if you want proof of that, you only have to ask Lord Slade. It was held at his country house in Buckinghamshire, and he very kindly allowed us to stay the night. I suppose it must've been near to midday when Vincenzo and I left.' This statement was accompanied by an evil grin, the reason for which became apparent later on.

'So there you have it, Chief Inspector,' said the solicitor. 'There are clearly no grounds for detaining my client. Police cannot go around arresting people on a whim when they have no evidence. Furthermore, consideration will be given to legal proceedings.'

'I'm afraid I have a bit of a disappointment for you,' I said. 'The City of Westminster magistrate has issued a warrant for Giovanni Maroni's arrest on an extradition warrant sanctioned by the Home Office.'

'On what charge?' demanded the outraged

solicitor. He obviously knew nothing of Maroni's shady background, or if he did, was making a damned good job of not showing it.

'Information has been laid by the Italian government to the effect that your client is wanted in Italy in connection with a murder committed in Palermo some five years ago. I shall therefore take him into custody on that warrant, and he will appear in court tomorrow morning.'

'They can't do this, can they?' Maroni, his face as black as thunder, turned to his legal adviser.

'I'm afraid they can.' The solicitor spoke wearily, as though tired of the whole business.

'Will I get bail?' demanded Maroni.

'I very much doubt it,' I said. 'Usually in these cases, the accused is remanded in custody.'

Maroni turned back to his lawyer. 'Is this true? Can't you obtain a writ of habeas corpus to get me out?'

'I shouldn't waste your money,' said the solicitor, as he stood up and stuffed his papers into his briefcase.

We were now left with a problem. Several problems in fact.

If Tom Bowyer's account was to be believed – and I saw no reason to disbelieve it – we had Foster and Goodwin remanded in

300

custody for crimes they had not committed. In that case, what should they be charged with? It seemed to me that Maroni had deliberately set up a smokescreen to shield the real murderers. I suppose that a conspiracy to waste police time might be considered, but I couldn't see the Crown Prosecution Service taking much interest in that. Even so, there was the little matter of the Beretta pistol that had been used – by someone – to murder Vincenzo Camilleri.

Secondly, we had to track down Lord Slade at whose country house, it was claimed, Maroni and Camilleri had stayed during the weekend of the murder. That, however, was an irrelevancy. A conspirator does not have to be at the scene of the murder in order to be indicted as a party to that conspiracy.

Once we were back at Curtis Green, I set Dave the task of finding Slade's London address, presuming he had one.

Dave Poole is what I call a good armchair detective. In other words, he will search every source possible before getting off his backside to go out and start looking.

'I've been to the Commissioner's library, guv,' he announced, entering my office with two cups of coffee.

'How nice,' I said.

'I had a look at *Burke's Peerage*, and found Lord Slade. He's the fourth Lord Slade, the previous three having been distinguished army officers. But, as far as I can find out from *Who's Who*, the present Slade doesn't do anything.'

'Except hold parties for villains,' I said. 'Do we have a London address for him, Dave?'

'We have, and we have the address of his club.'

'Good. Try his home number and see if he's prepared to see us.'

'Right, guv,' said Dave. 'By the way, Charlie Flynn's outside. He's got some useful information for you.'

'Send him in.'

A minute or two later, DS Flynn appeared in my office holding a small plastic-shrouded bottle in his latex-gloved hand.

'What have you got there, Charlie?'

'A bottle of Rohypnol pills, guv. After we nicked Finch this morning, I left a couple of the lads to search the premises, and they found this.' Flynn placed the small package on my desk. 'It's not been sent for fingerprint examination yet, but I thought you'd like to know that we found it in Finch's bedroom at the studio.'

'Yes, I know about Rohypnol. It's commonly known as a date-rape drug.' It was then that I recalled how distant and detached Sasha had been on the Sunday morning after she'd slept with Finch. Her state certainly indicated that she was affected by drugs of some sort.

'A couple of birds turned up while they

were there, saying they'd come for a session. I reckon he's running a brothel.'

'Nearly, Charlie. I expect they were porn actresses. Finch makes blue movies, but not very successfully from what Bowyer told us.'

I mulled over the find, and then it hit me. Bowyer had said that he picked up Finch at some time after three o'clock on the Sunday morning. But Sasha Lovell had claimed to have spent the night with him.

I returned the bottle to Flynn with instructions for it to be sent straight for fingerprint examination. Then I shouted for Dave.

'I've arranged for us to see Lord Slade at five this afternoon, guv,' he said.

'Yes, well that might have to wait,' I said. 'Right now we're going to see Sasha Lovell.'

Twenty

Sandra Roberts, the constable guarding Sasha, was making tea when we arrived. I got the impression that she undertook this task every half an hour or so.

'Sasha, you remember the night of Saturday the seventh of September.'

'I'm not likely to forget it,' Sasha replied.

'You told me that you'd spent the night with Dominic Finch.'

'That's right, I did.'

'Tell me exactly what happened.'

'I went round to Dom's place on Saturday afternoon. He spent about forty minutes taking shots of me, and then we went to bed. That evening we had a meal at a bistro in King's Road, then back to the studio, had a few drinks and went to bed. *Again*.' Sasha laughed outright at that, almost as if willing us to criticize her.

'What time would that have been?'

'I don't know. About eleven, I suppose.'

'What time did you first wake up the next morning, Sasha?'

'About nine, I suppose, when Dom brought me a cup of tea.'

'Are you sure he brought the tea, because he said you made the tea?'

'No, it was definitely him.'

'And what time did you leave Finch's place?'

'It must've been about half past nine, I suppose.'

'How did you feel when you got up on that Sunday morning?'

'How did I feel? Well, like I'd had too much to drink.'

'Like other occasions when you'd had too much to drink?'

'Not exactly, no.' Sasha furrowed her brow. 'I felt dizzy, and at first I didn't know where I was. In fact, it was the worst hangover I'd ever had.'

'Was Dominic there?'

'Yeah, I told you, he brought me tea. As a matter of fact, he asked me what was wrong, because he said I looked like a zombie. I was slurring my speech, like I was still pissed, and I felt sick. I'd never felt like it before, and I asked Dom what the hell he'd given me to drink.'

'I can answer that, Sasha,' said Dave. 'Finch slipped a Rohypnol pill in your drink. Maybe even two.'

'What the hell's that?'

'It's better known as a date-rape drug,' explained Dave. 'And the way you say you felt on that Sunday morning bears it out.'

'As does your behaviour that morning,' I added. 'A bottle of those pills was found at his flat when he was arrested.'

'Arrested? What for?'

'For the murder of Jack Harding,' I told her.

'But how could he? He spent the night with me.'

'That's what he led you to believe, Sasha,' I said, 'but I'll wager you didn't wake up once between going to bed at about eleven, and when Finch woke you up at about nine the following morning.'

'That's true. I went out like a light. But why should Dom have wanted to kill Jack?'

'Because Jack knew that Maroni was wanted for murder in Italy. Apparently he got to know a girl in Rome whose name was Sofia

305

Maroni, Giovanni's sister, and she told Jack where her brother was in London. Jack Harding tried to blackmail Maroni, but Maroni wasn't having any, and he paid Finch and another man to kill him.'

'My God! How awful. And to think I lived with a murderer. Two, in fact.' Sasha shuddered at the thought.

'There's one thing that puzzles me, Sasha: how did you finish up living with Jack Harding?'

'It was Dom's idea. I'd known Dom for a long time, maybe five or six years, and when I split from Gio, Finch said that a mate of his was looking for a live-in model. Well, I had nowhere to go, so I jumped at it.'

I'd no doubt that the idea of Sasha moving in with Harding came originally from Giovanni Maroni. And that, in my book, just went to show how long he'd been planning Jack Harding's murder.

We went straight from Sasha Lovell's place to Lord Slade's apartment – in a mews behind Park Lane – and arrived there at five o'clock that same afternoon.

'Come in, come in, my dear fellows.' Rupert Slade was a tall, foppish individual, about forty years of age. As if to emphasize his foppishness, he was attired in a plum-coloured velvet smoking jacket, a garment that would have been fashionable seventy or eighty years ago, and was smoking a cigarette in a long holder.

We followed Slade into his sumptuously furnished sitting room, and settled in one of the two leather chesterfields.

'I hope my making our appointment for five o'clock hasn't inconvenienced you, Chief Inspector,' Slade said, once introductions had been effected. 'I have to admit that I had a leisurely lunch at a gaming club.' He smiled ruefully. 'Unfortunately, I lost a few pounds.' He chortled at this. 'Pounds sterling, not pounds avoirdupois, you'll understand.' He chortled again, and patted his considerable paunch. 'Ever since we hereditary peers got thrown out of the House of Lords, I seem to have a lot of time on my hands. Now, then, what can I do for the police?'

I rapidly decided that his exclusion from the Upper Chamber was no bad thing; I couldn't see him contributing much to the legislative process.

'I'm investigating a case of murder, Lord Slade,' I began, 'and Giovanni Maroni is implicated. He told us a fanciful tale about having spent the weekend of the seventh and eighth of September at a party at your house in Buckinghamshire.'

'Nothing fanciful about it, Chief Inspector,' said Slade smoothly. 'He was there. It was quite a shindig. I'd arranged for a couple of willing girls of my acquaintance to join us, and as you say, Gio was there, and Vincenzo, along with some of their chums.' He paused to stare at a tasteful portrait of a nude hanging between the two large windows. 'Now, let me see. Ah, yes. There was an engaging fellow called Terry Foster, and a chum of his called Albert Goodwin. Salt of the earth, those chaps. And Terry brought along a charming girl called...' He paused, as if searching for the name. 'Yes, I have it: Cheryl Green. Quite a stunner, I can tell you. Have you met her?'

'Yes, we met her when we searched Foster's house, Lord Slade.'

This disturbing news was confirmation, despite what they had admitted, that Foster and Goodwin had *not* been involved in Harding's murder. Foster, Goodwin and Green had been charged with various offences, and two of them were in custody on remand. I had no doubt that if it came to the crunch, Slade's testimony would be accepted.

'You're absolutely sure that they were there, are you?'

'Quite definitely. Why? Is there some sort of problem?'

'Was that the first time you'd met Foster and Goodwin, sir?' asked Dave.

'Yes, indeed. But are you suggesting that they are criminals of some sort?'

'Not suggesting it,' said Dave. 'I'm telling you that they most certainly are. Both Foster and Goodwin are well known to the police as armed robbers.'

'Good gracious!' Slade made a passable attempt at being shocked by this revelation. 'I had no idea. They were friends of Gio, you see.' He forced a brief, humourless laugh. 'Perhaps I'd better have the family silver checked, eh what?'

'And how did you meet Maroni?' I asked.

'At one of his clubs, Chief Inspector. He has all these wonderfully sexy girls doing erotic gymnastics around chromium poles.' Slade lowered his voice to a conspiratorial tone. 'All stark naked, of course.'

'But you'd not previously met Foster, Goodwin, or Cheryl Green, I take it?' I asked again.

'No, I hadn't. But it seemed a good idea to invite Gio and some of his chums for the weekend. Sort of returning hospitality, if you know what I mean. Gio was always very generous whenever I visited his club.'

I'll bet he was. Slade was not the first peer to fall for such blandishments.

'Did Maroni suggest that particular weekend?' I asked.

'As a matter of fact, he did. I floated the idea of a party, and Gio said that that weekend would be ideal. How is he, by the way? Have you seen him lately?'

'I saw him this morning, when I arrested him on an extradition warrant for murder. He's a Mafioso, you see, and it's alleged he murdered a judge in Palermo five years ago.'

I suppose that I shouldn't really have told Slade that, the case being *sub judice*, but he needed to be told what a naive fool he was. Unless there was a cunning, conniving criminal mind beneath that dandified exterior.

'My God!' This time, Slade appeared genuinely shocked. 'I had no idea. When you said just now that Gio was involved in a murder, was that the one in Palermo?'

'No, Lord Slade,' I said, 'it was one committed the weekend of your house party.'

'Oh, well, he couldn't have done it, could he?'

Dave took a statement from a somewhat shaken Lord Slade, and we returned to Charing Cross police station.

'The prisoner Finch has got a solicitor with him, sir,' said the custody sergeant.

'Fat lot of good that'll do him,' muttered Dave as we made our way into the interview room.

The solicitor started the moment we got through the door.

'My client has a rock-solid alibi for the date you say he committed this murder, Chief Inspector.'

I ignored him, and directed my remarks to Dominic Finch. 'Shortly after you were arrested this morning, Mr Finch, police officers searched your studio and found a bottle of Rohypnol pills in your bedroom. I am certain that a fingerprint examination of the bottle will reveal your prints on it. Furthermore, I have reason to believe that you administered this drug to Miss Sasha Lovell at some time on the evening of Saturday the seventh of September. As a result, Miss Lovell has no recollection of anything between about eleven o'clock that evening and nine o'clock the following morning when you woke her with a cup of tea.'

'She made the tea, not me,' said Finch.

'Miss Lovell is adamant that you brought her tea, and she is willing to testify that she felt dizzy, that her speech was slurred, and she felt disorientated. All of which are symptoms of having been given Rohypnol. And I can confirm that; I saw her a little later on that same morning. So, in terms of an alibi, her testimony won't stand up.'

'I would like a moment to confer with my client, Chief Inspector,' said the solicitor, now much less hostile than he had been when we arrived.

Ten minutes later, the solicitor called us back. 'My client has something to say, Chief Inspector.'

'All right, I was there,' said Finch.

'Where?'

'When Jack was murdered, but it wasn't me who killed him, it was Tom Bowyer. He had the knife and he did the business. We weren't meant to kill Jack, and Gio Maroni said that he just wanted him beaten up a bit to teach him a lesson. He wanted us to give him a going over, and leave him some place so's he'd get the message. But Bowyer went mad. I think he's on drugs.'

This was a typical response to a murder committed by two people acting in concert. But as far as the law was concerned, it didn't matter much which of them had wielded the weapon. I dismissed Finch's statement that Maroni didn't want Harding killed as an attempt to row himself out of a charge of murder.

'Ah yes, drugs,' I said. 'Bowyer maintains that you supplied him with heroin, but he later said that he only met you immediately before the murder. Which is it?'

Finch scoffed, and made the expected reply. 'I certainly didn't supply him with drugs. He's trying to work one off on me, telling you that. Bowyer was one of the studs I employed for my adult DVDs. I've known him for over a year, but he was no bloody good, and the girls didn't fancy him. All in all, Bowyer was a bit of a tosser.'

'A bit of a dog's dinner, Mr Brock,' said the jovial lawyer at the Crown Prosecution Service offices. He was a refreshing sort of individual, evidence of which was his suit with broad chalk stripes, yellow socks, and an albert strung between the pockets of his waistcoat.

'I'm glad you're sorting it out, and not me,' I said.

The lawyer flipped through a few pages of my report, and then leaned back in his chair. 'Conspiracy to murder for Maroni, and murder for Bowyer and Finch. I had considered indicting Finch for administering a noxious thing, namely Rohypnol, but I doubt it would add anything to his sentence. Apart from which it would be damned difficult to prove.'

'What about Foster and Goodwin?' I asked.

'Ah yes, Messrs Foster and Goodwin.' The lawyer savoured the names, and peered at me over his half-moon spectacles. 'I think we ought to do them for conspiring with Maroni to waste police time. I doubt they'd get any porridge for it, but the judge might be persuaded to impose a hefty fine. Perhaps equal to the amount that Maroni paid them for their subterfuge.' He chuckled at the thought. 'Opportunity for the state to lay hands on some of their ill-gotten gains, eh?'

'Isn't there enough to indict them for conspiracy to murder?'

'Probably, old boy, but trying to persuade a jury of it would be a non-starter. Might as well do them for wasting police time. That way, they'll appear before a district judge, and he won't be fooled.'

'There is the question of Vincenzo Camilleri's murder,' I ventured.

'Bit of a problem that,' said the lawyer. 'I don't doubt that Maroni was responsible for

Camilleri's murder, but on the other hand, you say that the Beretta pistol was returned to Maroni *after* the murder.'

'Maroni said that Foster returned the pistol to him on Tuesday, the twenty-fourth of September,' I said. 'But we've only got Maroni's word for it. Personally, I think it was returned to him *before* the murder.'

'Yes, but even if we were able to get a contradictory statement from Foster, I doubt it would carry any weight, not with the string of previous convictions he's got.'

'Well, I'll try for a statement from Foster if you like,' I said.

'Worth a try, I suppose.' The lawyer nodded. 'On the other hand, the Italians are baying for Maroni's blood. I doubt they take too kindly to a chap who goes about killing judges.' He laughed. 'Mind you, Chief Inspector, there's one or two I'd happily strangle.'

'What do we do about Foster and Goodwin?' I asked.

'Oh, you can leave that to me. I'll get 'em sprung,' said the lawyer cheerfully.

A few days later, I saw Terry Foster at Ramsay MacDonald House.

'You and Goodwin are likely to get done for wasting police time, Terry,' I said.

'It was Maroni's idea, Mr Brock.' Foster was quite unrepentant, and seemed to have enjoyed putting one over on the police. 'He

314

reckoned that it would throw you off of the scent, so to speak. And we knew that we'd got a copper-bottomed alibi for that weekend that we was going to spring on you if we ever finished up at the Bailey.'

'Yes, I know about Lord Slade. Very amusing, Terry, and how much did Maroni pay you for your little charade?'

'Two grand apiece, and a thousand for Cheryl.'

'And Vincenzo Camilleri's part in all this?'

'Maroni got Vince to set up all that guff on his computer, and on his phones, knowing that you'd go for it. Never done him no good though. I reckon Maroni topped him because he knew too much. In fact, I wouldn't be surprised if Vince hadn't put the arm on Maroni for a few more shekels than he was promised, but as I've said many times before, Maroni's a nasty bastard.'

'Both Finch and Bowyer said that Maroni only wanted them to give Harding a roughing up.'

'Course he did, guv'nor. No, Maroni definitely wanted him topped. And I'll bet Bowyer and Finch will try to put the blame on each other.'

'Tell me, Terry, how did your dabs get on the Volvo? This story of robbing a betting shop in Fulham was a load of old moody, wasn't it?'

'Yeah. I put me dabs on it special like, so's you'd find 'em. Another of Gio's ideas, that

315

was.' Foster grinned at the thought he'd deluded us.

'So it was Harding that Maroni wanted sorted, was it? And the story that he was annoyed that Sasha Lovell had left him was a blind, I suppose.'

'Yeah, that's what he said, about the girl, I mean, but it was another bit of the smoke-screen. He set it up, but deep down he never give a toss about her.' Foster laughed. He was really enjoying himself.

'One other question, Terry. When did you return the Beretta pistol to Giovanni Maroni?'

'Return it?' Foster scoffed. 'I never had it, Mr Brock. Maroni give it to Cheryl on the Monday after Vince was topped, and the first time I saw it was when your lot turned it up underneath the bath. Want a statement, Chief?' he asked, and grinned.

For what it was worth, Dave took it all down in writing, but when we presented it to our lawyer at the CPS, he laughed. 'One villain's word against another,' he said. 'We'll keep that one on file in case you turn up any more evidence, but I doubt we'll see Maroni again, once the Italian judicial system has finished with him. Knowing what they're like over there, it'll probably be years before they get him to trial, let alone sentence him.'

Some months later we all trooped up to the Old Bailey for the start of several trials.

In the end, and after the usual jousting with defence counsel, Maroni, Bowyer and Finch received life sentences with varying tariffs. But the crafty old learned judge recommended that Maroni should be allowed to serve his sentence in his native country, thus saving the British taxpayer a substantial amount of money, and neatly circumventing all the palaver of extradition into the bargain.

Later, Foster and Goodwin were arraigned before the City of Westminster magistrates' court. They cheerfully acknowledged having taken part in a conspiracy – at the behest of Giovanni Maroni – to draw the police away from discovering the true murderers of Jack Harding. The district judge imposed a heavy financial penalty for wasting police time, but God knows whether they ever paid the fine. No one seems to bother too much about that sort of thing these days.

As for Cheryl Green, she was given community service for the unlawful possession of the Beretta pistol. She must have thoroughly enjoyed scrubbing the floors of an old people's home.

I later learned that James Porter was sentenced to ten years' imprisonment for sending an explosive device to Dominic Finch, and, oddly enough, he fetched up in the same prison as Finch, albeit briefly. I was told, even later, that Porter eventually went mad and was transferred to Broadmoor.

But I still wondered whether Maroni was behind the attempt to bomb Finch's studio. Perhaps he had paid Porter to do it with the intention of removing another conspirator who could have informed on him.

Maybe Bowyer would have been next. I certainly didn't think that Maroni was going to let him stay in his elegant Docklands penthouse for as long as he liked. I think it was the other way around: a case of Bowyer staying there for as long as *Maroni* liked.

Arresting Bowyer might just have saved his life.